Praise for Kristin Vayden and her novels

"Vayden never lets me down; always and forever a one-click author . . . every work a work of magic!"
—S.E. Hall, *New York Times* and *USA Today* bestselling author

"I've come across a genius with a gift in reading Kristin. I can't wait to read more of her books!"
—Kathy Coopmans, *USA Today* bestselling author

Praise for *Heart of a Cowboy*

"A touching tale of family, friendship, fated love, and everything in between. A sweet romance that will make you swoon!"
—Audrey Carlan, #1 *New York Times* bestselling author

"A wonderfully woven story that will have you laughing, swooning, and choking back tears."
—Molly McAdams, *New York Times* bestselling author

"Start to finish, *Heart of a Cowboy* sucked me in and didn't let go. Vayden put my heart through every emotion, especially love. Incredible story I already want to re-read. With lots of tissues."
—Jennifer Ann Van Wyk, bestselling author

"A breath of fresh air . . . Cyler and Laken's story warmed my heart and made my toes tingle with feelings. Beautiful. Five stars."
—Erin Noelle, *USA Today* bestselling author

Books by Kristin Vayden

Lyrical Press mass market
Gentlemen of Temptation series

FALLING FROM HIS GRACE

From Lyrical Press e-books

Elk Heights Ranch series

HEART OF A COWBOY

THE COURAGE OF A COWBOY

THE COWGIRL MEETS HER MATCH

Falling From His Grace

Kristin Vayden

Lyrical Press
Kensington Publishing Corp.
www.kensingtonbooks.com

LYRICAL BOOKS are published by

Kensington Publishing Corp.
119 West 40th Street
New York, NY 10018

All Kensington titles, imprints, and distributed lines are available at special quantity discounts for bulk purchases for sales promotion, premiums, fund-raising, educational, or institutional use.

Special book excerpts or customized printings can also be created to fit specific needs. For details, write or phone the office of the Kensington Sales Manager: Attn.: Sales Department. Kensington Publishing Corp., 119 West 40th Street, New York, NY 10018. Phone: 1-800-221-2647.

Lyrical and the Lyrical logo Reg. U.S. Pat. & TM Off.

First Printing: September 2018
ISBN-13: 978-1-5161-0568-7
ISBN-10: 1-5161-0568-0

eISBN-13: 978-1-5161-0569-4
eISBN-10: 1-5161-0569-9

10 9 8 7 6 5 4 3 2 1

Printed in the United States of America

I can't write a book without dedicating it to my husband. Without him, this book—any of my books—wouldn't happen. He's the inspiration behind all the romance, the security of my heart, and the maker of dinner when I'm holed up in our bedroom fitting in some time to write! I thank God for you each day. I love you!

Acknowledgments

Thank you, Kay Springsteen Tate, for all the years of correcting me on my Regency facts, and for always being there to answer some obscure question! Thank you, Paula, you're always saving me somehow with your eagle eyes in editing, and I'd be lost without you! Thank you, Rachel Van Dyken, for feeding my love for historical fiction and giving me the push I needed to write it myself! And thank you to Kensington Publishing, your faith in my writing is a blessing.

Prologue

London 1817

Lucas Mayfield, the eighth Earl of Heightfield, was a lot of things, depending on whom you asked. But chief amongst all the adjectives his peers or others might attribute to him, none was more accurate than the one with which he labeled himself.

Bored.

It wasn't a benign state either, rather a dangerous one—because boredom bred ideas, and the ones spinning about in his mind were of the scandalous, inventive, and daring variety. Ideas also necessitated risk, something with which he didn't dally lightly. Rather, he craved control—thrived on it, in every aspect of his life. Control prevented pain, prevented others from manipulating you—because you held the marionette strings. If you were in control, life couldn't toss you on your ear with blindsiding betrayal, death, or worse.

Because yes, indeed, there were always things worse than death.

Life, being one of them.

However, risk compromised that basic need for control, so it was with careful calculation that he even considered such a reckless and delightful diversion.

He would also need assistance, but that was easily afforded and solicited. Heathcliff and Ramsey were as bloody bored as he. Among the three of them, they had every connection and resource necessary to breathe life into this concoction of his imagination.

He tapped his finger against his brandy glass, the amber light of the fire in his study's hearth casting an inviting glow. Darkness was so predictable, so protective. Much easier to manipulate than light.

He took a long sip of the fine French brandy, savoring the burn. It was heavenly. The perfection leading to temptation . . . leading to . . .

He sat up straighter, the leather chair squeaking slightly from the abrupt movement. *Tempting.*

He rolled the word around in his mind, a grin widening his lips even as he shook his head at the audacity of such an idea.

It was the perfect irony.

His idea had a name—a bloody insightful one.

Different than all the other gaming hells about London—his would thrive on anonymity. No names. No faces. Masks and the uttermost exclusivity that no other hell could boast. No strings attached, where your privacy is also your security—your pleasure.

Temptation. Short, sweet, and directly to the point.

Where you could fall from grace and never want to go back.

He lifted high his brandy glass, toasting himself, and took a long swig. It would solve so many of his own problems, the problems of his friends as well. And no doubt, if he struggled with such things, countless others did too.

Unable to resist such a brilliant plan's lure, he stood and crossed his study in several wide strides, heading to the door. It was still somewhat early in the night, surely his friends would be still lingering at White's. So with an eager expectation, he rode off into the night, the irritation of his boredom long gone.

In its place, something far more hazardous.

Determination.

Chapter One

Lady Liliah Durary urged her mare, Penny, into a rapid gallop as she flew through Hyde Park. A proper lady should have a care about the strolling couples about the park. A proper lady should not ride at such breakneck speed. A proper lady should obey her father in all things.

Liliah was *not* a proper lady.

And hell would have to freeze over before she'd ever even try.

Tears burned the corners of her eyes, blurring her vision as she urged Penny faster, not caring that she was in a miserable sidesaddle—or that her speed was indeed dangerous for her precarious position. She wanted to outrun her problems—rather, *problem*. Because aside from the one damning issue at hand, life was otherwise quite lovely.

Being the elder daughter of a duke had its distinct advantages.

Of course, it had its distinct disadvantages as well. Like your father demanding you marry your best friend.

Who so happened to be in love with your other best friend.

It was a miserable mess . . . and she was caught in the middle of it all. If only her father would see reason! Yet asking such a thing was like expecting her mare to sprout wings and fly: impossible.

She slowed Penny down to a moderate walk and sighed deeply, the light breeze teasing the strands of unruly blond hair, which came loose from her coiffure as a result of her quick pace. She blew a particularly irritating curl from her forehead, and tucked it behind her ear. Glancing about, she groaned, remembering that she hadn't taken a maid with her. Again.

Thankfully, the staff at Whitefield House was accustomed to her constant disregard of propriety. Maybe Sarah, her maid, would notice and make herself scarce, giving the impression she was with her mistress. Liliah bit her lip, turning her mare toward home—even if that was the last place she wished to be—simply for Sarah's sake. It wouldn't go well for her maid if her father discovered the way his staff allowed his unruly daughter far more freedom than he did, and should he discover it, such freedom would end abruptly—and badly.

Being attached to the staff—especially her maid Sarah—Liliah increased her pace. Besides, running from problems didn't solve them. As she swayed with the steady rhythm of Penny's trot, she considered the situation at hand once more.

It made no sense.

Yet when had one of her father's decisions required logic? Never.

Her best friend Rebecca was delightful and from a well-bred and heavily pursed family. There was no reason for the family of her other best friend Meyer, the Baron of Scoffield, to be opposed to such a match. Yet Meyer's father refused to see reason, just as Liliah's father refused. Only Meyer's father, the Earl of Greywick, had threatened to disinherit his son and grant the title to a cousin when Meyer had objected to the arrangement.

It was wretched, no matter how one looked at it. Love matches were rare amongst the ton, and here was a golden opportunity for each family—squandered.

It was true, Liliah was quite the match herself. The elder daughter of a duke, she understood she was quite the heiress and pedigree, yet was her breeding of more importance than Rebecca's? She doubted it.

Apparently, her father didn't agree.

Nor did Lord Greywick.

As she crossed the cobble street toward her home, she took a deep breath of the spring air, feeling her freedom slowly sifting through her fingers like dry sand. As Whitefield House came into view, she pulled up on the reins, halting Penny's progress toward home. The horse nickered softly, no doubt anticipating a thorough brush-down and sweet oats upon returning, yet Liliah lingered, studying the stone structure. One of the larger houses in Mayfair, Whitefield demanded attention with its large stone pillars and wide, welcoming balcony overlooking the drive. It fit her father's personality well, as if magnifying his overinflated sense of importance. Reluctantly, she urged Penny on, taking the side entrance to the stable in the back.

Upon her arrival, a stable boy rushed out to greet her, helping her dismount. Penny jostled the lad with her head, and he chuckled softly, petting her velvet nose.

"I'll take care of Penny, my lady. You needn't worry." With a quick bow, the boy led the all too pampered horse into the stable, murmuring softly as they walked.

Carefully glancing around, once she was certain that no one lingered about, she rushed to the servants' entrance just to the side of the large manor. The heavy wooden door opened silently and she slipped inside, leaning against the door once it was closed. Her eyes adjusted to the dim light, and she took the stairs to the second floor, turning left down a small hall and turning the latch on the door that would lead to the gallery, just a short distance from her chambers. The metal was cool against her gloved hand as she twisted, then peered out into the sunlight-filled room. Breathing quietly, she listened intently for footsteps or voices. Just before she dared to step out, Sarah, her maid, bustled down the hall, a pinched frown on her face as she opened the door leading to Liliah's rooms.

After waiting one more moment, Liliah stepped from the servants' hall, rushing her steps till she approached her room, then slowed as if she weren't in a hurry at all, just in case someone noticed her presence.

Quickly, she opened the door to her room and swiftly shut it silently behind her, Sarah's relieved sigh welcoming her.

"My lady! You've not but a moment to lose! Your father is searching about for you! When he noticed me, he bid me find you, but I fear he is growing impatient. He was in the library."

"Quick, help me disrobe. I need an afternoon dress." Liliah started to tug off her gloves, exchanging them for ones that did not bear the marks from the leather reins, as Sarah made quick work of the buttons on her riding habit.

In only a few short minutes, Liliah was properly attired—all evidence of her earlier unchaperoned excursion tucked away. And with a quick grin to Sarah, who offered a relieved sigh, Liliah left her chambers and strode down the hall as if without a care in the world.

When in truth, the cares were heavy upon her indeed.

Because her father rarely spoke to her, unless demanding her obedience in some matter—and she knew exactly what he had on his mind.

Drat.

She clasped her hands, trying to calm the slight tremble as she took the stairs and walked toward the library. How she hated feeling weak, out of control in her own life! With a fortifying breath, she made the final steps to the library entrance, the delicate clink of china teacups drifting through the air.

"Your Grace." Liliah curtseyed to her father, taking in the furrow in his expression, drawing his bushy salt-and-pepper eyebrows like thunderclouds over his gray eyes.

"At last. I was about to begin a search," he replied tersely, setting down his teacup and gesturing to a chair.

"Forgive me, I was quite absorbed in my—"

"Book, I know. Your little maid said as much. And I'll remind you that you mustn't spend so much time engaging your mind. Fine-tune your other qualities. Your pianoforte could benefit a great deal from some practice." He sighed, as if already tired of the conversation with his daughter.

Liliah bit her tongue, not wishing to initiate a battle

of wills just yet; she'd save the fight for a more worthy cause.

The only worthy cause of the moment.

"Now that you're here, I need to inform you that Lord Greywick and I have decided on a date—"

"But, Your Grace . . ."

His brows knit further over his eyes, and he glared, his expression frosty and furious. "Do not interrupt me."

Liliah swallowed, clenching her teeth as she nodded.

"As I was saying . . ." He paused, arching a brow, daring her to interfere again. "Lord Greywick and I are tired of waiting. We've been patient, and your progress with Greywick's heir is apathetic at best. Therefore, tonight, at the Langford rout, Meyer will be asking you for two waltzes. That should set up the perfect tone for the banns being read in two weeks' time. Hence, you shall be wed at St. George's in two months. That is beyond generous and I—"

"It is anything but generous and you well know it!" Liliah couldn't restrain herself any longer. Standing, she took position behind the chair, her fingers biting into the damask fabric as she prepared for battle.

One she knew was already lost.

"How dare you!" Her father's voice boomed.

"Father, Meyer has no interest in me! How long will you imagine something greater than friendship?"

"I care not if he gives a fig about you!" her father roared, standing as well.

"I refuse." Liliah spoke softly, like silk over steel as she clenched her teeth.

Her father took a menacing step forward. "There is no other way. And consider this: If this arrangement is not made, your friend will lose his title. Do you think that Lord and Lady Grace will allow their daughter to be married to a man with no means? No title?" He shook his head, his eyes calculating. "They will not. So cease your reluctance. There is no other option." He took a deep breath and met her gaze. "I suggest you prepare for tonight; you'll certainly be the center of attention and you should look the part. You're dismissed." With a quick wave of his fingers, he turned and went back to his tea, sitting down.

Tears burned the back of Liliah's eyes, yet she held them in till she spun on her heel and quit the room, just as the first streams of warm tears spilled down her cheeks.

Surely there had to be another way?

Perhaps there was, but time was running out.

For everyone.

The Langford rout was buzzing with activity from London society's most elite, the *bon ton*. The orchestra's sweet melody floated through the air, drowning out most of the buzzing hum of voices. The dancers swirled around, a kaleidoscope of pastel colors amidst the gentlemen's black evening kits. Ostrich and peacock feathers decorated the main banquet table, along with painted silver eggs. But the beauty of the ballroom was lost on Liliah; even the prospect of a treacle tart didn't boost her mood. She meandered through the crush of humanity, swiping a glass of champagne from a passing footman. Sipping the cool liquid, she savored the bubbles as her gaze sharpened on her target.

Lady Grace—Rebecca—danced gracefully as she took the practiced steps of the quadrille. Rebecca smiled at her partner, and Liliah watched as the poor sop all but melted with admiration. Stifling a giggle, she waited till the dance ended, and made her way toward her friend. As she drew near, Rebecca caught sight and raised a hand in a wave, her overly expressive eyes smiling as wide as her lips.

"Liliah! Did you only just arrive? I was searching for you earlier." Rebecca reached out and squeezed Liliah's hand.

"I stalled," Liliah confessed.

Rebecca's smile faded, her green eyes no longer bright. "Did it work?"

"No." Liliah glanced away, not knowing if she could handle the heartbreak that must be evident in Rebecca's gaze.

"We understood it was a small chance. We must now simply seize every opportunity." Rebecca spoke with far more control than Liliah expected. As she turned to her friend, she saw a depth of pain, yet a depth of strength in her gaze.

"There's always hope," Liliah affirmed, squeezing her friend's hand.

"Always. And that being said, I must now seize this present opportunity." Rebecca's face lit up as only one deeply in love could do, and curtseyed as Meyer approached.

The Baron of Scoffield approached, but Liliah ever knew him as simply Meyer. Their friendship had been immediate and long-standing. Ever since Liliah, Rebecca, and Meyer had snuck away during a fireworks display at Vauxhall Gardens, they had created a special bond of friendship. But over the years, that friendship had shifted into something deeper between Meyer and Rebecca, while Liliah was happy to watch their romance bloom. Meyer's gaze smoldered as he studied

Rebecca, a secretive smile in place. As Liliah turned back to Rebecca, she saw the most delicate blush tint her olive skin. Liliah blushed as well, feeling like an intruder in their private moment. "I'll just leave you two . . ." She trailed off, walking away as she heard Meyer ask Rebecca for a dance.

Liliah sipped the remaining champagne, watching her friends dance. Their eyes never left each other's; even if they switched partners for the steps, they always came together, their love apparent for anyone who cared to look.

It was beautiful, and it was for naught.

As the dance ended, the first strains of a waltz soared through the air. What should have been beautiful was poisoned, and her heart felt increasingly heavy as Meyer walked in her direction, his lips a grim line.

He didn't ask, simply held out his hand, and Liliah placed hers within his grasp, reluctantly following as they took the floor.

"By your expression, I can only assume you had as much progress with your father as I've had with mine," Meyer said, his brown eyes sober as his gaze flickered away—likely looking for Rebecca.

"Your assumption would be correct," Liliah replied.

Meyer took a deep breath, meeting her gaze. "We'll figure something out."

"But Meyer—" Liliah started.

"We will. We just need to bide our time till the opportunity presents itself." He nodded with a brave confidence in his deep eyes.

"But what if we don't?" Liliah hated to give voice to her deepest fears, watching as Meyer's brave façade slowly fractured.

"Liliah, I—I can't think of that. I'm damned if I do,

damned if I do not. I'm sure your father reminded you about my title—"

"And how Lord and Lady Grace wouldn't consider you without a title . . ."

"Exactly. I have to hold on to hope. But I, I do need to tell you . . . Liliah, if we are forced . . . nothing between us will change." He lowered his chin, meeting Liliah's gaze dead on, conveying words he couldn't speak out loud.

"Thank you," Liliah replied, feeling relieved. As much as she hated the idea of a platonic marriage, it hurt far worse to think of the betrayal that would haunt them all should Meyer take her to bed. It hurt to think she'd never know physical love, yet what choice did they all have? Should they take that step, Meyer would be thinking of Rebecca during the act, Liliah would know, and would not only be betraying her friend, but how could she not be resentful? Far better for them to simply bide their time till an arrangement could be made—she would simply step aside. Maybe take a lover of her own?

How she hated how complicated her life had become.

Liliah took a deep breath, mindlessly performing the waltz steps. A smile quirked her lips as she had a rather unhelpful—yet still amusing—thought.

"Ah, I know that smile. What is your devious mind thinking?" Meyer asked, raising a dark brow even as he grinned.

Liliah gave him a mock glare. "I'm not devious."

"You are utterly devious." Meyer chuckled. "Which makes you a very diverting friend indeed. Now share your thoughts."

Liliah rolled her eyes. "Such charm. Very well, I

was simply thinking how it would be lovely if we could simply make the wedding a masquerade and have Rebecca switch places with me at the last moment! Then you'd marry her rather than me and it would be over and done before they could change it!" She hitched a shoulder at her silly thoughts.

Meyer chuckled. "Devious indeed! Too bad it will not work." He furrowed a brow and glanced away, as if thinking.

"What is *your* wicked mind concocting?"

"Nothing of import." His gaze shifted back to her. "Your mentioning of the masquerade reminded me of an earlier conversation with a chum."

Liliah grinned. "Is there a masquerade ball being planned?" she asked with barely restrained enthusiasm.

"Indeed, but it is one to which you will not be invited, thank heavens." He shook his head, grinning, yet his expression was one of relief.

"Why so?"

"It's not a masquerade for polite society, my dear. And I shouldn't have even mentioned it."

"A secret? Meyer, you simply must tell me!"

"Heavens no! This is not for your delicate—"

Liliah snorted softly, giving him an exasperated expression, before she slowly grinned.

"Aw hell. I know that smile. Liliah . . ." he warned.

"If you won't tell me, then I can always ask someone else—"

"You'll do nothing of the sort!"

"You know I will."

"You're a menace!" Meyer hissed, his expression narrowing as the waltz ended.

"So, you'll tell me?" Liliah asked, biting her lip with excitement.

Meyer was silent as he led them to a quiet corner of the ballroom, pausing beside a vacant alcove.

"This is a yes!" Liliah answered her question, squeezing his forearm as her hand rested upon it.

"I'm only telling you so that I can properly manage what you hear. Heaven only knows what you'd draw out of an unsuspecting swain. At least I'm immune to your charms and won't give in to your pleas."

Liliah almost reminded him that he was doing just that—but held her tongue.

"There is a . . . place." Meyer spoke in a hushed whisper, and Liliah moved in closer just to hear his words above the floating music. "It's secretive, selective, and not a place for a gently bred lady, if you gather my meaning."

Liliah nodded, hanging on every word.

"Only few are accepted as members and it's quite the thing to be invited. One of my acquaintances was far too drunk the other night and spoke too freely about this secretive club—mentioning a masquerade. That is all."

Liliah thought over his words, having several questions. "What's it called?"

Meyer paused, narrowing his eyes. "Temptations," he added reluctantly.

"And they are having a masquerade?" Liliah asked, a plan forming in her mind, spinning out of control.

"Yes. And that is all you need to know."

Meyer broke their gaze and looked over his shoulder at the swirling crowd.

"Go to her. We still have one waltz left and then I'll ask you all the questions you'll refuse to answer." She winked, playfully shoving her friend toward the dance floor.

"When you put it that way . . ." He rolled his eyes and walked off toward the crowd.

Liliah thought back over what Meyer had said, considering his words—and what they might mean. A masquerade—inappropriate for ladies.

It sounded like the perfect solution for a lady wishing to be utterly inappropriate. All she had to do was discover the location, steal away, and maybe, just maybe . . . she'd get to experience a bit of life before it was married away. Was that too much to ask? Certainly not, and as long as she knew the name, surely she could discover the location.

For the first time since this whole misbegotten disaster, she felt a shred of hope.

Utterly scandalous hope.

Chapter Two

"Lucas!"

Heathcliff's booming voice rattled about in Lucas's head. It had been a long night. Several club members had been removed from the premises, creating a large upheaval in the otherwise smooth production of last night's events. Tonight would hopefully be less eventful—yet masquerade balls usually presented their own risks—and rewards.

"I'm in here. Bloody hell, what do you want? And can you please keep your voice down?" Lucas's voice was thick from lack of sleep and parched from too much brandy the night before.

"There you are. You look like hell, get up. Busy day today. Last night was fun, eh? Nothing like a good brawl." Heathcliff Marston, Viscount Kilpatrick, was a large man, his Scottish brogue as thick as his arms and his smile as broad as his shoulders. A mountain of a man, he was one of Lucas's two greatest friends, and the largest pain in the arse.

Lucas slowly stood from his position behind his desk. He'd never made it to his rooms last night, simply surrendered to sleep at his study's wide mahogany desk. His back protested in pain as he stood. Wincing, he groaned. "I'm too bloody young to feel so bloody old."

"Speak for yourself." Heathcliff shrugged. Never one to be called by his title, Lucas had grown accustomed to the almost plebian manner of his friend. Most days it was refreshing—today it was annoying.

"Did you want something? Other than to irritate me to death?"

Heathcliff chuckled. "Tempting. But I'm pretty sure the devil can't die, so I'll take the second option—yes, I need something."

"And that is?" Lucas asked, rotating his neck, trying to work the kinks out of it.

"It would seem that . . . well. We have a leak."

"Leak?" Lucas blinked in confusion. "Damn rain. In the roof?"

"No. As in leak of information. Holy hell, you're slow this morning."

Lucas swore under his breath. "Tell me you didn't say anything to Ramsey."

"Do I look like an idiot?"

"Ye—"

"I'll answer that for you. No. I'm damn brilliant and I kept my mouth shut."

"For once."

"That and Ramsey would be hotter than Hades about this. You know how he hates anything that whispers the word *scandal*—"

"Which is the fullest of ironies, that he's participating in this club."

"I never said the man made sense."

"Here, here." Lucas knocked his fist on the desk. "But the man's brilliant with numbers—so let's just keep this bit of information to ourselves. What do you know?"

Heathcliff strode to a chair opposite Lucas's desk. Sprawling on the piece of furniture, he shrugged. "It would seem that last night several young men asked for entrance. None had paperwork or invitations, and neither were their families on the docket for invitation."

"Damn."

"Exactly."

"And right before the masquerade."

"This poses a bit of a difficult security threat." Heathcliff leaned forward. "I think we should simply double the guard in front, and check all vouchers. No one gets in unless they have their golden invitation."

Lucas pinched the bridge of his nose. "Several gentlemen will not appreciate that. They expect their level of membership to entitle them to—"

"It's the masquerade." Heathcliff shrugged. "We simply explain that such an . . . event . . . requires additional security. That way no one is the wiser."

"Yes. Yes. That might work. It has to. We've no other option."

"See? Problem solved. You're welcome. Now . . . get dressed. We have work to do and you smell and look like hell." Heathcliff rose, his loud footsteps echoing as he quit the room.

Lucas watched his retreating back, thankful to have solved the immediate issue. Yet the greater one at hand still plagued him.

Who was leaking the information—and how could it be controlled?

The clock chimed, reminding him of the ungodly hour, and with a groan, he twisted his back once more and then left his study. He ascended the stairs and proceeded to his rooms. "Duff?" he asked as he swung open the large double doors. Moments later his valet approached, a knowing quirk of an eyebrow as he assessed Lucas from head to toe.

"Study again, my lord?"

"Indeed. Now if you'll help me dress quickly, I'm in dire need of some hot tea." Lucas started to tug loose his white shirt.

"Of course," Duff replied, his hands moving far swifter than Lucas's.

"And you've prepared my evening kit for tonight?" Lucas asked as he shrugged into a new shirt.

"Complete with your mask, my lord."

"Brilliant." Lucas stifled a yawn. Dear Lord, he should have slept in his bed last night! With the added security this evening, he'd need to be exceptionally vigilant.

After Lucas refreshed his clothing, he gave a quick nod of gratitude to Duff and left for the dining room. Graves, his longtime butler, nodded as Lucas approached. "Everything is as expected."

Lucas nodded once, then heaved a sigh of deep satisfaction. *Familiarity, control, expectation.* They were beautiful words, ones that registered a loyalty deep in his very soul. Just like every morning, he walked to his place setting and took a seat. His glass was filled with water, his teacup with tea—two sugars, no milk—and a silver spoon rested upon his saucer. He lifted it and stirred the tea, watching as the steam swirled around his fingertips, warming them. Coddled eggs and three rashers of bacon sat upon a single piece of buttered toast, like every morning. He draped his napkin over his lap and proceeded to break his fast, his mind already spinning with what needed to be accomplished before that evening.

No less than ten minutes later, he was striding back to his study. He had taken a carriage home from the Barrots' residence, the location of their club, Temptations. The Barrots were long-standing friends who cared little for society's approval, and deeply adored a good party. They were the souls of discretion, and were the closest thing to family that Lucas had. It was brilliant to have the club at a residence rather than an actual hall. They could control the security, the members, and keep their privacy so much easier than if they had tried to establish the gambling hell somewhere else. As he opened the door to his study, he noted that while he had been breaking his fast, the room had been tidied, the fire built back up, and the used brandy glasses replaced with clean ones.

Damn, he loved efficiency.

He studied the lists of things that needed attending to before the party, and willed himself to have the same efficiency as his staff.

With half the sleep.

But it was true what they said: No rest for the wicked.

And tonight was going to be very wicked indeed.

Chapter Three

Liliah studied the slip of paper in her hand, telling herself to be brave. Because right now, she truly didn't feel that bravado. The hired hack swayed back and forth as the horses brought her closer and closer to her destination, and with each step she questioned her sanity.

For pity's sake, she wasn't even sure this was the correct address!

But desperation was the mother of invention, or stupidity. Perhaps both. And she was certainly feeling both, especially since she'd procured her information from Spencer Holloway. But he was the only friend of Meyer's who would not only talk but also most likely would have the information needed. All it took was a little batting of her eyes, a slight pop of her hip, and a warm smile, the rest was history.

And now she felt as if she were going to possibly be history as well. Well, at least if she perished, her father and Lord Greywick couldn't insist Meyer marry her.

She shook her head, astonished at her own melodrama. This was no way to go upon an adventure! Indeed not. Steeling herself against the unknown, she glanced outside at the passing dark London streets. She had expected to be taken to a lesser part of town, yet as the hack continued she noted that they were only several streets away from Mayfair—in a highly affluent residential district. Curiosity melted away her fear and she watched as the road continued to grow increasingly crowded. Thankful she had instructed the hack to drive past the address and then pull over after a few blocks, she watched in earnest as her carriage meandered around a few parked hacks, their drivers all waiting.

But for whom?

Light spilled onto the street from a house just ahead. Its size seemed overstated, and there were footmen at the entrance, speaking with the occupants of each carriage before it pulled up to the residence. Interest piqued, Liliah watched as a carriage was allowed entrance and paused before the stairs. Two men stepped out and up the stairs, another footman speaking with them.

But what solidified her suspicions?

The men wore masks.

It appeared as if Spencer had given her the correct address after all! She shifted to the inside of the carriage, lest anyone see her even through the darkness, and waited as the hack passed several houses before pulling over.

It was now or never.

But she couldn't very well go through the front door. She glanced out the window again. Certainly there was a servants' entrance. If she could gain entrance through there, then maybe she could find a room where she could change, don her mask, and blend in. Absentmindedly, she stroked the small carpetbag beside her, thankful for her foresight in bringing it along.

Taking a deep breath, she opened the carriage door, careful to keep her head down, her hat in place. Without a word, lest she give away her disguise, she handed the driver a few coins along with written instructions to wait for her return—with a promised bonus if he remained.

The driver eyed her curiously, as if not fully believing the story she'd initially given him.

But the lure of money must have been enough, and he gave a grunt with a swift nod and seemed to settle in.

Without wasting a moment, Liliah walked into the shadows, keeping a wary eye out. To anyone looking, she'd appear as a young lad. With her leggings and boots, she looked nothing like the daughter of a duke. Her golden hair was pinned tightly against her head, a hat hiding the gold beauty. Her hands felt cold as she gripped the carpetbag tighter, taking quick steps toward the house that promised escape—for just a night. An alleyway appeared ahead, and she studied the distance between the house and alley. It was indeed close enough that it could lead to the back of the residence. She paused, her gaze lingering on the dark cobbled alley. A slight breeze tossed a piece of discarded parchment across the cobble, giving a ghostlike appearance as it danced. One tentative step at a time, she slowly made her way into the darkness, sighing with relief when the path took a bend toward the house. Stepping quicker, she watched as several lads unloaded boxes from a cart and carried their contents through an open door.

"Hurry, lads!" a man called, and Liliah saw her chance. Rushing forward, she kept her head down and walked up to the door, hoping the light spilling into the narrow street didn't give away her disguise.

"I'm late, excuse me." She spoke in her lowest timbre, brushing past the man.

"Ach, you're going to be sorry, lad," he mumbled, but didn't stop her progress. Rushing inside, she kept her head down as she wove around servants, all rushing to and fro.

"Did ye get the champagne? The lord insisted it be served at eleven!" a woman shouted as she passed Liliah, her accent slightly Scottish.

"Ach, stop your worrying, woman!" another man called out, just as a lad about Liliah's size caught her shoulder as he passed, almost knocking her over.

"Watch it!" he ground out, but Liliah didn't turn, simply kept pushing through, relieved as she saw several doors. As she watched, one swung open, giving her a glimpse at her target.

Golden masks covered each face, and the sound of music like she'd never heard floated through the door, only to be shut off as it closed.

"Are ye just going to stand there and stare, lad? Get to work!" A woman blocked her view of the door, her expression impatient as she raised a dark brow.

Liliah nodded, not trusting her voice, and scurried on, unsure of where exactly to go. Her gaze darted from side to side, and as she moved forward, the hallway cleared up a bit from the sweltering crowd of people. Seeing a door slightly ajar, she glanced behind her. Everyone was far too absorbed in their own duties to take notice, and with a silent breath, she slid into the dark room.

Then gasped.

"I do believe you're in the wrong room, love," said a woman from the corner of the room, whose seductive voice matched her tight silk dress. Liliah blinked at the most scandalously beautiful woman she'd ever seen. Raven hair cascaded down her shoulders and around her back, hiding more skin than Liliah had ever dreamed of revealing.

"I, uh. I—" Liliah swallowed and stumbled back, only to end up closing the door fully rather than stumble through it.

"Oh!" The woman's lips created a perfect O as she slowly approached. "You're the new one, then. Lovely. Truly you'll make a splash. Is that your dress? Let me help you." the woman's movements were graceful, cat-like, and Liliah felt utterly wretched in comparison—a feeling that was entirely foreign.

"Can't you speak, love?" the woman asked gently as she took Liliah's carpetbag and opened it.

"Yes," Liliah answered, piecing together exactly what was going on. Dear Lord. The woman was a courtesan.

The woman thought that *she* was a courtesan as well!

A slow smile spread across her face. What luck!

She forced back the thoughts that questioned her sanity, offering a smile to the woman.

"I'm Lark, sweetling. What's your name?" the woman asked as she opened the bag and pulled out Liliah's somewhat wrinkled dress. "Oh dear, this will never do. Lord Heightfield will never approve of wrinkles. You must learn this now if you're going to make it out there." She gave a stern glance that softened. "Give me just a moment, I'll find you something. It was utter providence I took a moment to myself. I can't imagine if you had wandered out there ill prepared."

"Thank you." Liliah swallowed.

"Just what was your name?" Lark asked, pausing with her hand on the door.

Liliah scrambled for an idea, a grin spreading across her face as one struck her. "Delilah."

"Well, if that isn't the perfect name, I don't know what is. You just wait a moment, Delilah, I'll be right back."

As the door closed, Liliah gave a deep a sigh of relief. Well, she was in. She'd made a friend, and she was about to become a courtesan.

Well, at least pretend to be one.

What could go wrong?

Chapter Four

So far, so good.
Lucas scanned the ballroom below from the balcony, watching as the men cheered at the gambling tables off to the side, while others sauntered from one side of the room to another, studying the competition. While a small string quartet played, it was hardly heard above the constant yelling at the tables. Few danced, and when they did it certainly wasn't the kind of movement you'd see in a London ballroom. Glancing to his list, he checked off the name of every person who was anticipated. The footmen at the gate had turned away several young bucks attempting to sneak in, but so far there was nothing amiss.

Which made him more nervous.

Narrowing his eyes, he studied the golden masks that covered each face, yet certain signs gave each identity away. His gaze locked on Lord Warrington at the faro table, his knee bobbing slightly as he waited for the next turn. Shaking his head, Lucas wondered just how much of the lord's fortune was left after his immense loss just a week past. Moving on, he noticed Lord Kribe with Lark, his paramour—at least his paramour at the moment. He gave a sigh of impatience. Lark tended to be passed around among the gentlemen, and he knew she preferred it that way. Fickle as the day was long. He swallowed his irritation at the beautiful woman. He'd spoken with her concerning the possibility of causing a *disruption* within Temptation by allowing herself to be passed from protector to protector. After assuring him that all her protectors knew her nature, Lucas let it slide. But here was something deeper; he sensed it but didn't push her to reveal it. In truth, he simply suspected that her fickle nature was a form of protection. And he'd not begrudge her that.

They all had their own ways of protecting themselves.

Himself included.

Disregarding the raven beauty, his eye caught a woman in a tight red dress, but her demeanor made her stand out. Her face, though covered with a delicate golden mask, seemed far too attentive to the surroundings—as if seeing them for the first time.

Damn it all.

No courtesan allowed in the Temptations club would act in such a way. All of them had been screened, knew the protocols, and abided by the rules. Yet this woman gawked at every aspect of her surroundings. He needed to figure out just what was going on.

He took the stairs two at a time, thinking back over the list of guests. Had any of the gentlemen notified him of a new courtesan? He came up blank, sure that none had. As he reached the ballroom floor, he pulled his mask down over his face, lest he attract attention, and wove around the assorted tables of cribbage, faro, and hazard to where the woman in question waited, shadowing Lark.

Biding his time, he took the long way around the table, regarding the beauty with flaxen hair. Her dress wasn't overly tight, which was odd since the courtesans habitually wore clothing that revealed more than the ladies of the ton, and her gloved fingers caressed her bared shoulders, as if she found it strange to wear such a gown. Between taking in the party around her, she'd turn to Lark and mimic her movements, the pop of a hip, the slow caress from her neckline to her hip with a gloved finger—they were not the practiced flirtations of a courtesan. They were the awkward movements of the innocent.

Dear Lord.

Who in *hell* would bring an innocent here? Did she recently acquire a protector? Entirely possible—yet if that were the case, why did she not stand beside him? Why Lark?

There were far too many questions, and not enough answers. And he needed answers, damn it all!

Sauntering over to the faro table, he took an empty seat beside Lark, giving her a tight smile as he placed his bet. He watched as Lord Kribe won the round, and Lark squealed, hopping onto his lap and kissing him full on the lips.

A quiet gasp stole all his attention, and he turned. Eyes wide, the woman watched Lark as if astonished at her brazen behavior.

If that scandalized her, heaven only knew how innocent she truly was!

At that moment, she glanced away and met his gaze. He fully expected her to break eye contact, further confirming his suspicions. Yet she did not. Rather he found himself swimming in the depths of a sea-blue gaze, one that did not flinch as he arched a brow. Instead, her tinted lips widened into a welcoming smile that seemed to constrict the very air around him, making it difficult to breathe.

"You are?" he asked, narrowing his eyes and pulling himself into line. It was a bloody courtesan! A professional seductress and flirt. He must be going daft if he let someone like her toy with his emotions.

"Delilah," she answered, and even with the mask covering most of her cheeks, he could see the tinge of a blush.

Raising his suspicions once more.

He couldn't remember the last time he'd seen one of the demimonde blush. But damn it all, if her voice wasn't as welcoming as a silk-sheeted bed. He tried to ignore the way her voice seemed to caress the air, and turned back to the gambling table.

"I see you've met the new girl," Lark whispered into his ear, his body growing irritated at the close proximity. Damn, the woman had snuck up on him!

"New girl?" he asked, forcing his tone to be disinterested, when he truly was hanging on to each word, searching for answers.

"Indeed. I found her earlier. She was quite lost, but I took care of the little lamb. Delicious, isn't she?" Lark straightened, and Lucas relaxed slightly, appreciating the distance. Yet he wasn't finished with the conversation.

Turning to look over his shoulder, he asked, "Just where did you say you found her?" He cared not that the woman in question was just over his other shoulder, easily hearing every word.

"In the servants' entrance just past the kitchens," Lark replied, hitching a shoulder, causing the shoulder of her deep blue gown to slide from her body.

"Excuse me." Lucas nodded to the other men at the table and stood, but as he turned to address Delilah, she was nowhere in sight.

"Blast it all," he muttered, scanning the room. Catching a flash of red just across the ballroom, he started toward it. He watched as a door opened and closed, a glimpse of flaxen hair giving him the only clue he needed to give chase. He waited till he was through the thickest of the crowd, then darted around the last two tables, wrenching the door open. A vacant hall loomed to the left and right, and he paused, listening. Soft footsteps sounded from the right, and he took off, certain he'd catch up, only to come up empty as he reached the end of the hall. Listening, he slowly approached the nearest door. Gripping the handle tightly, he opened it quickly and discovered not a girl but a staircase. A soft gasp reaching his ears was all the encouragement he needed, and he was once again giving chase. The staircase stopped at a door that opened to the balcony he had only recently vacated, and sure enough, Delilah was slipping through one of the doors in the hall. A smile tipped his lips as he stalked his prey, knowing she had no means of escape. The few doors from the balcony held rooms of the private residence of Lord and Lady Barrot. Most were likely to be vacant at the moment, as the night was still young—

but there was no escape except through the door which she had just entered.

His hand closed around the cold metal of the door handle and he slowly turned the knob, opening the door silently. He stepped over the threshold and blinked.

"Did you enjoy our game of hide-and-seek, my lord?" the silken voice asked from her reclined position on the bed that dominated the room.

That was unexpected.

He was fully anticipating a woman in hiding, a woman keeping secrets.

Not a woman playing games.

A few candles illuminated the room just enough to make out her masked face. His gaze lowered to her shoulders, then to the soft swell of her breasts, the sight enticing him in ways he hadn't explored in years.

But far more distracting was her rapid breathing, and the way her leg trembled as it was tucked neatly behind the other. Knowing how to read people was one of the most crucial skills in operating a gambling hell—especially one as exclusive and illusive as Temptations—and Lucas prided himself in those particular skills.

"I must confess that I did not. Why were you running?" he asked at last, taking slow strides toward her, trying to ignore just how inviting the bed appeared at the moment.

She shrugged delicately, her gaze flickering to his left, then back to meet his once again. "Don't you ever tire of the predictable?"

He chuckled, shaking his head. "I would say no. I rather delight in all things predictable. It's so much easier to anticipate life that way, don't you think?"

"No. While I can understand the siren call of exerting control in one's life, you cannot expect me to believe that a man such as yourself, a man *here*, would rejoice in the mundane."

He hitched a shoulder, his knees almost touching the bed as he towered over her. "I never once said I enjoyed the mundane. Just the predictable. But you never answered my question. Why did you run? You had no expectation for me to follow . . . or did you?"

"You asked Lark about me, and I figured I had sparked your interest." She smoothed her skirts, a move that triggered a million memories of debutants in the ballroom, debutants in parlors awaiting swains— hell, even his own mother smoothing her skirt before she spoke when uncomfortable.

Surely not.

How would a deb know about the club . . . let alone find it?

Impossible.

Rather, it should be. The thought made his hot blood run cool. There was one way to find out for certain.

"You were right," he replied in his most seductive tone. It was foreign on his lips, but he pressed forward. Placing one knee on the bed, he leaned in closer to her, watching as her blue eyes widened. But rather than edge away, she sat motionless, watching him with an odd wonder, a strange curiosity that was utterly seductive in its innocent nature.

Tugging off his glove, he reached up and caressed her bare shoulder with his hand, the sensation of her skin against his hand was like touching a smoldering coal that threatened to bring his body to life in ways he'd rather ignore. Her red lips parted, a slight gasp at the contact, but she leaned into his hand as if the warmth, the touch were welcome. A pink tongue darted out to lick her plump lips, and without thinking, Lucas leaned forward, capturing them. All thoughts flew from his mind as his body ignited with a long dormant passion that burned from the inside out. Her lips weren't enough, and he closed the distance between their bodies, glorying in the way she immediately reclined onto the soft mattress. Every inch of his body hardened as he deepened the kiss, only to have the bloody masks in the way. A flick of his wrist sent his sailing across the room. He quickly removed hers as well, the metal making a slight clink on the wooden floor as it landed. His hands reached into her hair, his fingers trembling at the thick, soft texture of the golden locks, and he groaned as her hands found his hair as well, tugging, caressing—mimicking.

Bloody hell.

Mimicking.

He broke the seal of their kiss and met the confused gaze of the woman who had utterly shredded his prized self-control. She was even more beautiful than he had anticipated. Her skin was like lit alabaster, with the smallest hint of freckles across her nose. Dark lashes framed expressive eyes that were openly searching his.

"Why did you stop?" she asked, her tone thick with arousal, reminding him that, indeed, he didn't need to stop . . .

Yet in the same moment, his suspicions were more insistent than his very demanding body. "Who are you?" he asked, his body still poised over hers, his lips only inches away.

"Liliah," she whispered. Then swallowed. "Delilah," she finished.

But it was all he needed to break through the passionate haze and gather his thoughts.

"Which one is it?" he asked, his tone harsh.

She sighed. "Liliah, if you must know. What is your name?"

Liliah. Somehow it fit her, and it surprised him that she was honest. He rather expected her to continue with the charade. "Luc," he answered, giving only the barest of information.

"Luc." Her voice caressed his name, sending a demanding throb to his lower regions that demanded release. A pink tongue darted out as she licked her lower lip, inviting him. He knew he must ask the questions rather than succumb to the temptation—the irony wasn't lost on him—that she presented. Yet one more kiss surely wouldn't hurt? He leaned forward slowly, watching in satisfaction as her eyes fluttered closed as he met her lips, savoring her flavor for one more stolen moment.

"Lucas, damn it all, where is he?" Heathcliff's voice sounded from the hall, the sound sobering him like a jump into a frozen lake. Withdrawing from the kiss, he watched Liliah's eyes dart to the door, then back to him, worry etched in her features as she reached up a tentative hand and touched her maskless face.

"Having second thoughts?" Lucas arched a brow as he slowly stood from the bed.

Her eyes narrowed slightly. "No, but privacy is a commodity I prize."

"On that we can agree." Lucas shook his head and strode to the door, then paused before opening it, glancing over his shoulder. "Stay here."

He didn't wait for her to reply, simply opened the

heavy door and slipped into the hall. Heathcliff was at the end of the hall, wiping his hand down his face in an exasperated and frustrated manner.

"Do I even want to know?" Lucas asked as he approached his friend.

"Bloody hell, where have you been?" Heathcliff threw his hands up in irritation. "Damn it all, we have a bit of a situation. I addressed it as best as I can, but we have need to calm Ramsey the hell down. He's in Lord Barrot's office. Come."

Heathcliff strode away, yet Lucas paused, his gaze darting back to the room, then to his friend. "One moment."

Pausing, Heathcliff turned, giving his friend an impatient glare. "Yes?"

Lucas ran his hand through his hair, sighing. "I'll go to Ramsey and speak with him . . . but I need you to watch someone for me."

"Did someone get in?" Heathcliff took a wary step toward his friend.

Lucas blew out a breath. "Possibly. Though it's not what you're thinking. She's in the second room on the right. I'm not finishing questioning her."

Heathcliff's face split into a wolfish grin. "Is that what we're calling it? I can't remember the last time you actually 'questioned' a woman." He waggled his eyebrows and started down the hall.

Lucas rolled his eyes. "It's nothing of the sort, just don't let her out of your sight, there's something she's hiding." He waved his hand in a dismissive gesture and started down the hall, but damn it all if his ears didn't capture the soft sound of the door opening. And he sure as hell couldn't ignore the way his body all too clearly remembered her taste, her soft acceptance of his attention, the way rosewater clung to her skin.

Pushing the memories aside, he made his way to Lord Barrot's office, determined to focus on the problem at hand.

Only then did he realize he hadn't a clue what exactly that problem was.

Bloody hell.

Chapter Five

Liliah listened carefully for the sound of Luc's voice, inching her way toward the door. The voices were too far away for her to make out the words, but just as she was about to open the door, she heard footsteps. Rushing back to the bed, she held her breath.

She should be trying to escape, she should be putting on her mask and hiding—yet she traced the outline of her lips, reliving her first kiss. Surely he had heard the mad pounding of her heart, felt the slight tremble of her hands, but all she wanted to do was taste his kiss once more, reliving the maddening sensation of his body pressed against hers and the delightful pleasure it evoked.

The door handle turned, and Liliah held her breath.

Only it wasn't Luc.

The man's smile widened, then froze. "Please tell me you're not who I think you are . . ."

Closing her eyes, she wished she'd have donned the mask after Luc left, but it was too late. "That depends on who you think I am." Liliah forced a confident smile, standing from the bed and tilting her head. Dear Lord, she hoped she was playing the part well enough!

The imposing man practically filled the door, and he finished stepping through it, then closed it softly—the gentleness a complete contradiction to his size. "Perhaps I'm mistaken." He answered too quickly, raising her doubts. "Won't you come with me? Lord Heightfield wishes to"—he coughed—"question you." He bit back a grin. "Don't forget your mask . . . my lady." He winked and opened the door.

Drat.

Liliah sighed and walked over to her discarded mask, lifting it and carefully placing it back over her face. With a hesitant step, she followed the man into the hall. The hall opened onto a balcony and she glanced over the edge as they walked by, taking in the view. Away from home, practically compromised by a man she barely knew, and following another stranger toward a dark stairway weren't exactly the most ladylike or safe behaviors. The full weight of her predicament weighed on her shoulders. Escape was necessary, especially if the man in front of her knew her identity.

The last thing she needed was for word to get back to her father. Perhaps if she disappeared now, then no one could prove her attendance? It was worth an attempt.

They took the stairs and turned left down a shadowed hall. Voices filtered through the closed door as they approached.

"One moment." The man spoke quietly, opening the door and slipping inside.

Seconds later she was running down the hall and taking the door that she had used to slip from the ballroom when Luc initially suspected her. That first plan had worked brilliantly—and she only prayed her next plan would work equally well. She took the stairs swiftly, her feet going as fast as possible. Not knowing just how much time she had until she was missed, she burst through the door that led to the servants' hall, and almost collided with a woman carrying a basket of bread.

"Oh!" the woman gasped, lifting the basket high so that Liliah didn't unsettle its contents. Without pause, Liliah set her sights on the open back door, slowing only enough to not gain attention. She nodded to a few servants that passed, who gave her questioning glances but said nothing. Thankfully the door was unguarded, and she slipped out into the night. Running down the alley, she prayed that no one lurked about, and heaved a large sigh of relief when the hack came into view. The driver's snores reached her ears, and she broke into a wild grin. She pounded on the carriage twice, and the driver jerked awake and spun toward the noise. Liliah nodded once, stepped into the carriage, and closed the door, biting her lip as the carriage slowly pulled away into the dark night. She likely startled the driver with her change in attire, but at least she wore the mask to lend her some privacy. She accepted her left-behind carpetbag as a total loss, but she counted it a worthy price for the escapade of the evening.

A hysterical giggle started deep in her belly, transforming into a laugh born out of fear and adrenaline. What a fantastic adventure! Her heart pounded with residual fear, yet she relived each moment with utter joy. Especially the stolen moments with Luc.

Her heart pinched at the thought that she'd never know his kiss again, nor would she likely be able to return to the club. It was a pity, she rather liked her time there—with him. It was a beautiful thing, to be wanted, to experience passion. It gave her a new understanding of Rebecca and Meyer, and it brought her own future into sharper focus. As the carriage rolled on toward home, she grew increasingly contemplative. After experiencing passion, she wasn't willing to give it up so easily. One kiss, a few stolen moments weren't enough. Not when she was facing a very platonic marriage just over the horizon. Yet she didn't see a way to steal any more moments, nor did she want them with just anyone. It was a problem, one that had no ready answer.

The hack pulled up a block away from her home, and Liliah slipped into the dark, giving the driver the promised payment, thankfully stowed away carefully in her slipper. As she wound her way around her home to the servants' entrance, she quietly tiptoed inside, up the stairs, and down the hall before collapsing—fully clothed—on her bed.

Perhaps tomorrow she'd think of another brilliant plan.

Lord knows she needed one.

Chapter Six

Lucas pinched the bridge of his nose, breathing deeply. *I will not kill my friend, I will not kill my friend, I will not kill the idiot that is my friend.* "She's gone?" He whispered the words, afraid to release them into the air.

"I would say so." Heathcliff strode into the room as if having not one care in the world, and sat across from Lucas. He relaxed into the wing-back chair, the wood protesting under his weight.

"You're not taking this seriously," Ramsey remarked, his eyes narrowing.

"I always take everything seriously," Heathcliff replied, yawning.

"The hell you do!" Ramsey said, standing, his hands fisted at his sides. "We had two men name their seconds tonight at the hazard table, one of them my bloody uncle!"

"Hazards of the game." Heathcliff chuckled.

"You're not amusing," Ramsey replied icily.

"Both of you, enough. Ramsey, all is resolved, please relax. As for the girl, it's nothing of note. She's an unknown, so be it. At least it was a girl, not some young buck wanting to make a name for himself, eh?" Lucas shrugged, the lie tasting bitter in his mouth.

Ramsey ran his hand through his sandy blond hair. "Very well. I'm going out to check on the tables. Lord knows what other disasters will happen tonight," he mumbled, quitting the room promptly.

Lucas watched as the door closed, his attention arrested by the low chuckle from Heathcliff.

"What?" Lucas bit out.

Heathcliff arched a brow, a knowing grin spreading across his face. "I know who your friend is." He stood slowly, walking toward the fire burning low in the grate.

Lucas closed his eyes, controlling his reaction, his emotions. That encounter with the minx was still fresh in his mind. "Oh?"

"Indeed." Heathcliff glanced over his shoulder.

Lucas took a calming breath. "And are you going to tell me who the bloody hell she is?"

"I can tell you who she isn't."

"Helpful."

"She's not a courtesan, though I'll say she played the part shockingly well."

Lucas's blood heated at his friend's words. "Did you touch—"

"No, I have no business ruining an innocent." He gave a shudder. "Lord knows I'd have to pay for that sin. I much prefer sins I can commit without punishment." He turned to face his friend. "You, on the other hand . . ."

"Her virtue is intact." Lucas sighed dramatically, annoyed with his friend's conversation.

"If my assumptions are correct, only by a thin shred. She might not be bedded, but she certainly was compromised. Her gown alone attested to that truth. That, and, well . . . the fact that your mask was tossed clear across the room, as if you were quite impatient to discard it. I cannot imagine why . . ."

"What of it?" Lucas ground out, his patience wearing thin.

"I just thought you'd like to be fully aware of the situation before you know her name."

"I know her name. It's Liliah." Her name rolled from his tongue like honey, and his body responded.

"Calling her by her Christian name . . ." Heathcliff shook his head. "For shame. No daughter of a duke should give such license to a man not her betrothed."

Lucas froze.

He replayed Heathcliff's words in his head—twice. *No. No, no, no, no!*

"You're serious?" Lucas whispered, his gaze fixed on his friend's face.

"Lady Liliah Durary, daughter of the Duke of Chatterwood."

"Chatterwood." Lucas shook his head. The man was an arse, a political thorn in his side, and one of the most self-righteous, arrogant men with whom he'd ever had the misfortune to share a sordid and distorted past. And Lucas had almost bedded his daughter!

Could the evening get worse?

Of course. She was no longer here.

"You're sure?" Lucas asked, spearing his friend with an unwavering gaze.

"Quite."

"Blasted bloody wretched hell," Lucas swore passionately as he ran his hand through his slightly mussed hair.

Mussed by her hands.

His mind was quick to remember the welcoming sensation of her warm body pressed against his, and he bit back a groan. "What do you suggest we do?"

Heathcliff gave a slow shake of his head. "I'm quite shocked you don't see the real problem here."

Lucas glared at his friend. "Forgive me if there are too many problems at this point for me to be specific about solving one. If you have a brilliant idea, by all means, share it." He gave a wide gesture with his hand and stalked to the sideboard, pouring himself a healthy snifter of brandy.

Lord knew he needed it.

"What strikes me as the most important question is the one concerning how in the bloody hell she even knew about the club's existence," Heathcliff observed smoothly.

Lucas almost choked on his brandy.

As he cleared his throat, he watched his friend approach the table and pour himself a finger of brandy, lifting it in a toast.

"To your biggest problem. For once, it isn't me," Heathcliff teased, saluting his friend and taking a large gulp.

Lucas ground his teeth together as he thought over the situation. His gaze shifted to the remains of brandy in his glass. He swirled the amber liquid, the sharp and sweet scent floating up to his nose. "Motive. She had to have a motive to be here. Don't tell me it was simple curiosity." He glanced back to Heathcliff.

"Perhaps it was, but I would wager that she had

other reasons. And as much as I hate to say it, our best avenue for discovering how she learned of the club would be to ask her directly."

"Hell no!" Lucas backed away from his friend as if his words had been breathed in flames.

"Easy, old man." Heathcliff shook his head as if annoyed by Lucas's overreaction. "I'd rather think you'd be quite interested in seeing the delicate English flower. But if I must, I'd be happy to take your place." He offered a wolfish grin.

"Delicate English flower, my arse," Lucas grumbled. "And what do you expect to do? Waltz up to her doorstep during receiving hours and ask her the pointed question in front of some stodgy chaperone? Why, that will go over splendidly." Lucas chuckled with a sarcastic edge.

"You've no imagination. Your need for control and predictability has robbed you of any ingenuity." Heathcliff rolled his eyes. "We wait till some rout, make an appearance, which will no doubt be the talk of the week. Think of it, the scandalous Lord Heightfield attending a ball, and while you're there, you make conversation. She can't exactly give you the cut direct in such a crowded place, not without causing talk . . ." Heathcliff let the words linger.

Lucas sighed. "I rather thought we discussed your approaching the chit."

Heathcliff's lips tipped into a knowing grin. "I have a feeling she'll be far more amenable to speaking with you . . . if you gather my meaning."

Lucas did, in fact, gather his meaning. And the thought was both terrifying and tempting beyond words. But a ball—damn it all, he avoided those like the plague, rats, and mustard sauce.

"I knew you'd see it my way." Heathcliff downed

the rest of his brandy and set the crystal glass on the table.

"I never once said that." Lucas took a slight sip from his glass.

"Ye will," he answered in his thick brogue that came out when he was greatly amused.

Damn the man. "You can leave now." Lucas arched a brow at his friend, irritated at his cocksure attitude.

"And leave you alone with your thoughts? It always took you longer to process information. I see my presence in your life as a real blessing," Heathcliff said as he closed the door.

Lucas glared at his friend's retreat, then turned back to his brandy. What was going so well earlier had certainly gone to hell in a handbasket in a hurry. But he knew that he had questions.

And Lady Liliah Durary had the answers.

Chapter Seven

Liliah woke up with a pounding headache. After her adventure, sleep had been elusive and fitful. Each time she'd surrender to slumber, she'd be haunted by the face of Luc.

Drat. How she wished she knew his full name. It sounded less real to have such limited information. But in her fitful sleep, she had come to accept two important facts.

First, Luc was somehow involved in the management of the secretive club. Second, she needed to see him again.

Execution of the second act would be far more difficult. Sneaking into the club wasn't going to work a second time. If only she knew more about Luc. With a start, she sat up in bed, a grin spreading across her lips. Meyer. He would know! She wouldn't have to give him all the details either, just enough to gain the much needed information. From there, she could ascertain her next step.

As she rose from bed and rang for her maid, the thought that Luc would seek *her* out filtered through her mind. Yet she dismissed it quickly. Why would he? While she assumed he was at least marginally attracted to her, she didn't delude herself into thinking he had any real connection to her. But, sadly, that was exactly what she needed. An escape, an encounter, and Luc would be a prime candidate to fulfill those needs.

And after her experience last night, those were, indeed, needs.

Sarah knocked gently, and entered at Liliah's welcome. Her hazel eyes carefully studied her mistress. "How are you this morning, my lady?"

Liliah smiled at Sarah's gentle inquiry. "Well enough for the late night we had."

Sarah nodded understandingly. She had waited up for her mistress and helped her quickly disrobe after the escapade. Yet Liliah was careful to not confide all the details of her excursion to her dear maid, lest Sarah be questioned by the duke. Less information was far more prudent for both of them.

"I already arranged for your hot chocolate to be brought up directly," Sarah said, and stood by the vanity, waiting for her mistress.

Wordlessly, Liliah nodded. Sarah picked up a brush from the marble-topped vanity and started to unwind the plait in Liliah's hair. Sighing contentedly, Liliah took a seat at the vanity and closed her eyes, enjoying the sensation of her hair being brushed. As she opened her eyes, she glanced to the wardrobe, considering what she wished to wear for the morning. Sarah made short work of coiffing her hair and was offering options for Liliah's day gown. After she selected a gown of soft green muslin, her hot chocolate arrived. Soon

Liliah dismissed Sarah and strode to her desk. Sending a missive to Meyer was not a wise idea; it could be used against them by their fathers, since only betrothed couples could exchange letters. The duke and earl would leap at the opportunity to move their impending betrothal along quicker. *Drat*.

Liliah worried her lip, then thought over her schedule for the day. The Lyman rout was tonight, and Meyer was sure to attend. The issue was her impatience in waiting that long to speak with him.

Yet there was nothing for it, she must be patient.

And hopefully that patience would pay off in the end.

That evening as her father ignored her presence in the carriage on the way to the Lyman rout, the imp in her was tempted to simply announce that she had been compromised. But the problem came from not knowing the real identity of the person who had compromised her. With her luck, her father would claim it was Meyer and then they'd all be worse off than before. Yet it would be a delight to see her father's expression, knowing that his daughter had dared defy him in such a manner. A slow smile stretched her lips as she tried to keep it from showing. But her smile faded as she considered that her defiance would only serve to punish her sister, who hadn't a rebellious bone in her body. Their father would tighten the leash on Samantha, who was already afraid to even whisper her thoughts into the world. No, Liliah needed to keep her secrets to herself.

The carriage rolled along the cobbled London streets

quickly, and Liliah resigned herself to the silence in the carriage. Silence was preferable to scolding, and truly those were the only options.

They arrived fashionably late, and as soon as she alighted from the carriage, her father gave her a stern glare to serve as warning, made sure more than one matron was available to serve as a proper chaperone, then disappeared into the growing crowd. Relieved to be rid of him, Liliah strode down the hall of the Lyman estate to the open ballroom. The enchanting sound of the string quartet aided in raising her spirits as she took in the swirling sight of dancers gracefully performing the cotillion. Her gaze shifted across the room, taking note of who was in attendance. It was always at this point she wished her mother was still alive, feeding comments and insights into her ear as they entered a ballroom. But wishing didn't erase the past, and her mother had died around four years ago from pneumonia.

Liliah straightened her shoulders, smoothing the soft silk of her sky-blue gown. As she strolled among the people milling about, she caught sight of Rebecca. A welcoming smile brightened her friend's face as she spotted Liliah. Careful to meander around a footman carrying champagne, Liliah started toward Rebecca, meeting her halfway. "Late, as usual," Rebecca teased, her sharp gaze sparkling with intellect.

"I enjoy sneaking in while others are otherwise engaged," Liliah returned with a cheeky tone. "Have you seen Meyer? I have a question for him." Liliah's gaze shifted from her friend to the crowd behind her.

"Have you news?" Rebecca's hopeful tone immediately put a damper on Liliah's impatience.

As she met her friend's expectant gaze, Liliah gave a slow shake of her head, her chest constricting when Rebecca's countenance fell. Reaching out, she grasped Rebecca's gloved hand and squeezed affectionately. "How I wish that I had the news you so long to hear, sweet friend. We shall continue to work toward that end."

Rebecca nodded once, her shoulders straightening with determination. "Indeed. But if that is not what you wish to discuss, what is it that you have on your mind this evening?" Rebecca's green eyes glinted with curiosity.

Liliah bit her lip and glanced away, feeling her face heat with a blush.

"You're simply blooming with color! Tell me! What are you not telling me, and how in the heavens does Meyer know something of which I'm not aware?" Rebecca placed her hands on her hips as Liliah's gaze flicked back to her friend.

"He'd have a fit if he only knew." Liliah grinned widely, giggling under her breath. "He made a slight slip about some information and I took it upon myself to investigate. Apparently there are many venues that gently bred ladies are not allowed to attend," she whispered conspiratorially.

Rebecca's eyes grew wide. "What have you done, Liliah! And don't you dare skip a single detail." Rebecca tugged on her friend's hand and led her toward the edge of the ballroom.

Liliah followed willingly. When they reached the spot that Rebecca deemed satisfactory, Rebecca released her hand and gave her an impatient gaze.

"Well, it truly wasn't Meyer's fault, so you mustn't be cross with him," Liliah explained.

"Very well, continue."

"I learned the location of an exclusive gentleman's club, snuck in, was mistaken for a courtesan—"

Rebecca's gasp was loud enough to attract the curious and disapproving gazes of a few nearby people. Liliah gave a tight smile to her friend and waited till the unwanted attention faded.

"Pardon," Rebecca whispered, her face a mask of shock. "Do continue."

"Only if you promise to not make a spectacle of yourself," Liliah scolded.

Rebecca nodded with emphasis.

"However, I must not have played the part well, for the manager, or some sort of gentleman involved with the club, began to question me. So I fled, but he followed me." Liliah leaned forward, enjoying the retelling of the story.

"And? Did he catch you?" Rebecca asked, then glanced around to make sure their conversation was not overheard. Upon reassuring herself that it was indeed a private conversation, she met Liliah's gaze with an expectant one.

"Yes." Liliah widened her eyes, grinning wildly.

Rebecca gasped, covering her mouth with her white-gloved hand.

"I had snuck into a bedroom—"

"No!" Rebecca whispered a little too loudly, and Liliah gave her a disapproving arch of her eyebrow.

"Carry on." Rebecca lowered her hand and waited with wide eyes.

"He questioned me, then kissed me—and Rebecca,

it was utterly heavenly. I never expected it to feel like that, to make me feel—I don't even know how to explain it. Surely you know, surely you've kissed—" Liliah's words trailed off as she watched her friend's gaze falter.

"Surely not," Liliah almost scolded.

"We have, but it's been . . . a length of time since we've had the opportunity," Rebecca replied softly, her tone thick with disappointment.

"I'm sorry." Liliah gently touched her friend's shoulder.

Rebecca forced a brave smile, then asked, "So who was the man who stole your first kiss?"

Liliah grinned. "Luc, and I haven't a clue as to the rest of his name. Which is why I wish to speak to Meyer. Surely he will be able to help me identify this mysterious man."

Rebecca replied, "This party has become very exciting indeed! Let's go seek him out. Surely neither his father nor yours would begrudge it!" She spoke dryly, her gaze already searching the *bon ton* for her love.

"You always seem to find him before I can, so I'll leave the searching to you," Liliah teased.

"There, over by the faro room." Rebecca nodded toward the other side of the ballroom and started in that direction. Liliah followed, skirting around the edge of the dance floor. As she nodded to several gentlemen, an odd prickling sensation trailed up her spine. Glancing to the left, then to the right, she couldn't find a reason for the strange feeling. Hurrying her steps, she stayed close behind Rebecca as they approached the length of wall where Meyer conversed with several of his chums from his days at Eton.

Liliah curtseyed along with Rebecca as they stopped. Meyer halted his conversation and reached out, taking Liliah's hand first, kissing it quickly. He turned then to Rebecca, and taking her hand with gentle care, he lingered in kissing her gloved fingers. Liliah glanced away at the intimacy in their secretive grin for one another.

Meyer's friends made their introductions then excused themselves, leaving the three of them in relative seclusion. "To what do I owe the honor of two lovely ladies trekking across the ballroom to find me?"

Rebecca blushed prettily under Meyer's intense gaze, and Liliah waited patiently for them to finish.

"It would seem you have information that our dear friend requires," Rebecca replied after a moment, her gaze flickering from Liliah, then focusing back on Meyer.

"Oh?" Meyer arched a brow, turning to Liliah. "I pray it's nothing to do with our previous conversation."

Liliah grinned unrepentantly in response.

"Why do I have an ominous feeling?" Meyer lamented, shaking his head.

"Because you know me well," Liliah answered cheekily.

Meyer waited, his gaze suspicious.

"What do you know about the gentlemen who are involved with the management of the place we mentioned before?" Liliah asked in a roundabout way.

Meyer narrowed his eyes. "I'd say they were a loose interpretation of gentlemen, in the way of their morality. But titled men, powerful men . . . men I'd not wish to cross." He tilted his head. "Why do you ask?"

Liliah tugged on her glove, straightening it. "Does one of them go by the name Luc?"

Meyer's gaze darkened with concern. "Indeed. Why?"

"What is his full name? Or title, if he has one," Liliah asked, her heart pounding with anticipation.

"He would be Lucas Mayfield, the eighth Earl of Heightfield. A dark history if there ever was one. Did you happen to meet the gentleman in question?" Meyer asked slowly, as if afraid to hear the answer.

Liliah bit back a grin. Lucas Mayfield, Earl of Heightfield. A name, she knew his name! It was a small victory, but it seemed quite large at the moment.

"Liliah?" Meyer asked, his tone concerned.

She nodded. "I've met him." *Kissed him, lay on a bed with his body*—She forced her thoughts to halt as a blush crept up her neck and warmed her face violently.

"Do I dare ask *how* you met him?" Meyer asked cautiously.

"No," Liliah answered succinctly, her gaze lingering on the ground a moment before meeting Meyer's puzzled and alarmed expression. "I'm quite certain you don't wish to know."

"I'm quite certain I don't wish to know either, yet part of me wonders if I should at least be aware so that you aren't left to your own devices." Meyer muttered under his breath, his gaze shifting to Rebecca. "Are you aware?"

Rebecca nodded once. She was biting her lip as if trying to keep her silence as she watched Meyer.

Meyer's gaze lifted heavenward as if petitioning the Almighty for aid in dealing with his situation. As he turned his attention back to Liliah, she noted that his gaze shifted to just over her shoulder. She was about to turn when Meyer met her gaze. "Liliah, I need you to be utterly honest with me."

Liliah's brows pinched as she nodded.

"Is there any way that the gentleman you met could be aware of your identity? For the love of Mary, tell me you wore a disguise." Meyer's gaze was worried and he shifted his attention over her shoulder once more.

"I wore a disguise."

Meyer's shoulders relaxed.

"But I think it's also possible that he knows who I am," Liliah finished.

Meyer's expression sharpened as he studied her. "I suggest you skirt around the ballroom to the left, then seek out your father directly, just in case." Meyer's gaze was over her shoulder again, watching someone.

"Why?" Liliah asked, turning to follow Meyer's gaze.

"Why don't you just listen?" Meyer hissed, but it was too late.

Liliah's eyes widened as she took in the dashing figure of Lucas Mayfield, Earl of Heightfield. His midnight-black evening kit seemed far darker than everyone else's in the room, drawing attention to the way the cut of the cloth accented every line of his body. Liliah watched as he turned to his companion, and Liliah recognized him as the man who had attempted to escort her to the study. He was just as tall and broad as she remembered, even more so as the cut of his evening kit accented his wide shoulders.

"Friends of yours?" Rebecca asked softly.

Liliah nodded, unable to speak as she greedily took

in the sight of Luc. It wasn't love, but it certainly was *something*. Attraction, maybe? But it felt more . . . insistent. Was this what lust felt like?

"I've never seen them before," Rebecca commented.

"That's because they don't attend the parties that are of the more proper variety," Meyer commented dryly. "There must be some reason they came out of their self-exile. I can't imagine what that might be."

His tone caught Liliah's attention, and she noted his glare in her direction. "Me? You think they are here on my account?" Liliah asked, though her body warmed at the idea. Yet she didn't expect it to be true. "Rebecca, I'm concerned about Meyer, he's acting quite delusional." She gave a quick wink to Rebecca, who just watched her with wide eyes. Liliah's attempt to lighten the mood had apparently failed.

"What if he is correct, Liliah?" Rebecca asked, her gaze on Meyer, then Liliah, then the two men in question. Her gaze widened, as if trying to take in all the small details.

Liliah didn't blame her. As she scanned the room, she noted that most of the attention of the ton was focused on the new gentlemen in question. Whispers were heard echoing through the hall, as matrons whispered to their charges. Likely warning them, yet secretly wondering if the gentlemen were entering the marriage mart. For if the men were as notorious as Meyer believed, then they were dangerous and delicious—true catches of the season for any unmarried lady of breeding. Their clothing spoke of substantial wealth, and at least Luc was a titled earl. The London social sphere had grown far more interesting.

"You need to stop staring!" Meyer whispered, scolding.

Liliah lowered her gaze, then like a moth to the flame, she hazarded a glance back, watching as Luc's gaze scanned the crowd. His chin was tipped up slightly, as if finding the attention of the ton beneath him. Restlessly, his eyes searched the crowd with each step deeper into the ballroom. Those around him gave a wide berth, all whispering secrets behind gloved hands, as the gaze of the ton moved as one, focused on the two men.

"Who is the other one?" Liliah asked, turning to Meyer.

Meyer sucked in a deep breath, his expression irritated and concerned, as if realizing his advice to avoid the gentlemen was going to be ignored. "That would be the Viscount Kilpatrick. He's a titled Scot, so not one of us, but none of the gentlemen here would dare speak it to his face. Liliah . . ." Meyer drew out her name. "He is not a man to be trifled with, neither of them are. Do you understand me?"

Liliah nodded once, for she did comprehend the danger. But the risk didn't negate the reward. As she searched Meyer's face, it was as if fate were staring back. Her future played out in a flash—holding Meyer's arm as his wife, never holding his heart. Always knowing that he was destined for another woman, knowing she was destined for another man. No love, no passion, no secret jokes, no thrilling jolts of electricity through her system with a heated gaze. Nothing.

It wasn't a future she could resign herself to, ever. As she met Meyer's gaze, it was as if he saw the same thing, only the reversal. Rebecca gasped beside them, pulling Liliah's attention to her friend.

"What is it?" Liliah asked, watching as Rebecca's gaze widened.

"Liliah," she mouthed, and Liliah turned to see what had caught her friend's attention.

The air whooshed out of her lungs as she met clear blue eyes not more than ten feet away. A flicker of amusement flashed across his expression before Liliah was frozen by the icy chill of his regard. She glanced to his side, noting the attention of his friend, the Viscount Kilpatrick. But rather than a chilly stare like that of the earl, the viscount's expression was amused. Full lips spread into a wide grin as he arched a brow in her direction.

Against her better judgment, she grinned back. The viscount gave a slight shake to his head, as if unable to believe her audacity.

She couldn't quite believe it either.

"Baron Scoffield, isn't it?" Luc addressed Meyer, even while his gaze was trained on her. Her face heated with a blush and he raised an eyebrow, then turned his attention to Meyer.

"Indeed." Meyer extended his hand. "Lord Heightfield, is it not?" Even as his greeting was formal, his tone bordered on incivility. Liliah glanced at her friend, shocked and concerned at the potential social implications it could create. Turning to Luc, she watched his reaction.

A corner of his mouth lifted in a half smirk. "Indeed. Would you please introduce us to your companions?"

Meyer's jaw ticked as he ground his teeth, and Liliah held her breath, wondering what course of action Meyer would take. She exhaled as he gestured to Rebecca.

"This is Lady Rebecca Grace." She dipped a slow curtsey.

Meanwhile the crowd around them had grown thick with people wanting to hear what was taking place. Liliah swallowed compulsively, then glanced back to Luc.

"And this"—Meyer sighed—"is Lady Liliah Durary."

Chapter Eight

Luc studied the beauty in front of him as she dropped into a graceful curtsey. Damn it all if that wasn't the same minx who had been haunting him since her abrupt disappearance from the club. Heathcliff was right about her identity, but what was most confusing was why the daughter of a duke would deliberately seek out the dark shadows of his club, presenting herself as a courtesan. Her perceptive blue eyes flashed with intelligence, daring him to call her out.

He wouldn't . . . yet.

He resisted the urge to tug on the collar of his stiff white shirt. The damn ton were circling him like vultures, all fighting for a delicious piece of gossip to take away and titter about with their friends. It reminded him anew of why he avoided these parties and these people like the black plague. Irritation rose within him as he considered his situation. It was Heathcliff's idea, and he had no one to blame but himself for agreeing.

Although a measure of his irritation melted in the heat of his curiosity directed toward the woman before him, he still didn't feel at ease.

Heathcliff was too bloody comfortable with the situation; rather, he was too bloody amused. Which he made blatantly apparent when he stepped forward.

"I don't believe I've had a proper introduction, my ladies. I'm Heathcliff Marston, Viscount Kilpatrick. You may call me whatever you wish." His brogue made the scandalous words even more seductive, and Luc barely resisted rolling his eyes. The crowd whispered loudly behind them, conveying his rakish ways to the rest of the ballroom.

Delightful.

"A pleasure, Lord Kilpatrick." Liliah gave another delicate curtsey, her expression amused.

Which pulled Luc up short.

What in damnation did she have to be amused about? They had figured out her identity, and any association she had with them would serve to scandalize her situation. Yet she didn't seem concerned, and that was troubling, it was odd, it was . . . challenging. Either she was daft, or she had nothing to lose.

If she thought this was amusing, would she allow other liberties? The thought was delicious, and utterly impossible. She was an innocent—at least innocent *enough.* She wasn't one to trifle with, at least without unnecessary risk. And that risk wasn't simply the ire of a scorned woman, it was the social constraints of being forced to marry, of entering into the very convention that turned his heart cold.

Hell would need to freeze over first.

And it would have to be a damn solid freeze.

Heathcliff's voice pulled his thoughts back to the situation at hand. "Lady Liliah, would you do me the honor of this next dance?"

Luc's gaze shot to his friend. Clearly the man was daft. First, because they had shown up to a party, unannounced and probably uninvited—since Luc made it a point to toss out any invitation that dared cross his threshold. Second, because Heathcliff was to bloody prance around in the quadrille? Luc tried to remember the last time he'd seen his friend dance.

And failed to remember one instance.

This ought to be interesting.

"Of course." Lady Liliah blushed prettily, even as her gaze lingered on Luc, causing a strange sensation to rise up within him before he determinedly tamped it down.

She placed her delicate hand in Heathcliff's monstrous one and strolled off toward the dance floor. Luc scoffed silently at the reaction of the ton. As if Heathcliff had become Moses, the ballroom parted like the Red Sea. As the first notes of music hung in the air, the dancers took position. The men cast wary glances toward Heathcliff, while the women's gazes lingered appreciatively. It was nauseating.

"Would you care to dance?"

Luc glanced behind him, watching as Meyer, the Baron of Scoffield, reached out and extended his hand toward the other lady beside him, whom Lucas had utterly dismissed the moment he'd made her acquaintance. Yet the intensity of the gaze between the two people caught his attention. It wasn't the gaze of interest; it was the gaze of desperation.

He'd seen it hundreds of times before. When what you want is just out of reach. You can touch it, but cannot grasp it. Gamblers, men with broken hearts, women offering their love . . . only to have it rejected—it was the same for each one.

Something seemed off.

And he couldn't help but wonder if the lady dancing with his friend was the keeper of many secrets.

Lucas watched as the couple danced past him. The woman ignored his presence, but the man studied him, as if taking his measure. It wasn't the gaze of a man studying a competitor; it was the gaze of a man looking out for a friend.

And as they walked into the center of the room, Lucas's mind filled with questions.

He only hoped that Heathcliff was having better luck finding answers than he.

Chapter Nine

Liliah could feel the gaze of the ton on her back like an open flame. Rather than focus on the attention she was receiving, she kept her focus on the man before her. His ready smile was a contradiction with the size of his frame. He *should* be formidable, yet wasn't. It was his eyes, she decided. They crinkled just enough to put her at ease. He truly was a handsome man, but his appearance was easily glossed over when he stood beside the raw beauty of Luc. Heat simmered just below her skin and she glanced away to the other dancers.

"Ach, why are you grinning so?" Lord Kilpatrick asked, just as they passed one another in the quadrille. Liliah grasped hands with another partner, nodding to the gentleman before releasing his hand and grasping another's and doing a turn. Across the circle, the viscount's expression implied he was more than willing to patiently await his answer.

As the music continued, Liliah again found herself grasping the viscount's hand. "You seem to be a keeper of secrets, my lady," he whispered quickly before releasing her to her next partner.

Liliah wasn't certain how to reply to such a statement, but was blessedly relieved from giving an immediate response as the dance continued. It was several turns later that she was once again with the viscount.

"Perhaps, or maybe you are assuming much where no foundation for truth lies," she answered, then released his hand, taking another's.

An amused smirk tipped his lips, and Liliah wondered how long he'd dance around the topic in which he was likely most interested: how she'd escaped.

It was ironic how they were dancing with their bodies and their words, as the flow of the music prevented a full conversation. As the final strains ended, Liliah curtseyed to her partners, and held her breath as the viscount came to escort her.

"My lady." He offered his arm.

She could have walked away . . . but her curiosity was too strong—far stronger than her good sense—and she took his arm delicately.

She broached the topic boldly. "You wish to know how I escaped?"

The viscount gave her a sidelong glance. "Amongst other things."

"What other things?" Liliah questioned as he took her for a turn about the outside perimeter of the ballroom. The hungry gaze of the ton followed them, but the interest was diminishing.

How fickle society was.

Not that she minded.

"I would think it would be quite obvious, my lord. I ran. However, it leads me to my first question: How were you aware of my identity?" Liliah studied his face, curious if she'd have any inkling if he attempted to lie.

"Running. Why didn't I think of that?" he joked sarcastically, rolling his eyes. It wasn't exactly gentlemanly behavior, but it suited him somehow. "I was more curious as to which exit you took, since they were all heavily guarded."

"Ah, were you expecting trouble, then?" she asked, arching a brow.

The viscount shot her an approving gaze. "Perceptive, aren't you?" He chuckled. "Perhaps, but apparently we weren't vigilant enough."

"If I speak of how I found entry, then I can't come back."

The viscount's caramel-colored brows shot up. "So you're planning to return? Why not use the front door?" he teased.

"I was told that ladies of breeding weren't welcome," Liliah answered cautiously.

He halted his steps, regarding her shrewdly. "That is because ladies of breeding leave as ladies of the night, if they darken the halls."

A shiver of fear trailed down her back, followed by a thrill of excitement. "I shall remember that, and remember to avoid the front door."

"Which begs the question, why were you interested in our little soirée?" the viscount asked, resuming their leisurely walk.

Liliah shrugged slightly, using the gesture to stall and collect her thoughts. She wasn't quite certain how much information she wished to divulge.

"Isn't a lady allowed her secrets? Why, what mystery would I hold if I came clean on all accounts, my lord?" she asked with a cheeky grin.

"Then maybe you'll answer the most pressing question from our perspective," he said, flickering his gaze to her.

"Perhaps."

"How did you even know the club existed?" His words were casual, as was his tone, but the way his shoulders froze momentarily gave away his level of curiosity.

Liliah debated, but figured that it wasn't truly a secret she needed to keep. "A friend slipped, and then when that person refused me additional information, I asked a more . . . enamored friend . . . for further details. It wasn't difficult from that point. You truly should be more careful about who is aware of your little club if you wish to remain so exclusive that even the dandies don't speak of it," she uttered quietly.

"I see." The viscount nodded. "And you'll give me no more information on the topic?"

"I have truly nothing to give. I'd rather think the largest liability you have is me." She shrugged, biting back a grin when the viscount halted his steps abruptly.

His expression registered surprise before quickly being schooled into indifference. "Pardon?"

Liliah took a slow breath, measuring her words, knowing that this was the pivotal point at which she laid her wager on the table, hoping he wouldn't call her bluff. "Of course, my silence would come at a price." She faced him fully, tilting her head and offering a smile.

The viscount grinned slowly, amusement flickering across his expression. "And what price would that be? Surely the Duchy of Chatterwood isn't destitute."

She leaned in, waiting till he followed suit. "But, sir, there are some things that ladies cannot purchase . . .

with their father's money." She leaned back, watching as confusion, then curiosity shifted across his face.

"I see. I wasn't aware I made such an impression on you, my lady."

"Are you certain I'm referring to you?" Liliah asked, embarrassed at her own brazen behavior, yet unrepentant nonetheless.

"I see." His grin widened. "Isn't this interesting?"

"And possible?" she questioned.

"Perhaps," he answered enigmatically, tossing her previous response back at her.

The strains of the cotillion started, and the viscount shifted their position. "Would you do me the honor?"

"Two dances? You certainly wish to cause talk tonight, don't you?" She smiled archly, even as her pulse raced with the excitement of their conversation.

"As I'm already causing talk, why not make it worthy?" he answered. Yet his gaze focused just over her head, as a wicked gleam illuminated his green eyes.

She was about to turn, but he led her toward the dance floor. As the music started, she hazarded a glance in the direction he had focused on earlier.

Luc's heated gaze seared through her, and she wondered if maybe she had just made a deal with the devil.

After all, he was a fallen angel.

And no angel was more beautiful than the Earl of Heightfield.

Chapter Ten

Lucas edged around the dance floor, his gaze trained on his friend, his mind overworking as he considered Heathcliff's curious expression a moment before as he was leading the lady in question back to the dance floor.

Two bloody dances.

He might as well have announced his interest in the *Times*.

Certainly the ton would not expect him to offer for her hand—no . . . there had been no waltz. That would have been the fatal error.

His gaze lowered and he noticed a fleeting brush of Heathcliff's hand along Liliah's waistline as they passed each other in the dance. Hot blood raced through his veins, and there was but one word that echoed in his mind.

Mine.

The possessive nature buried deep within caused all

other emotions to recoil. It was only as he took a step forward that he came to his senses.

Marching out on the dance floor and stealing her away from his friend wasn't going to solve any of their problems; it would simply add to them.

And he had quite enough problems at the moment.

So he bided his time, watching, waiting, and cursing himself a bloody fool for even reacting in such a way.

Hadn't he been down that road once?

Caring for another only led to loss.

Marriage bred betrayal.

And beautiful eyes only told even prettier lies.

Forcing his gaze away, he studied the room. The buzz had died down and he wasn't the center of the gossip at the moment, or it at least seemed that way. A footman passed, and Lucas lifted a glass of champagne from the silver tray, sipping the cool refreshment as he ambled toward the game rooms. Yet as he moved closer, his interest was redirected as he heard Liliah's name mentioned as he passed a brood of dowagers, all cackling amongst themselves.

"Chatterwood is going to have forty fits—"

"If he ever leaves the faro table," another woman chimed in, her gaze sliding to the gaming rooms and then back to her companion.

"True enough. Hadn't you heard that she was betrothed to the Earl of Greywick's son? Is that what you told me, Mary?"

Liliah betrothed? Somehow he doubted the validity of that claim, especially with the man in question utterly desperate for the other lady.

"Well, that is the talk from the duke. Heaven only knows if it's accurate." There were a few titters and

Lucas's interest waned. As he pushed off from the pillar, he heard his name.

"You didn't miss Lord Heightfield's entrance, did you?"

He suppressed a groan.

"Delicious, if I say so myself. But rather untouchable, if you gather my meaning. That's a rake if there ever was one."

Lucas gave his head a shake of amusement, and noted that the music had shifted to a waltz. He ambled around the edge of the pillar and made his way back toward the dance floor, the gambling rooms all but forgotten. It only took a moment to find her among the crowd, her hand regally set up on Heathcliff's arm as they left the dance floor. Lucas sighed in relief, even as he told himself it was because Heathcliff had used sound judgment in not keeping the lady on the dance floor. Heathcliff met his gaze and nodded in acknowledgment. As Heathcliff guided Lady Liliah toward him, his gaze greedily took in her form, his memory all too accurately recalling the shape of her in his hands. Her expressive eyes met his in the most direct manner, and a faint blush tinted her porcelain skin. "My lady." He bowed mockingly.

Her brow pinched slightly, yet she held her head high, nodding once. "My *lord*." She emphasized the word, as if saying it out of courtesy, not respect.

Anger and frustration warred within him at the slight, yet it wasn't unwarranted, he simply wasn't used to being challenged by women. Nor did he appreciate the onslaught of emotion that she provoked within him.

Lucas was about to add to his insulting sins when

the gentleman he'd met earlier all but interrupted. "Lady Liliah?" He held out his hand, and Lucas studied his face.

The man's gaze was severe.

His lips were pressed into a firm line.

His expression resigned and painful.

Yet he took Liliah's hand tenderly, his response at war with everything readable on his visage.

Lucas stepped back, giving the couple room, and turned his attention to Liliah. The teasing light in her eyes was extinguished like a rain-soaked flame, and her shoulders caved in, as if defeated; with a longing in her expression, her gaze flickered to his, then shuttered as she followed the man's lead.

"Interesting," Lucas mumbled, studying their body language. On the dance floor, they kept more than a proper distance between their bodies, their expressions broken in various degrees. It was utterly pathetic and depressing at once.

Heathcliff came to stand beside him. "Odd."

"Indeed," Lucas replied.

Heathcliff shifted his weight to inch closer and leaned forward, whispering quietly. "Our lady friend is quite fascinating."

Lucas tamped down the immediate affirmation, and settled for a simple nod. "Were you able to find out any pertinent information?"

Heathcliff gave a light scoff. "Indeed. And I do believe our greatest threat is not those who sneak in, but ladies who sneak out."

Lucas tore his gaze from Liliah and turned to his friend, confused. "What can you mean by that?"

"I'll explain later." Heathcliff gave a pointed look to the crowded ballroom.

Lucas nodded, though he was curious to the point of distraction. He settled for keeping an eye on Liliah, studying the way she moved and the various expressions shifting across her face, when her back wasn't turned as she danced. Of one thing he was certain: He wasn't finished with her yet.

The idea both thrilled and terrified him, because things were never as they seemed, and it appeared that Lady Liliah had many secrets.

And if she kept many secrets, she also had much to lose.

He'd bet money she was taking a gamble with life.

But it was unfortunate that ladies weren't taught that the house always wins.

Chapter Eleven

Liliah's gaze lingered on Luc's form at the edge of the ballroom. Closing her eyes, she imagined that he was her partner—not Meyer. Her body leaned into the music, and a faint smile touched her lips.

"Escaping." Meyer breathed the word, a cold laugh escaping his lips. "I know the feeling."

Liliah opened her eyes and studied her friend. "I shan't take it personally." She arched a brow, trying to lighten the utterly depressing mood surrounding them like a rain cloud.

Meyer studied her, his eyes narrowing slightly. "Who were you imagining me to be?"

Her gaze flickered to the perimeter of the ballroom, giving away her answer before her lips uttered a word.

Meyer scoffed slightly, and as Liliah focused back on her dance partner, she waited.

"Do I dare ask which one? Or both . . . no . . ." Meyer's brow pinched as he considered the options.

"Heightfield, am I right?" An amused grin tipped his lips even as his gaze grew wary.

"I refuse to answer," Liliah replied cheekily, keeping the conversation lighthearted.

When her heart was anything but.

"Minx, it's in your eyes. I see it clear as day. The question is . . . why the sudden interest? You have some nefarious plot afoot, and I am at a loss as to what it is." Meyer's gaze narrowed.

"I'll leave it to you to uncover my schemes," Liliah teased, thanking heaven as the music ended.

Meyer released her abruptly as soon as it was polite, but it was his voice that stopped her short. "Did your father—"

"Yes," Liliah answered quickly, in a clipped tone. She didn't want to revisit the earlier conversation with her father, let alone speak of it out loud. The weight of the world settled back on her shoulders.

"One of two." Meyer whispered the words.

"An announcement," Liliah echoed in the same tone.

Meyer took her arm and escorted her to the refreshment table with slow, purposeful steps. Rebecca was nowhere to be seen, as Liliah searched for her friend.

"She left." Meyer answered her unspoken question as he offered her a glass of Madeira, then took one for himself.

Taking the beverage, she sipped it thoughtfully. "I do not blame her."

"I told her as much," Meyer replied tightly. "Damn, I hate how helpless I am. At the mercy of my father's will, and Rebecca—" He snapped his mouth shut as if barely stopping from spilling a secret.

Liliah tilted her head. "What have you two been keeping from me?" she asked quietly.

Meyer's guilty gaze was all the confirmation she needed. "Nothing that would change our current malady." His gaze fell to his drink. Closing his eyes, he lifted it to his lips. As he lowered the glass, he sighed, his lips forming that now familiar grim line. "I'll come find you for the last waltz." With a curt nod, he left her by the refreshment table.

The air escaped her lungs in a rush as she thought over the implications. Not only was her best friend hiding something, but the nail in the coffin of her and Meyer's betrothal was to be secured tonight.

Two waltzes.

They might as well leave the ballroom married.

All that was left was the announcement in the *Times*, and the reading of the banns.

Time was sifting away like sand in an hourglass.

And soon it would be too late.

There had to be a way out.

If only she could find it.

If only.

Chapter Twelve

Lucas circled the ballroom a second time, scanning the crowd for Liliah. His gaze narrowed at the stricken expression on her face a moment before she all but darted from the crowded ballroom, heading toward the darker hall. Frowning, he searched for the reason for her abrupt departure. Meyer's visage was strained, and Lucas questioned if perhaps Meyer had upset Liliah. Yet his expression was just as distraught. Meyer didn't strike him as a severe type of fellow, yet in a short span of time he'd seen him do little more than scowl.

He stepped around the milling people, heading toward the hall where Liliah had disappeared. The gears of his mind worked tirelessly with each step. Perhaps the titter about Meyer and Lady Liliah held some validity. True, many marriage arrangements were based not on emotion but on practicalities of wealth and position It was simply how things were done, was it not? Why would it create an issue of this magnitude? Clearly

they were friends; was that not more than most mar-
riages had with which to begin? Granted, even the
thought of marriage had Lucas's stomach clenching
with dread, but he had the good sense to realize that
others didn't have his same visceral reaction to matri-
mony.

Except maybe Meyer.

And Liliah.

Which still was utterly confusing, and he found himself anxious to solve the mystery.

He skirted around the edge of the ballroom, avoid-
ing Meyer, and picked up his pace to where the shadows ran into the light of the ballroom. The darkness
beckoned him, and he focused on the line between illumination and shadow. As he crossed the threshold, his
whole being relaxed and a smile curved his lips.

Odd how the dark had become his sanctuary.

Odd how he felt more at home there than he ever
had in the light.

As his eyes adjusted to the lack of light, he scanned
the small alcove. Sure enough, Lady Liliah had her
back turned as she walked out onto what appeared to
be a deserted balcony. Shoulders straight, he allowed
his gaze to seductively outline her silhouette. Delicate
curves were simply hinted at by her gown, but he was
all too aware of the luscious figure hidden within the
fabric. His hands burned to touch her, to feel her lips
caress his. As he stealthily strode toward her, he was
about to offer a greeting when she paused against the
balcony wall. Bracing against it with her arms, she
dropped her head, defeated.

Lucas halted his progress, studying her in the starlight.

She stilled, then angled her head like a bird listening
for a predator.

Lucas grinned at the mental picture, and its accuracy.

"Sneaking up on ladies?" Liliah glanced over her shoulder, her tone wry.

"Only ones that are suspect." He shrugged and strode forward, pausing to lean his shoulders against a nearby pillar.

"Am I suspect?" Liliah turned to face him. Half of her face was more deeply shadowed than the other, and he found it difficult to read her expression.

"Yes, and I must say I've learned a few interesting details about you this evening, yet none of it makes sense."

"Ah, well, if it helps at all, you're not the only one who is unable to make sense of it all." A ghost of a smile faded across her lips.

"If you're looking for pity, I must warn you that you'll find none in me."

Liliah tilted her head. "Then it is a good thing I wasn't expecting, nor searching for, pity. Do I strike you as the type of woman needing your sympathy?" She stood fully and stepped toward him. "No. And while I'm indeed searching for something from you . . ." She let the words linger in the darkness. "It most certainly is not pity."

Lucas watched her slow approach, each step filled with purpose till she paused an arm's length away. "And what are you searching for? I must say I'm insatiably curious, a character flaw that has both served me well, and . . . not," he replied in a careless tone.

"I do not find that disclosure surprising, my lord."

After a moment, Lucas asked again. "But, my *lady*, you still haven't answered my question."

She was close enough for him to see her shadowed

tongue dart out and lick her lower lip. The gesture was utterly seductive, yet he instinctively knew it wasn't meant as such.

It was a gesture of indecision.

And damn it all if every shred of his curiosity smoldered further.

"I propose . . ." Liliah glanced behind them, assuring herself of their privacy.

If anyone should find them, it would go very badly indeed . . . for her.

He'd never be brought up to scratch, and she'd be a ruined woman.

Yet the gentleman within had died long ago, so he simply waited for her to continue.

"You need me to remain silent, and to keep my distance from your club, is that right?" She changed tactics.

Would he be forever in warfare with women?

"Yes and no. While it would not be . . . convenient for you to disclose information about the club, I can just as easily turn your blackmail on its ear, and threaten to ruin you." He hitched a shoulder in a blasé manner.

Liliah's lips bent into a grin. "Odd you should mention that . . ." She glanced to the floor.

Lucas narrowed his eyes. "I'm listening." He shouldn't be, he should be leaving her in the darkness, finding his damn friend and heading back to the club.

Yet he was rooted to his spot.

Why would the daughter of a duke resort to such extreme measures?

He had to know.

"If I'm to be relegated to a platonic marriage for all my days, then I want to at least taste pleasure before my future is decided." She lifted a delicate shoulder, her gaze flickering up to meet his.

"What a lovely picture you paint, yet I find it hard to believe that a betrothal to your acquaintance would be platonic. Unless the gentleman prefers his own kind?" He arched a brow, stepping forward, lazily reaching out and tracing a single finger up her arm.

"For learning much, you have seen little," Liliah replied, her tone soft. Her body gave a delicate shudder.

And his body hardened painfully.

He needed to step back, regroup, retreat—yet he had never done such before.

And against his better judgment, he took a small step forward.

"Meaning?" he asked.

"You've ascertained that I'm all but betrothed to a friend, true, but that certainly isn't the trial of which I'm speaking. It goes deeper. Lord Heightfield, what do you know of loyalty?" she whispered, leaning into his touch as his hand cupped her shoulder possessively.

"Not much."

She sighed, only it wasn't a sigh of pleasure but of impatience. "You misunderstand. Loyalty to friends. You must understand that idea, for do you not have a friendship with Viscount Kilpatrick?"

Lucas paused, nodding once. "Continue."

"Would you steal away the one thing he lived for, simply because it was expected of you?"

Lucas released her shoulder and took a step back. "No." Frowning, he tried to follow her train of thought.

"Then you'll understand why my potential marriage

to Meyer will never be more than a scrap of paper."
Liliah breathed.

The gears in his mind clicked into place. "Lady Rebecca."

"Indeed."

The evening's events suddenly shifted, adding up into a scene that caused him to wince slightly. Indeed it was unfortunate, he could see that.

But it still was not his problem.

"And why am I part of this melodrama? What do I have to gain from . . . assisting you?"

Pleasure, satisfying my curiosity, feeding my lust.

"My silence, and my word to never darken your door," she answered, leveling her shoulders as her chin lowered in a regal regard.

It wasn't enough. It shouldn't tempt him.

He could easily leave the ballroom, never think of her again . . . yet part of him took pause in the tenacious nature he'd uncovered in Lady Liliah Durary.

He had the sneaking suspicion that while not dangerous, she could easily be a pain in the arse.

And he needed to eliminate problems, not add to them.

His gaze raked over her.

Bedding her wouldn't be a challenge.

He even doubted if her inexperience would be dull; rather she would probably be a quick learner.

His body responded enthusiastically, and damn it all, he was going to have to linger in the darkness before he could walk out into the light.

"I'm not sure—" he began, but halted his refusal as soon as a shadowed figure walked toward their cozy balcony.

"Lady Liliah?" Meyer's voice called warily.

"Do you need something from the lady?" Lucas ambled toward the gentleman, purposely leaving off the courtesy title.

"Meyer—"

Lucas lifted a hand to silence Liliah, and studied the man before him. "I don't think she will be needing your escort. Not *this* night." He arched a brow in a challenging manner, knowing Meyer would allow him to escort her back to the ballroom, away from the shadows that whispered secrets of ruin; especially since Meyer would surely follow close behind.

Then turned to face his ill-thought-out fate.

Lady Liliah met his gaze. Apprehension shifted to acceptance, then illuminated into victory.

And in that moment, as Lucas took her arm and led her out into the light of the ballroom, he was certain of two things.

He was a bloody idiot.

And Liliah Durary was about to be thoroughly ruined—in more ways than one.

Chapter Thirteen

L iliah forced a calm she didn't feel as she walked into the bright ballroom on the arm of one of the most notorious rakes in all of London.

Her father would be furious.

Her reputation would be questioned.

And she didn't care a fig.

As the strains of the waltz played, amazement and delicious anticipation filled her when Lucas led her onto the dance floor. His warm hand possessively settled on her hip, spanning her curves deliciously. And even through her gloved hand, she could feel his warmth radiate against her palm. With graceful movements, he led them into the throng of dancers. The sound of whispers filtered through the music of the string quartet. A wicked gleam illuminated his eyes, and Liliah didn't shrink back, but firmly held his gaze.

It was far different to dance with Lucas than with Meyer. Her body was drawn to his, so much so that she had to make a conscious effort to maintain a proper distance.

And when his hand pressed into her back, pulling her in closer, she willingly obeyed.

Little did he know he was already beginning the seduction.

Or maybe he did know, but it mattered not. It was delicious. It was sinful. It was everything she had hoped it would be.

And it was only a dance.

Heavens, she might not survive the act!

Of course, there were worse ways to die.

"Penny for your thoughts?" Luc asked, a smoldering grin turning her insides to jelly.

"Thank you," she uttered, settling on the words of primary importance.

"I don't think I've ever been thanked for a tryst before it's taken place," he whispered quietly, his expression amused.

"Ah, but I wasn't thanking you for that, just yet." Her face heated, and she glanced behind him, for the first time seeing the amount of attention their dancing had drawn.

"Then why the thanks?" Luc asked, pulling her focus back to him.

He led her effortlessly, and she allowed herself to enjoy the dance, when all the other times she had dreaded it. "Because this dance was to have been with Meyer, as an announcement of sorts. You quite neatly allowed us to dodge it. I'm quite certain there will be hell to pay—"

"And here I thought gently bred ladies didn't swear." He tsk-tsked.

"And here I thought that men with a reputation of your caliber wouldn't be so offended by a small slip," she replied, grinning.

"Well played, continue." His full lips cracked a smile.

"Our fathers will not be amused. Let us leave it at that."

Lucas nodded. "So it is not just your father who wishes the union?"

Liliah twirled, then stepped back into Luc's embrace, her body relaxing slightly, as if she had found home. She brushed off the sensation and focused on her words. "No, it's quite a stubborn endeavor on the part of both our fathers. What Meyer and I cannot fathom is why, especially when the titles of both our families are amply wealthy." She shrugged. Was there any more powerful reason than money? She couldn't think of one.

"It is curious," Luc replied. His gaze trailed along her face, then dipped lower as he studied her unabashedly. Her skin flushed where his gaze traveled, as if he were touching her, not simply looking.

"You're deceptively attractive, Lady Liliah," he replied after a moment. "Innocent, yet . . . not."

The music ended, and he slowly released her from their dance. "It has certainly been a pleasure." With a slow bow, he took her hand and kissed it softly, then turned on his heel and strode into the crowd. They parted as he walked toward the viscount, and without a backward glance, the two men quit the ballroom.

Liliah's breathing slowly returned to normal as her heart ceased its pounding rhythm.

She had done it.

He'd agreed.

And while it was possible for him to go back on his word, she rather trusted that he wouldn't.

Such a realization sent her heart to pounding once more, but the heat in her veins chilled immediately as the crowd parted.

This time it wasn't in admiration of a rake's reputation.

It was in the fear of a furious father.

Apparently her father wasn't at the faro table any longer.

Without a word, he simply raised his arm, his expression daring her to refuse him.

Liliah placed her hand on his arm and kept her eyes straight ahead while the whispers surrounded them as they made an exit from the ballroom. The music played behind them, but all she could hear was the silence.

The calm before the storm.

She only hoped the price she was paying was going to be worth it.

Chapter Fourteen

Hours later as he swirled what was left of the brandy in his glass, he waited for the verdict from his friend. Heathcliff had listened to the whole sordid disaster silently, which was exceedingly out of character for the man. It was making Lucas twitch.

"You'll have to repeat that last part again." Heathcliff set his brandy down on the table beside the hearth. His expression was an odd juxtaposition of amusement and hesitancy.

"I'm an idiot." Lucas shot back the rest of his brandy, setting the crystal glass down on the sideboard with too much force, making a loud clank.

"Well, I've known that for years. What I'm referring to—"

"Yes. I said yes. As if I needed to add another person's problems to the list of my own."

"She has bewitched you from the first moment, has she not?" Heathcliff lifted his brandy in a salute.

"I wouldn't call it bewitching," Lucas grumbled.

"No? I wish you could have seen yourself when I was dancing with her. The bloody cotillion, and you were ready to engage in fisticuffs." Heathcliff chuckled darkly.

"I—"

Heathcliff cut off his friend's words. "No, if you lie, then lie to yourself. You are the only person in this room who will believe it."

"Aptly spoken." Lucas sighed.

"Besides, why are you complaining? You get to ruin a very beautiful, willing, and eager woman. One who stirs your blood and engages your mind—and yet you complain?" Heathcliff arched a dark brow.

"The scandal—"

"You're starting to sound like Ramsey," Heathcliff remarked with irritation.

"Am not," Lucas bit out, offended, then his emotions shifted to shame as he realized the accuracy of his friend's statement. "Damn and blast. This, *this*, is why I'm regretting this decision! Because it is creating an environment in which I have no control."

"Ah." Heathcliff nodded once, then refilled his glass of brandy. The sound of the liquid splashing in the crystal glass was obnoxiously loud to Lucas's already frayed nerves.

"Is that all the insight you have to give?" Lucas asked.

Heathcliff sipped his brandy in response, then hitched a shoulder. "Perhaps. Rather, I have a different question. How are you supposed to ruin Lady Liliah when you are here"—he gestured to the grand office—"and she is cloistered in luxury in her father's residence in Mayfair?"

Lucas's lips bent into a grin, his body relaxing as he considered the challenge. "Details." He hitched a shoulder. "Honestly, I wouldn't put it past the minx to waltz into the club once more, or somewhere just as improper. It's almost as if she views her predicament as if she has nothing to lose." He muttered the last words to himself.

"One can never comprehend the logic of a female." Heathcliff raised his glass in a salute.

Lucas nodded in agreement.

"But that still doesn't answer my question," Heathcliff remarked after a moment.

Lucas frowned. "The first step is attending another blasted party."

"I suppose there are worse things. It did seem to attract an uncommon amount of attention—this will only be good for business, you know."

"True," Lucas agreed, "as much as I loathe admitting it."

"What is your timeline?" Heathcliff asked, setting down his empty glass on the sideboard. He leaned his shoulder against the wall and regarded Lucas.

Lucas's brow pinched. "This isn't courting. Thank heavens. I expect to take care of the situation within a week."

"*Situation?* Is that we are calling seduction?"

"This isn't seduction. This is sex. Not lovemaking, not anything romantic. This is—is ruination."

"How in heaven's name you took something as delightful as sex and turned it cold, I'll have no idea. Do try to at least enjoy yourself." Heathcliff rolled his eyes.

"I doubt that will be an issue." Of all the concerns

he had with the arrangement, lack of enjoyment was the least.

"Then at least make it good for her. You know it is the gentlemanly thing to do," Heathcliff responded with a chuckle.

"Ah, and here I thought ruining an innocent wasn't exactly a gentlemanly act. Odd." Lucas arched a brow.

"You know what I mean." Heathcliff raised a hand dismissively. "You do remember how to please a woman, don't you?"

Lucas narrowed his eyes. "Some skills don't require practice."

"You would know," Heathcliff shot back, grinning unrepentantly. "Who would have thought the mastermind behind a gentleman's pleasure club would be a self-denying monk?"

Lucas rolled his eyes. "I'm not nearly as holy. And I'm quite certain that my lifestyle wouldn't be considered religious."

"That's vastly accurate; however, it does beg the question . . ." Heathcliff took a step toward Lucas, his gaze sharpening to the point where Lucas began to feel uncomfortable.

"The question?" Lucas asked, holding his ground.

"How did a slip of a girl, innocent to boot, single-handedly ended your dry streak? Because it isn't as if women haven't tried before . . . yet they all failed where she . . . succeeded." He arched a brow and walked past Lucas to the door.

Lucas watched his retreat, his words hanging heavy in the air.

"Remember what I said, Lucas. Lie, but don't expect anyone to believe it but you."

As he closed the door, Lucas wondered if perhaps he was doing just that—lying to himself.

Because he wanted her, when he shouldn't.

He said yes, when he normally would have said no.

And bloody hell, if he wasn't absolutely determined to make good on his word.

Perhaps more than once.

Chapter Fifteen

Liliah glared at her door.

Her father's words had been bitter, cold, and unfeeling. How was it possible to have children and act so hateful toward them? She simply couldn't fathom it. Yet, she would never know firsthand.

Not if her father got his way.

If she married Meyer, she'd never know the joy of having a child, never experience the love one has for a daughter or a son.

It wasn't as if she wanted a child now, but . . . it seemed extra cruel to take away her choice to have one in the future.

Hot tears stung her cheeks as she considered her father's scolding. He had waited till they were secure in the carriage before he had spoken with dark, low tones.

Wicked.

Rebellious.

Shameful.

Harlot.

All the words flooded back, yet she imagined herself like the ducks swimming in the Serpentine during the rain—all the water rolling down their backs and dripping back into the pond. She imagined her father's words having the same effect.

Yet, try as she might, there was still a slight sting.

How she hated him.

She heard a slight knock on the door, far too timid to be a maid or one of the guards her father had posted outside her room.

Damn the man.

It could only be one person.

"Samantha?" Liliah called out. "Come in."

The door slowly cracked open, and her sister entered, casting a wary glance behind her as she shut the door.

"Guards, Lil? Whatever did you do this time?" Samantha asked softly, without accusation.

Liliah sighed, scooting over on her bed to make room for her sister, younger by two years. "It's a long story."

Samantha arched a light brow, taking a spot beside Liliah and facing her fully. "I do believe we have the time to spare." A small smile tipped her lips.

Where Liliah had lighter features, Samantha was her opposite: dark hazel eyes were framed by long dark lashes the same tint as her hair, the color of richly brewed tea and just as comforting.

"You are certainly aware of my current predicament with Meyer." Liliah flopped back in an utterly unladylike manner onto her bed, staring at the ceiling of her room.

"Indeed," Samantha replied timidly, following her

sister's example and reclining in a much more ladylike fashion.

Liliah turned to meet her sister's questioning gaze. "I didn't meet his expectations last night, and he is quite put out."

Samantha nodded. "Put out might be an understatement. He's never posted guards outside your door, Liliah." Samantha's gaze was wary.

"True, it is quite irritating." With a huff, Liliah blew away a strand of stray hair from her lips.

"I find it quite alarming. What exactly happened?"

Liliah studied her sister, wondering just how much to tell her. It wasn't that she didn't trust her; it was that she wished to protect her.

If their father cornered her sister, she would feel the need to protect Liliah's secrets, even to her own detriment. Frowning, Liliah chose to keep the story rather generic.

"I didn't dance the final waltz with Meyer, and the duke is quite angry that he must wait till tomorrow's rout at the Brighamns to finalize the details he wished to already have accomplished." Liliah turned her gaze upward to the ceiling so that Samantha wouldn't suspect that her story wasn't complete.

"I see," Samantha replied simply.

Liliah's tense body relaxed as she realized her sister wasn't going to question her further. Yet she mourned the ability to divulge all her secrets! To explain the delight and powerful experience that it was to waltz with Luc! To explain the way her heart pounded fiercely, and how her body heated with a touch—it was incredible.

Yet, she dare not speak a word of it.

At least not yet.

"Then I'm assuming you're not going to accompany me to Bond Street to shop today," Samantha replied with a disappointed tone.

Liliah closed her eyes in remorse. She had forgotten she'd made plans with her sister.

"Perhaps we can ask?" Liliah said with a hopeful tone for her sister's benefit, almost certain their father would refuse such a request.

"No. Let's not risk his ire further. I do not need another bonnet, or another dress for my come-out next season."

At the mention of Samantha's first season, Liliah turned to her sister to study her. She would be one of the Incomparables of the season for sure. With her beautiful features and large dowry, it would be a season to remember. Yet a cold chill shivered down her back.

What if their father had already made plans for Samantha's match, just as he'd made plans for hers?

What if Samantha's season was nothing but a sham?

And who would be the object of their father's schemes? It was troubling.

"Why are you frowning so?" Samantha inquired, rising up on her elbow to regard her sister.

"It is of no consequence. Tell me, what did you do yesterday?"

Samantha's expression brightened. "Lil, I indulged in the most fascinating book! It was a detailed description of India!" Samantha continued to give the details of her reading, and Liliah considered her sister's immense joy in study.

Truly, it was a shame she wasn't able to attend Eton and further her studies. If there was a book to be had, her sister would devour it. It was a joy for their governess to tutor Samantha, while it had been a trial for the governess to tutor Liliah. But that was the case for most things.

Samantha didn't rebel.

Samantha listened.

Samantha was the perfect daughter.

And rather than be jealous, Liliah's heart pinched with fear as she listened to her beautiful sister. Because when the Duke of Chatterwood controlled your future, obedience was the one thing that might destroy you.

Chapter Sixteen

The Brighamns' estate was one of the oldest in Mayfair, and as such, it was a stone monster in size while lacking some of the more modern comforts. Lucas ascended the marble steps as his carriage pulled away, cursing Heathcliff for refusing to attend the rout with him.

Lucas had inquired as to why he declined.

"Do you need assistance in seduction?" Heathcliff had replied, his tone thick with insinuation.

Lucas had left him in the study as he growled out an inarticulate response to his friend's idiocy.

Yet now, as he faced the stone palace, he reluctantly admitted he missed his companion.

Damn the man.

The hall was bustling with the lords and ladies of the ton as each filtered into the grand ballroom in the middle of the residence. The crystal chandelier sprayed fragments of candlelight across the foyer, making the room sparkle with a soft glow. A lady with a heavily feathered hat brushed against Lucas, nearly making him sneeze.

He stepped away, almost bumping into another lady. Her catlike expression reminded him of a drawing he'd seen of the mountain lions of the Americas—fierce, calculating, and predatory. He'd seen the expression many times before.

And each time it made his stomach revolt. Unless she wished to work for him, he had no use for her . . . services.

Because every time he saw the predatory gaze, he thought of Catherine.

Blood cold, he strode ahead, his mind churning with memories he'd rather forget.

Memories he wished could remain buried with his dead wife.

May the bitch rot in hell.

He searched for a distraction. Damn it all, this was why he refused to attend parties.

It was better when he could control the environment, the people, the situation.

Then nothing could remind him of his past.

Rather, he could live as if it never happened.

Rather, pretend that it all had happened to someone else.

Which was partly true, because the day everything went to hell, the man he once was, died.

May that poor bastard rest in peace.

Lucas walked across the threshold of the hall into the ballroom. The estate had been updated with gas lights, which was likely the only update the old place had recently experienced. It wasn't that the Brighamns were poor in pocket, but it was well-known that they happened to spend the majority of their time in Ireland, not London.

Lucas studied the room, his gaze coolly searching for Lady Liliah. It was some sort of temporary madness for him to have had such a powerful response to her last time—one he was certain he wouldn't experience again. It was dangerous to give a woman control of your emotions.

Control of anything.

He'd be wise to remember that.

Scanning the crowd, his gaze narrowed as he saw the Duke of Chatterwood, Liliah's father. There was another ghost from his past. Except for a few occasions at parliament, he hadn't seen the bastard for years. Not only was he one of the most arrogant men he'd ever met—and he had met quite a few—he was also a constant thorn in the Tories' side, a true Whig to the core. The man was a pestilence wherever he went.

A tall, wiry man, it was odd how such a severe person could be the father of the vivacious Lady Liliah. As if thinking her name conjured her, the Duke of Chatterwood stepped to the side, revealing his daughter in a beautiful yellow gown that was the perfect mix of innocence and seduction.

Lucas's blood pounded with desire as he studied her perfect form hidden artfully within the folds and tucks of her gown. Yet as he studied her, he noticed how her expression held no joy, none of the exuberant nature he'd come to expect in the short time of their acquaintance.

Moving closer, he circled their position, keeping the pair in view as he evaluated the situation. The duke was speaking with another gentleman of his own age, yet every few seconds, he would subtly reach over and grasp his daughter's wrist.

Holding her close.

Holding her hostage.

The man was either brilliant or a tyrant.

Certainly Lady Liliah was trouble and more than a hoyden, but taking into account all that Lady Liliah had said regarding her and Meyer's entanglement, he suspected that the man was a tyrant.

Running his household much like he ran his politics.

Controlling the circumstances and the secrets he held captive.

Under his thumb, able to be manipulated.

Lucas understood the need for control.

Yet as he watched the duke's hand squeeze Liliah's wrist, Lucas's blood boiled.

Mine.

Again the simple yet damning word filtered through his mind.

So much for the emotional stoicism he was attempting.

Yet with her father closely guarding her, there was precious little he could do without provoking the duke's ire, which in turn would prove to distress Liliah further.

He was damned if he did something.

And damned if he didn't.

This was why he wanted Heathcliff present. Surely he'd have some idea as to how to address the conundrum.

Lucas meandered away from Liliah's position and instead searched for Meyer. Sure enough, he found him beside Lady Rebecca, speaking in low tones. To the left and several paces away stood a silver-haired man with an ample paunch and a neck that nearly drowned his cravat. His study of the two young people was overly attentive, and Lucas's curiosity was piqued.

Leaning against a pillar, Lucas ignored the whispers of the people who took not-so-discreet glances up and down his person as they passed. As if aware of the scrutiny, Meyer's gaze met his. A flicker of curiosity flashed across his features before he bowed smartly to Lady Rebecca and made his way toward Lucas.

Lucas gave another bow, then simply nodded to Meyer, then shifted his gaze to the man with the silver hair, still watching from his post. "Friend of yours?"

Meyer's quizzical expression shifted to anger as he turned to follow Lucas's gaze. "No. That would be my father."

Lucas nodded. "Can't say I see the family resemblance."

"Good heavens, I hope not," Meyer replied with emphasis, then he adjusted his cravat slightly. "He's been overly . . . attentive."

"Ah, so you noticed his study of you and your lady?" Lucas said, studying Meyer's reaction.

Meyer's eyes widened ever so slightly, giving away more than his words could. "Speaking of . . . friends." Meyer squared his shoulders, regarding Lucas coolly. "What of Lady Liliah? You seem to be quite curious?" He spoke the statement as a question.

"Lady Liliah is none of your concern, unless you wish to rescue her from her overbearing arse of a father, who keeps assuring himself that she is not fleeing the scene. It's as if she's suspected of a crime." Lucas studied his nails, then gave a bored expression to Meyer, waiting for his response.

"In some circles, defiance is a crime," Meyer replied,

but without heat, only a defeated tone. "It is unfortunate for Lady Liliah, however I'm quite certain that any intercession I might try would only make the situation worse."

"Is that so?" Lucas replied, irritation growing for the man before him. "You could offer to dance, could you not?"

Meyer tilted his head slightly. "Of course, but—"

"And it is impossible for another gentleman to intercede?"

"No—"

"You certainly are slow, are you not?" Lucas was losing his patience. "Next waltz, save the chit from her tyrant and I'll rescue you—will that suffice for a plan?" he enunciated through clenched teeth.

"Of course," Meyer replied readily, his expression shifting from surprise to appreciation. "Many thanks."

"Was that so difficult to cultivate, as far as plans? Dear Lord, and you are the future Earl of Greywick. God save us all."

Meyer reared back slightly, his brows pinched. "I take offence, sir."

"You should take notes, rather. Now, go and make sure you follow directions like a good lad." Lucas pushed off from the pillar, watching with delight as the verbal barb hit its mark.

Without waiting for a response, he left Meyer and wandered back toward the door, giving him a better view of Lady Liliah.

Her color was high, as if just on the edge of mutiny, and Lucas bit back a grin. He doubted he'd have needed to spell out the plan to her like he had to Meyer. No. She'd have run headlong into the fray with her own twist to the plot.

It was devious.

It was delightful.

It made him want her even more.

Damn it.

As if feeling his regard, she tilted her head ever so slightly, much like she had when he had found her in the balcony at the last ball. Glancing behind her, her intelligent gaze scanned the room before meeting his. Arching a brow, he waited for her response.

Her father's hand squeezed her wrist.

She winced—but rather than turn away, she lifted her chin defiantly, meeting Lucas's gaze with a boldness that made him painfully aroused.

Her gaze shifted to her father, and she nodded once as the strains of the first waltz lilted through the air. She glanced back at Lucas, and he nodded once to her, a slow, intentional movement.

I remember.

And remember he did. The Duke of Chatterwood might make their tryst slightly more complicated to arrange, but as far as Lucas was concerned, that made it all the sweeter.

May it never be said he didn't rise to the challenge.

Rather, he welcomed it.

Meyer approached the duke, bowed politely, and offered his arm to Liliah.

Lucas was too far away to hear the words, but the intention was clear. Liliah's shoulders froze, even as her chin lifted in an almost rebellious tilt, yet she followed him out onto the dance floor. Lucas made his move. Maneuvering around the ballroom, he skirted the edge where the milling people met the open dance floor, and selected a location opposite the duke, who, with any luck, wouldn't notice that Meyer would be replaced with another gentleman. As the dancers swirled around in a circular motion, Lucas spotted Meyer, and waited for his notice. As soon as he made eye contact, he nodded toward the farthest corner, and upon Meyer's small nod, he stepped closer to the dancers. Meyer was quicker to catch on than before, and led Liliah closer to the edge of the dance floor, and as he held his arm out for Liliah to twirl, Lucas stepped in, grasping her hand and setting Meyer free.

"Good evening," Lucas said, grinning unrepentantly.

Liliah's expression widened with surprise. "Well, good evening!" she remarked, her beautiful face illuminated with delight, the frozen posture of her shoulders relaxing ever so slightly. "How unexpected, and in the best of ways."

"I do aim to please." He spoke with double meaning.

Liliah blushed slightly. "How fortuitous for me."

Lucas chuckled as he led them back into the throng of dancers. Yet he sobered as he glanced at her wrist. "Are you injured?"

"Pardon?" Liliah asked.

"Your wrist."

"Ah, you miss little, do you?"

"Perhaps."

"I'm quite well. The injury is to my will, not my body. He fears my open defiance."

"I'm certainly glad I could accommodate it," Lucas replied, arching a brow wickedly.

"So am I." Her smile broadened and a faint rose hue tinted her cheeks, and Lucas studied the color, enjoying immensely the fact that he was the cause of such a lovely reaction.

Yet even as he thought it, he cursed himself for

being so easily enamored. What was it about the chit that made him go soft? It was disconcerting at the least and damn terrifying at most.

"What concerns you?" Liliah asked, pulling his attention from her lovely mouth to her curious expression.

"Nothing of consequence."

"I doubt that," she replied, almost too quietly to hear.

Lucas changed topics, feeling the need to distract her as much as she distracted him. "You are utterly ravishing in your innocent gown, but may I say that I much prefer your earlier attire—when we first met."

Liliah's eyes widened as she glanced around the swirling dancers, no doubt checking to make sure no one had overheard such a forward remark. Yet, rather than scold him, she arched a dark brow and grinned. "Why am I not surprised? Would it shock you then, to know the gown was borrowed?"

"And no longer in your possession?" Lucas asked, then spun her in perfect time.

Liliah's full lips tipped in a crooked grin. "Ah, but that is for me to know—"

"And for me to discover?" Lucas finished, flashing her his most flirtatious grin.

"Perhaps."

"Ah, and here I thought you were bent on"—he leaned in close enough to whisper—"seduction." Then retreated back to the normal expanse between dancers.

Liliah's color heightened. "What gave you the impression I'd changed my mind?" she dared.

"Then why are we tarrying in a crowded ballroom, my lady?" Lucas allowed his hungry gaze to lower from her expressive eyes to the perfect bow of her lips. His gaze traced the line of her jaw to her neck and the graceful curves below. The heat in his body pulsed to his lower regions, demanding that he partake of the pleasures promised.

"What do you have in mind, my lord?" Liliah asked, her expression brave, yet Lucas detected a hint of trepidation. It satisfied him to see her show some hesitancy before running headlong into ruin. Perhaps she had more sense than she cared to admit. Yet the folly was indeed to his advantage, his very tempting and desirous advantage.

"Could you not visit Lady Rebecca?" he asked, hinting at something more.

"Or I could simply . . . find you."

Lucas shook his head. "We've taken far more . . . elaborate . . . security measures. Besides, I do not mix business with pleasure, love."

"Love? My, we're progressing quickly," Liliah teased. "It might interest you to know that I have an appointment at the modiste's tomorrow around two in the afternoon. Perhaps—"

"Done," Lucas answered, his body tight with anticipation.

"Done," she echoed.

The music ended, but Lucas was loath to release her, yet he noted the arrival of Meyer, and so he stepped out of the way and gave a curt bow. He let his gaze linger on her form as Meyer held out his arm to her, wordlessly.

As if noticing Meyer for the first time, she hesitated for a moment, then placed her delicate hand on his wrist. Lucas's chest tightened with an unwelcome emotion as he watched them walk away.

He swore he'd never feel that way again.

He damned the feeling straight to the pit of hell.

Because the last time he felt its surge, it had practically killed him.

Jealousy—thou art a heartless bitch.

Chapter Seventeen

Liliah was wary on the carriage ride home, studying her father to determine if he realized that Lucas had taken Meyer's place. For if he had noticed, her plans for tomorrow would be much harder to keep. Yet as the carriage rolled away down the London streets toward home, her father didn't remark on anything; rather the silence kept her company.

It was well into the next day when she started to lose the wary edge to her emotions and the feeling shifted to a rather panicky sense of anticipation. Each moment ticked closer to the time she'd arrive at Bond Street and, consequently, her assignation with Lucas. She held no doubts that he meant to follow through on his word, and she was both terrified and delighted.

Terrified because she truly didn't know what to expect.

Delighted because she truly thought it would be remarkable.

"You do realize you're still on the same page, Liliah," Samantha remarked quietly, her gaze flickering to the library door as if to make sure their father wasn't eavesdropping.

Heaven knows he'd probably stoop to that level.

Liliah sighed and turned the page. "Now I'm not."

Samantha huffed. "Indeed." She edged closer, closing the distance on the couch and whispered, "Why are you so distracted?"

Liliah bit her lip, wishing she could speak of it to her sister, but knowing she hadn't the freedom. She wouldn't dare put her sister in such a position, not with their father so demanding. "It is of little consequence. Simply pondering the future," she answered honestly, albeit it a little cryptically.

"I see." Samantha nodded sagely. "If I could somehow . . . fix the situation, please know that I would." Samantha's warm hand touched Liliah's knee through her muslin dress. Tears pricked her eyes as she met Samantha's earnest gaze.

"Thank you, yet I would not wish this on you, my dear. No. You"—Liliah reached out and squeezed her sister's hand affectionately—"were made for love. Heaven owes us that, for we've been far too long in its absence."

Samantha nodded once, a lonely tear slipping down her cheek. "Indeed. Perhaps someday. Until then, I do have you."

"You have me. Always." Liliah nodded, swearing the truth in her heart. The one silver lining in the whole disaster of marrying Meyer was the knowledge that he'd understand the need for Liliah's involvement in her sister's life, and would encourage meddling rather than discourage it. It wasn't much of a silver lining, but she was determined to hold on to whatever she could grasp.

"Now then." Liliah changed the subject. "Are you ready for our appointment this afternoon? I'm only thankful that our father hasn't restricted those outings."

"I hate the fittings," Samantha grumbled, her hand sliding from her sister's as she slouched in a rather unladylike manner against the couch cushions.

"They aren't too terrible." Liliah gave a dramatic sigh. "Surely you want your gowns to fit well, not as if they were purchased for someone else?"

"Indeed, yet it is simply tedious."

"I'm quite certain you'll survive the experience," Liliah teased her sister, then took a fortifying breath. "I'll take along Sarah to accompany us on our trip. I have a few errands to run." What Liliah didn't mention was that she would be leaving Sarah with Samantha.

"Oh, very well," Samantha replied, not asking further questions. "I had better ready myself. What time is the appointment?"

"Two, so we should make haste and leave in half an hour." Liliah's heart pounded with anticipation and anxiety. How was it possible for a half hour to seem like both an eternity and a moment?

"I'll have the carriage readied." Liliah stood from her position on the couch and paused a moment before quitting the room, allowing the butterflies in her stomach to settle and the tingling in her spine to dissipate.

As she strode down the hall, the flutter in her belly gathered momentum. Once the carriage was ordered, she retired to her room to make herself ready. As she studied her reflection in the mirror, she wondered if there would be any perceptible difference after she was ruined. The thought was certainly sobering, yet it didn't change her resolve.

No.

She wanted this.

Needed it.

A knock sounded on her door and she jumped in response. As her heart pounded its frightened rhythm, she called out, "Yes?"

Sarah peeked in, her expression sober. "The duke wishes to see you, my lady."

Liliah swallowed the fear that rose in her throat and nodded.

"He is waiting in his study, my lady." Sarah curtseyed and left, closing the door softly.

Liliah smoothed her skirt and strode to the door, a million reasons for why her father wished an audience all fluttering through her mind. As she traveled the hall and descended the stairs, her footsteps echoed on the marble floor. The brass handle of her father's study door was cold, hard, much like the man within. She pushed the handle slightly, opening the already slightly ajar door.

"Liliah." Her father spoke authoritatively. He stood from behind his desk and walked toward the fire burning low in the grate.

"Yes." Liliah raised her chin slightly, taking a deep breath as she waited.

"The announcement has been sent to the *Times*, and will be published in tomorrow's paper." He turned from facing the fire and studied her, daring her to speak.

Liliah's heart pounded out a desperate rhythm; demanding she flee, react, do something other than just stand there like a lamb to the slaughter. Yet her feet wouldn't move, so she simply waited for whatever came next.

"The date has been set for three weeks hence. I've gone to St. George's and procured a date for the wedding. I'm notifying you, since tomorrow night's party at the Winharts' will be the confirmation of the announcement."

She wouldn't cry, she wouldn't let him see her heartbreak—not only for herself but for Meyer, for Rebecca, for the future they were all sentenced to. She gave a slow nod. "Is there anything more?" she asked, cursing him to the depths of hell for his heartlessness.

"No." He narrowed his eyes, then smirked. "It is, however, pleasant to see you obey for once."

It was too much. Liliah opened her mouth, about to give the most scathing retort she could think of, yet she paused a moment before she let loose her anger.

No.

One false step and her afternoon plans were for naught.

Her father would send men to guard her door once more, or worse, guard her and Samantha on her afternoon excursion.

It wasn't worth the risk.

So Liliah held her tongue, allowing the silence to speak for her.

"You're dismissed." Her father gave a gesture with his hand and then presented his back to her.

Spinning on her heel, she turned and measured her steps out of the study, forcing herself to keep in control when what she wanted to do was run.

Far away.

As she entered her room, she allowed one tear to fall. As she wiped it away, she rang for her maid.

By the time Sarah knocked, Liliah's determination and anger had risen to the point of coloring her skin as she studied herself in the mirror. "Sarah, I require assistance . . ." Liliah walked across the room to a chest of drawers and withdrew a carefully wrapped package. Last year she had purchased some underthings from the French modiste, and as of yet hadn't had the courage to wear them.

Today that was going to change. She set the package on the bed and untied the red ribbon. The softest chemise lay folded on top of the small pile. The muslin was an ultrafine weave that took on the hue of the skin beneath it. The lace that curved around the edges was delicate, feminine, and quite scandalous. The rest of the underthings were equally sheer, soft, and wanton.

"O-of course, my lady," Sarah replied, her tone hesitant. Yet she didn't make any other comments as she helped Liliah undress, and then put on a new day gown. Liliah had chosen a soft blue that highlighted the hue of her eyes, and was also easy to put on without assistance.

She was quite proud of her forethought.

And equally scandalized.

Yet completely unrepentant.

"Also, Sarah, I will require you to accompany Samantha and me to Bond Street. We are to leave in ten minutes' time," Liliah said as she tugged on her gloves.

"Yes, my lady."

The last ten minutes seemed like an eternity to Liliah. Finally, Sarah, Samantha, and Liliah all entered the carriage and started down from Mayfair to Bond Street. Liliah found that she was quite unable to remain still. Her fingers shook slightly, and her toes had the strangest need to tap incessantly. Pulling her wits about her, she focused on the passing scenery. It was a common day in London. The smoky stench of coal fires hung in the air much like the ever-present clouds. The sunlight filtered through them, illuminating the Town, but it was dreary and dull. Thankfully there was no rain, but that didn't mean that it wouldn't rain within the hour.

As they approached Bond Street, Liliah's gaze scanned the lined-up carriages. Would she recognize Lucas's? Likely not, as she had not seen it, yet that didn't stop her from searching. As her carriage pulled up beside the modiste's storefront, Liliah took a shallow breath. "Shall we?"

Samantha arched a brow, clearly disenchanted with the idea of a fitting, but stepped from the carriage. The bell dinged as they walked into Whittlemen's ladies' shop. The scent of vanilla and scented soaps filtered through the air, perfuming the stale atmosphere.

"My ladies." The clerk curtseyed lower than necessary. "It is a pleasure to serve you today." The woman was Mrs. Whittlemen's usual assistant and, as such, was quite familiar with the duke's daughters—and their available pin money.

"We are ready for you, Lady Samantha." She gestured to the back of the shop, then turned her attention to Liliah. "Is there something we can offer you, Lady Liliah, while you wait? Perhaps you'd care to see the new designs we've created?" the woman asked, her expression hopeful.

Liliah demurred. "Thank you, but I have another errand to attend to while my sister is fitted."

Samantha glanced at her sister, narrowing her eyes ever so slightly to convey her displeasure at being left alone.

"Sarah will stay with you," Liliah added, trying to make it seem as if she was being helpful to her sister, being sensitive to her dislike of being alone—rather than the truth.

"Of course, Lady Liliah." The clerk nodded sagely, then turned to lead Samantha toward the back.

"Sarah, I have several errands. Please see that Samantha is properly attended to in my absence?" Liliah asked, widening her eyes as if communicating unspoken meaning.

Sarah studied her mistress, then gave a slow nod of understanding. Sarah had been long familiar with Liliah's antics, even if she didn't always agree with them.

"Very well." Liliah nodded, exhaling a tense breath. Samantha gave one long look behind her as she followed the clerk, then disappeared behind the velvet curtain that separated the main shop from the fitting area.

Sarah followed, and soon Liliah was standing alone.

The prospect was thrilling, yet she found herself slightly reluctant to exit the shop. Instinctively, she knew that when she returned, she would be different.

It was a deliberate and very large step in her life, yet as she pondered Luc, she found she had more anticipation than trepidation.

Especially after the conversation this afternoon with her father.

The bell rang once more as she exited the shop. Glancing up and down the street, she searched for

Lucas, wondering just how he planned to find her. Inwardly she chided herself for not giving him more information, yet she suspected he'd find a way to seek her out. After debating for a few moments, she took a left and started down the cobbled street away from the more popular shops. When Luc found her, she didn't wish to have witnesses. She wanted to be ruined in body, not necessarily in reputation.

And she was quite certain there had to be a difference.

She glanced at the carriages rolling by, her attention drifting from the road to the shopkeepers lining the street, and her body started to relax.

"Having second thoughts?"

Liliah startled, then turned to smile at Luc as he gently touched her elbow.

"Not yet. Maybe if you'd waited a few more minutes . . ."

"Ah, then I'm just in time." His clear blue eyes danced with a mischievous delight as his gaze lowered, studying her shamelessly.

Liliah's body grew feverish with his study, and she grappled for something to say. "I must say, I had wondered how you'd locate me."

"You're difficult to miss," Luc replied. "And if I'm not mistaken, our stolen minutes are numbered, are they not?"

Liliah swallowed. "They are."

"Then let's not waste them." Luc arched a dark brow and glanced behind them. "I hired a hack, which I felt was in your best interest, since my carriage is quite recognizable. I'll meet you at my residence . . . the driver knows where to go." He nodded meaningfully, then paused, his expression guarded as he continued. "And should you change your mind, the driver will heed your request." As he finished speaking, he waved a hack over toward them. Liliah was thinking of a witty reply when the carriage stopped, and Luc opened the door for her, offering his hand.

"I'm not so frail of heart, my lord," Liliah replied as she took his outstretched hand and stepped into the carriage.

"Perhaps," was all he said, then closed the door and tapped the side. The carriage lurched forward and Liliah leaned back, closing her eyes.

For a moment she thought of perhaps changing her mind, even after she spoke her brave words.

Yet the indecision was fleeting, and soon was replaced with tenacious resolve. If she were to learn about the act of love, then there was no other man she wanted to experience it with than Lucas Mayfield, Earl of Heightfield.

He was indeed a rake.

But he was an honest one.

And she held no delusions that he'd form some sort of attachment to her—which had to be for the best, did it not? She wasn't expecting love—and he wasn't offering it.

What she did expect was pleasure.

And if there was one man that personified carnal pleasure, it was he.

Chapter Eighteen

Lucas took his own carriage to his residence. He had considered a more neutral location, yet he resisted the idea. His servants were trained and trustworthy, silent as the grave. It was best to meet her at his London residence, where he could control the situation. As he stepped from his carriage, he took the steps to the door two at a time. The door opened immediately, as his butler was vigilant, and he gave but a curt nod before traveling down the hall and making his way to the back entrance of the house. Sure enough, the black carriage he'd hired turned the corner and started toward the assigned drop-off.

Lucas studied the carriage, both relieved and slightly surprised that Lady Liliah had followed through. Even for her brave words, he suspected she was slightly reluctant, as she should be! Yet he was sufficiently a rogue to hope she made good on all her talk.

His body agreed, enthusiastically.

As he took the last few steps to the carriage, he wondered at the wisdom of such a tryst. Liliah was no merry widow, nor was she a fortune hunter. She fit into none of the categories he'd assigned women to, which was both refreshing and confusing. In fact, his life had become exponentially more confusing since they'd met.

But after today's encounter, there would be no more interactions.

At least that was the plan.

He opened the carriage door and held out his hand for Lady Liliah. Her white-gloved hand grasped his firmly as she stepped down from the carriage. He noted a slight tremble in her touch, and a twinge of tenderness hit him, yet he pushed the offensive emotion away.

"Welcome," Lucas murmured as she glanced up at him, her blue eyes full of expectation and a hint of fear.

"Thank you." She demurred, yet it wasn't coy, rather it hinted at a shyness ignited by a passion that had been smoldering for days.

With a gentle tug, he led her toward the back door of his residence. The sound of the hack leaving punctuated their footsteps.

Lucas opened the heavy wooden door for Liliah, and waited a moment for his eyes to adjust to the dim lighting of the servants' entrance. He made a mental note to see to its improvement later. Yet his attention was arrested by Liliah. The scent of rosewater perfumed the air around them, and he wordlessly led her to the back stairs. "I hope you don't mind the more private route," he remarked delicately.

"I'd much prefer it," Liliah replied, offering a brave smile.

Lucas grinned. "I can only assume you're familiar with your servants' entrance as well . . ."

Liliah laughed softly. "You would assume correctly, my lord."

Lucas paused at the top of the stairs, waiting till she glanced at him. Lifting a finger, he pressed it against her lips, watching as her expression grew curious. "From this moment on, I'm only Luc."

Liliah nodded slowly, her soft lips rubbing against his sensitive finger. As he slowly withdrew his hand, she murmured, "Then you must address me as Liliah, no 'lady' before it."

Lucas nodded once, then grasped her hand, leading her from the servants' staircase into the main hall of the second floor. Their footsteps were soundless as they walked on the rich carpet. He glanced at Liliah, watching her study her surroundings. "Does it meet with your approval?" he asked with a slight edge to his tone. Was she finding his situation lacking? After all, she was the daughter of a duke.

"Offended easily?" She turned the remark back to him. "I find it surprising that you'd think any part of your person lacking." Her tone held a teasing lilt.

"I do not. But I, however, cannot account for other people's taste."

"La, but you are a wicked one, are you not?" Liliah narrowed her gaze, her lips bending into a grin.

"I'd rather thought you'd be aware of that side of my nature—I'd rather think it was painfully apparent, given our current situation." Lucas watched as the blood flooded to her face at his brazen implication.

Dear Lord. If she blushed so powerfully with insinuation, heaven help them once the door was closed.

Lucas glanced down the vacant hall once more, then opened the door to his private chambers. He had debated mightily about where to bed Liliah, and while his private chambers wasn't the most prudent of choices, he found it was exactly where he pictured her when he imagined the event.

The room was dominated by his mahogany bed with red velvet curtains at each corner. A fire burned warm in the hearth, and the scent of sandalwood and cedar permeated the air, relaxing the tautness of his nerves, erasing the last of his hesitation.

As he turned to Liliah, her gaze scanned her surroundings, taking the details into account.

"Is it as you expected?" Lucas asked, curious.

"Oddly, yes. It suits you." She turned to face him as she pulled her lower lip between her teeth.

"Nervous?" Lucas asked, releasing her hand and starting to slowly circle her.

"A bit," she answered honestly.

Lucas nodded, studying her as he made a lazy circle around her. He'd considered many different ideas for her seduction, and as he gazed at her, he debated among several.

Did he go in for the easy target? Use her passions against her to make the experience quick and effective?

Did he use the opportunity to coach her to benefit his own pleasure?

Or take it slow, building up the climax to the fevered frenzy his body craved?

"I rather feel like you're a tiger and I'm your helpless prey." Liliah arched a brow artlessly. "I wasn't aware that this took so much forethought."

Lucas chuckled, pausing in his stride. "That, my

dear, is where you are most certainly incorrect, and where your innocence bleeds through your wit."

"Is that so?" Liliah tipped her chin daringly.

"Indeed. And while I do not have to take my time in this area, I find that it pleases me to do so, and as such, you are quite at my mercy." Lucas reached up and slowly unfastened his cravat, sliding the silk off his neck. Liliah watched with open interest as he set the garment on the side table.

"Should I . . ." Liliah tugged on her gloves.

"No." Lucas shook his head. "Wait. It's all about anticipation," he stated, answering his own question concerning methods.

Slow and erotic.

His body almost wept in delight.

"Very well," Liliah answered, her brow pinching slightly as he slowly unbuttoned his white shirt. As he stripped off his shirt, he tossed it to the side, his body pounding with heat at the fascinated expression in Liliah's eyes.

Her gaze roamed his chest freely, exciting his body further. "Oh my," she breathed, taking a slight step forward.

"Ah, no. Look only," Lucas instructed, slowly striding toward her. Her chest rose and fell in quick succession, giving a luscious view of the shape of her breasts. With a mischievous grin, Lucas leaned forward just enough to feel the heat from her skin, to smell its fragrance, to breathe her air, yet not touch. Tilting his head, he moved from her hairline down to the curve of her neck, breathing out against her skin, grinning when she shivered slightly.

Her hands twitched as if to move.

"Wait, love," he scolded teasingly. Breathing out against the sensitive space just below her ear, he leaned back and walked around her. Her gaze followed him, glancing behind her shoulder till he leaned in once more, this time nipping ever so lightly against her neck.

A soft gasp escaped her lips. "I—I thought we could not touch," she challenged, but the effect was lost in the breathy nature of her tone.

Lucas chuckled lightly against her skin. "I said you could not touch, nothing about myself."

She sighed softly as he nipped her again. "It hardly seems fair."

"I care not." He retreated slightly and carefully unfastened the few buttons at her back, belatedly realizing she'd had the forethought to wear something easy to remove, and replace.

Her forethought pleased him greatly, adding another layer of need to his already pulsing body. As he slipped the dress off her shoulders, his fingers tingled as they brushed the softest chemise she wore beneath. It was innocent and arousing all at once in its design and simplicity. Leaving just enough to the imagination to drive a man wild.

The dress pooled at Liliah's feet, and as she shivered slightly, he ran his hands down her arms, savoring the smooth texture of her skin. "Turn," he commanded quietly.

Liliah stepped from her dress, then turned, her expression wide and full of wonder. "When you touch me, it is like holding an open flame against my skin— yet no pain . . . I've never experienced the like." She spoke with quiet awe and artless honesty.

Lucas nodded once, then tugged on her hand, pulling her in close. Lowering his head, he brushed his lips against hers, once, twice, and a third time before retreating. "Imagine that . . . but all over." He used his nose to move her cheek to the side as he nipped her ear, then traced her jawline with his nose before capturing her lips once more.

He swallowed her reply with a searing kiss. His body strained against his remaining clothes, demanding he remove them and end the sweet torture of anticipation.

Yet he paused, and suffered and burned while he slowly tugged at Liliah's chemise, only breaking the kiss long enough to remove it fully. He captured her lips once more, not wanting to give her a moment to think about what was taking place, his body growing fearful he'd not experience his own release should she back down from their agreement.

His body trembled with impatience, reminding him of how long it had been since he'd experienced the soft submission of a woman's body. Willfully, he forced back his galloping passions and focused on the seduction—needing her to be as desperate as he.

He nipped at her lips as he reached up and cupped her breasts, glorying in the beautiful weight of them in his hands, the perfect shape of them against his fingers. She gasped as he touched her, but he silenced her shock with another kiss, then kneaded her artfully into submission. When he sensed her need growing, he released her delicate skin and quickly unfastened his breeches, stepping from them. His fingers caressed up her bare back and then moved back down, slipping around the last of her underthings and carefully removing them.

Liliah leaned back, her gaze unfocused, her breathing coming in soft gasps. "Dear Lord."

"And we've only just begun." Lucas grinned unrepentantly and spanned her hips with his hands.

Liliah glanced down as Lucas rubbed his most sensitive part against her. "Oh my." She blinked and met his gaze.

Lucas simply grinned and met her lips once more, knowing that her mind was spinning; yet all she needed was to *feel*.

Damn, it was all he needed too.

With a chuckle, he released her from the kiss and lifted her in his arms. He muted her gasp with his lips before he set her on the bed and promptly covered her body with his. If she had any thoughts, she didn't voice them as Lucas nipped at her lower lip, then traced his tongue against them, mercilessly devouring her as she opened her mouth to him. He situated himself just above her; feeling her hips reach up to meet him, he struggled against the primal need to go deep and hard into her. Grasping her hands, he twisted his fingers around hers, then slowly slid inside her, his body damn near coming apart at the warm and wet sensation. Her grip tightened on his hands and he paused, waiting for her body to adjust and welcome him. Bloody hell, he had to remember she was an innocent.

He was her first.

The idea was so damn erotic that he almost climaxed right then and there.

Breathing hard, he felt her relax slightly and he pushed in farther, swearing under his breath at the pleasure of her surrounding him. He wanted to push in deep, move against her, empty himself utterly—yet he resisted. Bloody hell, this was her first experience, he didn't want it to be miserable.

He wanted it to be profound.

So profound that none after would compare.

So with Herculean strength, he waited till she was ready, and then without warning, he slid all the way in, flinching when she gasped slightly at her slight tearing.

"The worst is over," he murmured against her lips, breathing in her breath, making it his own as he nipped at her lips, feeding off of their delights.

"It's over?" Liliah gasped, her gaze focusing on his and blinking in confusion.

Lucas gave a small laugh, then kissed her sweet mouth simply for the pleasure of it. When was the last time he'd laughed during sex? He couldn't quite remember.

"No. It's not finished . . . but, if I'm correct, you are quite close, love." He nuzzled her neck and then began to move his hips.

Liliah sucked in a shocked breath, then gave a soft moan of pleasure, causing his body to tremble with the need to release—yet he knew that he couldn't let go within her, he'd need to pull out. His body and mind fought against one another, fighting what was right versus what was wanted.

And damn, he wanted to ruin her fully, utterly, and irrevocably.

"Luc," Liliah whispered, burying her face against his neck as he moved swifter, harder, deeper inside of her as her hips rose up to meet him, their bodies mating with unreserved passion.

Her body stiffened slightly for a moment before she cried out, her hands clenching his as her breathing became great gasps as she slowly descended from her first climax.

Lucas ground his teeth as he waited for her to come

back to herself, yet it wasn't enough, his self-control had met its limit and he pulled out just before he spilled himself within her. His body shook with the power of it, his throat dry from the way it stole his breath, his arms trembling to hold him up over Liliah as he came back to himself from the soaring pleasure of sweet release. He sucked in a tight breath as the final spasms rocketed through him, and with jerky motions, he rolled off her and onto the bed beside her. His heart pounded out an excited yet sated rhythm as he turned to meet her wondrous gaze.

"I . . . have no words." Liliah blinked, her expression one of marvel.

"I should hope not," Lucas answered, studying the beautiful blush of lovemaking on her face. She was stunning, and his body grew hard with the idea of knowing her once more. Yet rather than follow his instincts, he rose from bed.

"As heartless as I sound, we must get ready and return you to Bond Street before anyone is the wiser." Even as he said the words, his body demanded he hold her prisoner, keep her in his bed.

"I suppose you're correct," Liliah remarked, and slowly sat up, then paused, glancing to her belly. "Why?"

Lucas pulled on his breeches. "So there will be no child."

Liliah blushed then nodded.

"I'll assist you." With gentle motions, Lucas helped Liliah not only clean herself, but tenderly buttoned her dress. When he finished, he placed the slightest kiss to her neck, lingering in the moment, wanting more yet utterly afraid of wanting more.

"Thank you." Liliah glanced over her shoulder and met his gaze warmly. "I'm sure I'll never quite recover."

Lucas chuckled, yet it was a sad sound to his ears. "I should hope not, Liliah." He watched as she walked to the mirror and tidied her hair. In short order they were walking down the servants' back stairs, toward a hack that he'd requested arrive around that time. As Liliah strode to the carriage, Lucas kept her arm firmly upon his, selfishly wanting the last few moments of their encounter. As she stepped up into the carriage, she met his gaze. "I'm a woman of my word. You need not concern yourself with my sharing information about your club . . . Luc."

Lucas nodded. "Thank you."

"In that, I do fear that you've given me far more than I've given you," she added, then sat back in the carriage.

"I rather think the opposite, Liliah. Farewell." He tapped on the carriage wall and it lurched forward, rolling down the street.

Lucas watched till it was out of sight, then returned to his residence, his body satisfied yet his mind utterly restless.

He had the strong suspicion that Lady Liliah was not going to be easy to forget.

And that scared him more than the devil.

Because in his experience, of the two evils, women were far more dangerous than hell itself.

Chapter Nineteen

Liliah leaned back against her carriage as she ignored the glare from her sister.

"I still don't believe that you were lost."

Liliah sighed. "You are free to believe whatever you wish."

Samantha huffed, but didn't reply. After Liliah had returned from Luc's residence, she had made her way back to the modiste's shop, only to run into her sister and Sarah. They, of course, had been concerned when she hadn't returned, but she'd simply lied and said she'd been lost.

Samantha was already in a vexed mood because of her fitting, and she wasn't inclined to believe, or forgive, Liliah's tardiness.

Liliah attempted to take the attention off of herself. "What do you think I should wear to the rout tomorrow night?" Yet even as she tried for a lighthearted approach, her stomach clenched in dread. It would be the first ball where it would be announced and become common knowledge that she was betrothed to Meyer. At least now she had experienced the physical act of love, but the elation and excitement she'd experienced were fading. Rather she found herself unsettled and rather depressed.

It was like experiencing heaven, and then realizing it was only for a few moments and you had to live out the rest of your life without experiencing it again.

It had been magical, truly the stuff of fairy tales. Yet rather than feel satisfied with the experience, she feared it would only create a hunger she didn't know how to fill.

Especially married to Meyer.

Her brilliant plans were coming to naught.

Samantha's voice interrupted her musings. "You can't exactly wear black, though it would be appropriate."

Liliah cracked a smile and giggled. "I don't see that going over well."

"No, and I'm assuming since Father wished to speak with you, that he announced your betrothal in the *Times*?"

"Yes."

"Then more's the pity you can't wear black—you, Meyer, and Rebecca."

"How true." Liliah shifted to the side as the carriage hit a bump. "The Winharts' ball will at least be diverting; they usually employ some sort of entertainment with the dancing. I shall focus on that."

"A wise idea," Samantha remarked.

As they approached home, Liliah was pleased to have an evening to herself without any plans. Heaven only knew she would have more than enough to deal with tomorrow—but for tonight, she simply wanted to remember.

As she alighted from the carriage, she quickly made haste to her room, dismissing Sarah from any assistance, and promptly lay on her bed. An amused smile teased her lips and she touched them delicately, wondering if they would ever recover from Luc's sweet assault.

Rolling off the bed, she walked to the mirror and studied herself. Though it was almost imperceptible, she could see a difference—it was in her eyes. There was awareness, a knowledge that hid within their green depths that wasn't there earlier.

She touched her face, then traced her lips. Closing her eyes, she gave herself over to the memories. Her heart pounded an excited rhythm as she remembered the feel of his skin on hers, the strong muscles of his back as he arched into her, the way he spoke her name . . . it was the highlight of her existence.

She was afraid it might also be her undoing.

For how did one survive the experience of making love and know it was once again out of reach?

Yet, even as she considered her words, she wondered: Was it the act, or was it Luc?

Her heart whispered the truth to her, even as she tried to silence it.

She had no idea that inviting ruin would not only compromise her body—but her heart as well.

Liliah sighed, knowing that any answers she sought wouldn't be given this evening. And she refused to feel sorry for herself. She chose to remember that she was given exactly what she asked for, and in that, it had to be enough.

So that night as she lay down to sleep, Liliah decided that if she had to live with Meyer as a husband in name only, then it wouldn't be so terrible if Luc was the one who loved her in her dreams.

That could hardly be sinful; rather she looked upon it as a gift. And she drifted off to sleep with Luc's name on her lips.

That very same name was on her lips the next morning, and throughout the day as she readied for the Winharts' ball. It became her touchstone, her safe place as the world spun out of her control. She had refused to look at the announcement in the *Times*, and she refused to dwell on the affirmation of the betrothal at the ball. Instead she allowed her memories to soothe her. Yet she soon discovered that memories were not enough.

Even when she told herself repeatedly that they had to be.

She focused on the scent of Luc, as Sarah coiffed her hair.

She remembered the sensation of his fingers brushing her skin, as Sarah helped her don her gown.

She remembered the way he spoke her name, as her father demanded she be at the carriage by eight p.m. sharp.

And she focused on the memory of Luc's smile as she stared at the passing town as they made their way to the Winharts' residence.

The stone estate boasted thousands of candles illuminating the entrance, all dancing in the soft breeze. Liliah was enchanted. Even given the miserable circumstances that awaited her within, she chose to find joy in the middle of it. As she strode into the ballroom, she noted the stares of several ladies and the whispers that followed—certainly affirming the announcement in the *Times*. They would all see a smart match, an ideal situation—they would also be utterly wrong.

Liliah lifted her chin as she walked around the ballroom, searching, yet hesitant to find Meyer or Rebecca. How miserable. Her two best friends were no longer a source of delight and joy, but a reminder of pain and sorrow. The delight of the candlelight faded quickly, leaving Liliah in a thick, dark cloud of her own misery. Her father had quickly abandoned her for the faro table, where he'd speak of politics all evening, and for once, Liliah felt very alone.

A tear pricked her eye and she willed it to stay. She refused to feel sorry for herself, it would do no good. Angrily, she squared her shoulders and determined to meet her fate head-on, not shrink away as if defeated.

Liliah took a deep breath and determined to find her friends, and somehow mend the friendship. It was possible, was it not?

Rebecca walked into the ballroom then, and Liliah started toward her. When Rebecca met her gaze, indecision, hurt, and anger flashed across her face and she turned away.

Liliah paused, then all but charged toward her friend.

As she grew closer, she called out politely, "Rebecca?"

But her friend ignored her.

"Please?" Liliah asked, then relaxed slightly when Rebecca paused and turned. Her eyes were cloudy with frustration and pain.

Liliah took a few steps and nodded toward a more private area of the ballroom. Rebecca nodded and they found relative privacy.

"I will not take Meyer from you. He will remain

yours, even if I must bear his name. I'll not bear his heart, or his children. You must understand that." Liliah took Rebecca's hands and squeezed them.

Rebecca closed her eyes. "I thank you for that, but is it wrong for that to not be enough?" She opened her eyes. "When you love someone, as I love Meyer, it is not enough to just own their heart—I wish to own every part of him. To know that it is my face that he will wake up to. That it is my name that changes to his, that it is my body that will bear his children—mine alone. I find I cannot even stomach the idea of sharing even the smallest part of him." Rebecca glanced down, a tear rolling down her face.

Liliah sighed. "I don't want to lose you, Rebecca. You are one of my dearest friends, and I fear that this whole problem is not only robbing us of our future, but of our friendship as well."

"Liliah . . ." Rebecca released her hands. "That is a problem I know no solution to, because I don't want to lose your friendship either, but nor can I stand by when you marry the man I love. Please don't ask this of me." Rebecca gave her head a small shake and walked away into the ballroom, leaving Liliah even more distraught than before.

For truly, what hope had she left?

None.

Meyer would come to resent her—in fact probably already did.

Rebecca couldn't remain her friend.

Nor could she change the announcement or her father's will.

Liliah blew out a sobering breath, collecting her emotions and forcing them into submission. As she walked into the throng of people, she wished Luc would attend. It was a pointless hope, their agreement had been satisfied, yet hope had never been rational, had it?

While she didn't see Luc, she did spot Meyer, his father ever vigilant behind him, and Lady Rebecca watching from a distance. Thankfully the first waltz wasn't expected for a while, yet that didn't stop the dread from pooling in her belly. It wasn't as if it changed anything, the announcement in the *Times* had already sealed the deal, but it was more the idea that every dance she danced with Meyer was one that Rebecca wouldn't have, and so Liliah had the sense that she was slowly stealing her friend's most prized possession: Meyer's time and attention.

Even if he was loath to give it to her.

Liliah took a flute of champagne and walked about the room, studying the décor and doing her best to ignore the chatter about her. And in far too little time, the strains of the first waltz rose, and Liliah sighed and looked up. Sure enough, Meyer was approaching her, his expression ever grim. How long had it been since she'd seen her friend smile? Far too long. It was as if his strained expression were frozen, unable to alter or change. Liliah breathed deep and extended her hand wordlessly as he offered his arm. As he led them into the swirling dance, Liliah met his gaze. "What is becoming of us?"

Meyer's expression pinched and he glanced away. "I've heard that life is what you make of it, yet, Liliah, I find I have not the strength of character to find the hope in our circumstance. As such, I fear I'm an abominable friend. For that I apologize." Meyer met her gaze once more, sincerity echoing in his eyes.

"I don't want to lose you, or Rebecca, and I feel as if

I'm fighting a battle that's been ordained for me to lose," Liliah whispered, twirling and stepping back into the frame of Meyer's arms.

"I feel utterly the same, my friend. But let us converse on a brighter topic, shall we? Enough of the self-pity, let us delight in conversation as we once did." Meyer put on a brave smile, and Liliah felt her lips twitch in response.

"Very well, what did you have in mind?"

Meyer glanced to the dancers, then back. "Your admirer isn't present. Is there a reason for that?"

Liliah's face burned at the thought of Luc, and all the wicked sensations her body felt as echoes of yesterday's events. "I did not expect him tonight."

"Ah, so you know of whom I speak?" Meyer asked with a hint of smugness in his tone.

"Of course." Liliah resisted the urge to roll her eyes. "But I wouldn't call him an admirer, rather . . ." Liliah searched for the correct and proper word. Because all she could think of was a more scandalous description. She settled for, "An acquaintance."

Meyer arched a brow in an expression of disbelief. "My dear, Heightfield isn't known for his acquaintances with women . . . rather his penchant for knowing them"—Meyer cleared his throat—"well."

Liliah bit her lip and glanced away, yet even as he said it a white-hot jealousy seared her veins. She didn't want to think of Luc sharing himself with any other—not that she had any claim. It was utterly irrational, yet present nonetheless.

"Your face bears an odd expression," Meyer commented.

"It's an odd comment to a lady," Liliah retorted, but softened her words with a smile.

"Interesting," was all the response Meyer gave.

Liliah studied him. "What are you thinking, for your expression is quite smug."

Meyer shrugged slightly as the song ended, not answering.

"Utterly irritating," Liliah huffed as he led her from the dance floor. Meyer chuckled in response, and bowed to take his leave.

Liliah watched him retreat, narrowing her eyes. The music began again, and rather than allow another partner to seek her out for the dance, she strode to a more quiet location in the ballroom. The potted plants in the corner kept several wallflower ladies company, and Liliah took a vacant seat. Several of the young ladies watched her with open interest—Liliah had never been amongst their ranks. Rather, as the daughter of a duke, she had far too many suitors—till recently. But she refused to think on it—instead she found rest in solitude. There would be another waltz, and no doubt there would be more conversations with her father, but for now, this stolen moment of peace was enough.

It had to be.

Chapter Twenty

Lucas studied the gentry as they walked into the main entrance of the club. The rout at the Winharts' was certainly winding down and the need to fulfill their more wicked natures was surfacing as the elite members of Temptation came to feed their desires. Lucas glanced at his pocket watch; it was nearly four in the morning, but the party would easily continue past daylight. As he moved from the balcony of the estate, he took the back stairs to the main level. He scanned the ballroom, where he noted that every courtesan was in place, along with the tables perfectly set for the many games that would feed or starve men's fortunes.

He tugged on his collar, then cleared his throat. Passing the ballroom, he ran into Ramsey.

"Bankroll is set, and I must say that so far the gentlemen are placing quite substantial bets on one event in particular." Ramsey arched a brow. His penchant for numbers made him the logical choice for overseeing the bank and betting aspects of the club.

"Oh? And what event is that? Pistols at dawn for some poor idiot?" Lucas snapped, his lack of patience bleeding through. Though he knew it had nothing to do with Ramsey.

Rather, it had everything to do with that bloody chit who haunted him day and night.

It had only been a day, yet he couldn't purge her from his mind.

"No need to snap at me, old man. I just remember you and Heathcliff mentioning some innocent deb's name, and she came up in the betting book tonight."

Lucas fixated his gaze on Ramsey. "What did you say?"

"Nothing as of yet, for fear of your damn aggression. What is your problem tonight? You're like a caged tiger." Ramsey crossed his arms, his spectacles making his eyes appear overly large as he studied his friend.

"Forgive me," Lucas ground out.

"I didn't need you to grovel, just back off a bit," Ramsey replied. "It would seem that the Duke of Chatterwood, bloody pain in the arse—his daughter is betrothed to Greywick's son. It's all quite common if you ask me, yet the gentlemen are betting large sums against one another that the marriage will or won't take place. I tell you, Greywick himself bet that the match will be made, and in two weeks, no less. Which, of course, is likely to be true—given he's the father and all. Can't say why anyone would bet against him." Ramsey shook his head. "Though I shouldn't be surprised. Last week, Lord Hawthorne placed a bet on whether it would rain for six days in a row. Bloody asinine."

"You don't say." Lucas clipped the words, jealousy pounding through him like a wild and irrational beast. Even though he knew that a marriage to Meyer would be in name only, he loathed the idea of her belonging to the man.

"Indeed. Shockley placed a few thousand pounds on the betrothal going to hell before the altar, and from there it spun out of control like mad."

"Greywick placed a bet." Lucas tilted his head slightly, studying his friend, his mind coming back into clarity from the jealous haze.

"Indeed."

"Of what amount?"

"It was large, substantially so. Ten thousand pounds." Ramsey whispered the words, likely in reverence for such a mammoth sum.

"Dear Lord." Lucas frowned. "Is he good for it?" It was a logical question. How often had a lord over-betted his worth and ended up not only penniless but in debt?

"I believe so, but only barely. My guess is that he'd lose his estate in the country, the one in Sussex."

"Interesting." Lucas twisted his lips. "Did Chatterwood place a bet?"

Ramsey shook his head. "You know he's not a member, why ask such a question?"

"Just curious. Did anyone else place a substantial sum on the marriage going through?" Lucas prodded suspiciously.

"A few . . ." Ramsey paused. "I think it would be best if you saw the list for yourself. Perhaps tomorrow when all the bets are placed. Would that satisfy your curiosity?"

Lucas nodded. "And you are checking for validity

of the funds that have been wagered, correct? No gentlemen's pass, verify. Agreed?" Lucas switched gears
into business mode.

"I'm quite aware that a gentleman's word holds as
much water as a fishing net. I'm double-checking,
Lucas," Ramsey replied with a hint of irritation.

"Well done."

"Thanks for the confidence in my abilities," Ramsey replied with sarcasm and strode away, back toward
the betting books.

Lucas frowned as he considered this new information. It was common practice for the men of nobility to
place gentlemen's bets. How often had White's taken
bets on some of the most foolish things? On when the
rain would fall, or if a servant would win in fisticuffs
against another—yet occasionally, the betting took a
different turn. Lucas had his suspicions in this case, yet
he dared not speak of them, not till he had proof. He
shouldn't care, he should leave it alone—let the men
bet and pay the betting fee and line his pockets. Yet he
found he didn't wish to simply walk away. Rather it
gave him the perfect excuse. A prospect that brightened his spirits immensely.

Yet even as he considered it, he tried to ignore his
better judgment, which was whispering *danger*. Because any further entanglement with Liliah would certainly be a threat to his sanity.

But if tasting her again meant he forfeited his sound
mind—it was almost worth it.

Almost.

Because he'd rather forfeit his mind than his heart.

And that was the danger of which he was most
afraid.

She was dangerously close already, and it had been just one night.

Heaven help him if he pursued more.

Yet the pursuit of more was the only rational thought in his mind, more of her skin, her flavor, her body in his bed, warming it.

As the night wore on, Lucas formulated a plan—one that was as selfish as it was selfless. If Heathcliff knew, he'd think Lucas had gone daft. Yet it was without a care that Lucas approached his friend as the party in Temptations came to a close.

Because if Lucas was going to pull it off, he needed help.

And if you couldn't depend on your friends, then you were in poor shape indeed.

However, that didn't justify your friends laughing at you, which is exactly how Heathcliff reacted.

"You've lost your bloody mind, and I can't say I regret it. I always knew she'd be the death of you," Heathcliff commented as he lounged on the settee in the study.

"Thank you for your encouragement." Lucas sighed, his lack of sleep catching up with him and his sanity slowly slipping.

"So what part of this diabolically stupid plan do you wish me to play?" Heathcliff asked, his brogue emphasizing the words.

Lucas glared.

Heathcliff raised his hands in defense. "Forget not that you are basically going against the Duke of Chatterwood and the Earl of Greywick. I'd not be surprised if he found a way to get you tossed in the Tower of London."

"We don't use the Tower for torture any longer." Lucas rolled his eyes.

"That wasn't my point . . ." He let the words linger.

"We all have dirt on us, Heathcliff . . ." Lucas spoke meaningfully. "Some more than others."

"True enough, though do not expect me to believe you're doing this out of the goodness of your heart— no, this is for the favors of a lady. But I'm quite surprised that you'd suggest that anyone dig into the sordid past of the duke, when you're one of the few who know it well." Heathcliff wiggled his eyebrows.

"Yes, well, there's a time for all sins to come to light, is there not? I do believe that's in the Bible somewhere."

"And yes, you're quite the authority on religion." Heathcliff chuckled. "Although, that does remind me of a different question, since we're on the topic of sin."

Lucas arched an irritated brow.

"You've been quite tight-lipped on your promise of seduction. I can only assume that since you're more . . . chivalrous?" He tilted his head. "I'm not quite sure that's the word. Perhaps the more lustful side of you has come forth and the deed has already been done?" Heathcliff grinned wolfishly.

Lucas opened his mouth to give a heated retort, but withheld. There was no need to come to her aid, not here. "The agreement was satisfied."

"Listen to you, going about and making sex sound sterile. Tell me, did you even enjoy the experience?" Heathcliff shook his head as if pitying his friend. "No, do not answer. I know full well that you did, because of your current plans. Rather . . ." Heathcliff stood from the settee and slowly approached Lucas, a calculating glint in his eye. "I'd wager that you were taken off guard, utterly disarmed, and fighting yourself even now because you both want her and fear her. Am I correct?" He waited, studying his friend.

"Damn you," Lucas swore.

"Bloody hell, how the mighty have fallen." Heathcliff chuckled, grinning wildly. "And Chatterwood's daughter to boot. Well, if you wish to have her, all you need to do is publicize that she's been ruined—you did thoroughly ruin her, did you not?"

"Quite thoroughly." Lucas arched a brow, his body heating in response, desperately wanting to repeat the experience.

Again and again.

"Good man. I knew you'd remember how." Heathcliff gave a wink.

"Don't wink." Lucas shook his head.

"Regardless, you can easily—"

"I don't wish to marry the chit, I simply want to bed her—repeatedly." Lucas sighed and walked toward the fire. "No commitment, no publicity, just—"

"Sex. Understood," Heathcliff said. "Then, why do you wish to upset her marriage to this Meyer fellow? Didn't you say it was more of a . . . platonic affair?"

Lucas shrugged. "Yes. Likely, or so she said, and my own assessment as well. He's rather smitten with the daughter of Lord and Lady Grace."

"Ah, a bloody Greek tragedy."

"Indeed." Lucas glanced over his shoulder at his friend.

"But that is my point." Heathcliff came to stand beside Lucas. "Clearly there is no obligation for her to remain faithful to her husband in name only, so you would be free to take her as mistress. No one would be the wiser, and it certainly seems that since Lady Liliah was willing to run headlong into ruin before marriage, she'd be willing to participate in it after."

Lucas studied the flames as they danced in the hearth. "You make a valid point. I'll consider it."

"There's little to consider. Either you wish to make a chaotic mess with Chatterwood and Greywick, or you wish to let things take their natural progression and you swoop in to snatch up your mistress."

Lucas nodded. "When have I ever taken the easy road?" He studied his friend.

"Never. Damn it. How I wish you would, just once in a while." Heathcliff sighed. "Very well, I assume we're going out tonight?"

"You would assume correctly."

"Should I tell Ramsey?"

"No, he'll hate the idea. Let him make love to his numbers."

Heathcliff shook his head. "Don't speak of it that way."

"How well you know that our friend loves his work above all else."

"Indeed, but I can remember a time that someone else did as well . . . now look at us?" Heathcliff spoke meaningfully.

"Damn you," Lucas retorted.

"As I said, how the mighty have fallen. Just be sure that you don't take me down with you, old man." Heathcliff slapped his friend on the back and strode from the study.

Lucas studied the fire a few more minutes, piecing the plan together in finer detail in this mind, then took his carriage home from the club.

One thing was for certain, he needed his rest—for tonight he planned on other activities.

Wicked, delightful, and erotic activities—and Lucas fell asleep with a grin.

Chapter Twenty-one

L iliah was loath to dress for the evening party at the Ganders'. It would be a small affair, and as such she had requested to decline the invitation. Yet her father held fast, requiring them to attend. It was as if he wished her and Meyer to be seen in every venue, at every opportunity, even if it had only been a few days since the announcement.

The idea of it was like a millstone around her neck, holding her down, oppressing her usual delight in life. So it was with great reluctance that Liliah entered the carriage with her father to attend the soirée. The idea that she'd no longer see Lucas only added to her disenchantment with life. Though he'd awakened her body in ways she'd never imagined, she rather found that the seduction was only a part of the reason she missed him. Lucas was a delight to converse with, and he withheld no honesty from his words—it was refreshing, and in a world where her friends were becoming more and more distant, he had been a welcome distraction and addition to her life. Yet that was over, and she didn't resent his disappearance. It was their agreement, and she would honor her side of it. No matter how it hurt.

The Ganders' estate was a white stone structure in Mayfair with a long gravel drive that was illuminated by Chinese lanterns. It was a lovely sight that momentarily lifted Liliah's spirits. The great stone pillars held up the portico, which was reminiscent of Grecian architecture, and Liliah studied them as she took the white stone steps along with the other guests. Music from stringed instruments floated through the air, welcoming the ton into the ballroom. As Liliah glanced around, she was surprised that it was more heavily attended than she had anticipated. Normally the Ganders' parties were of the smaller, more intimate variety. Of course, being the daughter of a duke, she was always invited. Whether the party be large or small—it was ever about *who* attended.

And she was of the notable variety.

Sure enough, she quickly spotted Meyer in his evening kit, and for once a smile illuminated his features. Her heart pinched in both sorrow and delight. Sorrow for how long it had been since she'd seen it, and delight because he had found his smile once more. Meyer was conversing with a dark-haired gentleman, but the crowd obstructed any more detail, and Liliah moved on in search of Rebecca. She'd resolved to make amends in their friendship, however impossible that might be. A footman passed with a tray of ratafia, and Liliah took a glass. Sipping the sweet concoction, she approached her dear friend Rebecca. Placing a hand on her shoulder, she waited for her friend to notice her presence.

"Hello," Liliah offered when Rebecca met her gaze.

Rebecca smiled, her expression holding a twinge of sadness, yet her eyes were clear as she reached out and grasped Liliah's hand. "Let us have a moment to speak." She turned to the other ladies in the circle. "Please excuse me." With a delicate curtsey, she tugged on Liliah's hand and led them toward the refreshment table.

"Liliah, I owe you a sincere apology," Rebecca began, then met her gaze with an earnest one of her own. "Yes, I'm heartbroken, but that is not your fault, and if anything, you've done your best to ease my pain—while I've done nothing to consider yours. For that I'm truly sorry." Rebecca spoke tenderly.

Liliah blinked, never once considering her friend's actions as needful of forgiveness, yet deeply touched that she'd offer herself in such a way. "Thank you, yet there is nothing to forgive," Liliah replied emphatically.

"Indeed there is, but it is ever so kind of you to overlook it. You are my dearest friend, Liliah, and I don't wish to lose you. Ever. Come what may." Rebecca squeezed Liliah's hand and Liliah returned the gesture.

"Nor I."

Rebecca offered her friend a watery smile, then glanced toward Meyer. "Have you seen who Meyer is conversing with? I haven't spoken to either gentleman tonight, but I'm assuming that it is of import to you." Rebecca grinned mischievously.

"No, who is it?" Liliah asked, rising on tiptoe in an effort to see over the people in the way.

"It's the gentleman that you danced with . . ." Her brow pinched as she thought of the name.

Liliah's heart pounded, her body tingled with hope, and she gasped, about to speak his name.

"Viscount Kilpatrick! I knew I'd remember the name after a moment," Rebecca finished.

Liliah's heart sank, the glimmer of hope fading as quickly as it appeared. "That is certainly of note, but I do not expect that he is speaking of me in any capacity."

"Oh? And what of the other gentleman? I must say, Meyer was quite concerned at his interest in you. He's not of the worthy variety." Rebecca spoke in hushed tones.

"Worthiness is in the eye of the beholder, my friend."

Rebecca studied her carefully, then nodded wordlessly.

"Come, let us find something sweet, and then we can discuss the latest gossip, for certainly you have something of note that I've not heard yet!" Liliah turned the topic and was rewarded with a grin from her friend. The country dances had begun, and Liliah almost wished to partake, but instead was quite pleased to spend the time conversing with Rebecca. It had been weeks since she had enjoyed her artless company with such freedom, without the dark, oppressive cloud covering them.

Yet even while the future still loomed, Liliah found she was able to not let it overtake her with weariness; rather, with her friendship restored, she was hopeful that they would come up with some sort of solution.

Two great chandeliers gave yellow light to the room,

illuminating it greatly compared to the candlelight that was employed last year. Even Rebecca remarked on the great expense the Ganders must have incurred for this improvement.

As each set came and went, Liliah knew that the dinner waltz was quickly approaching, and as such she expected her father would abandon whatever game he was participating in, to watch over her, make sure she accepted Meyer's offer to dance.

For certain, he would offer.

As the strains of the ever-scandalous waltz began, Liliah glanced to her friend, and reached out to squeeze her hand. "If it helps, I won't enjoy it."

Rebecca chuckled, giving her head a delicate shake. "I know. And as horrible as it sounds, that does help."

Liliah smiled, then rose from her seat. Meyer approached and bowed to the two ladies. "Lady Liliah"— and much more quietly—"Rebecca." He caressed her name with his tone, and Liliah grinned at the obvious affection, and the way Rebecca's color heightened.

Liliah took his arm and frowned slightly as Meyer gave her a daring grin. "What are you about, Meyer?" Liliah asked as he led them toward the center of the room.

He nodded over toward the left, where her father watched vigilantly.

"I see nothing amusing," Liliah retorted.

"That is why it is called faith, Lady Liliah. To believe in what you cannot see, as if it exists," he said cryptically. Liliah frowned as he glanced over her shoulder. "Just in time."

Confused, Liliah watched as none other than Luc

stepped around her person and tapped Meyer on the shoulder. "You don't mind, do you?" he asked.

Meyer shook his head and stepped out of the way as Luc's hand grasped her waist while his other tenderly took her hand. "Shall we?"

Liliah forced a blink as she stared at Luc, his devastatingly handsome features even more beautiful than in her dreams. "Of course," she answered belatedly.

Her gaze flickered behind him to where her father watched from across the room, far enough away to do nothing to intercede, but close enough for her to read the fury on his features.

"Eyes on me, Liliah," Luc coached as he led her into the dance.

Liliah focused on his crystal gaze, her body warming as if he were a fire. "I didn't expect you . . ." she whispered.

"Ah, which is why it was delightful to use the element of surprise." Luc grinned wolfishly. "And your friend was quick to accept my interruption."

"That is not surprising at all. Rather he will be free to ask Rebecca to dance."

"Exactly." Lucas nodded over her shoulder and turned her just enough for her to notice that indeed, Meyer had wasted little time in stealing Rebecca for the waltz.

"This is not going to go over well." A slight tingle of fear crawled up her back. "Yet I find that I care not."

"Why am I not surprised?" Luc teased. "So tell me, Lady Liliah—"

"I thought we had moved past my courtesy title," Liliah interrupted archly.

"Ah, but to protect your reputation—"

Liliah arched a brow bravely.

"Your reputation isn't always a reflection of the truth, Liliah. And while circumstances may have changed, your reputation need not," Luc whispered softly.

"I see. Then you are quite the champion this evening," Liliah remarked with a smile.

"I have my moments. Do not expect them often," Luc flirted.

"As you wish."

His hand grasped her in a firmer hold, his fingers slowly flexing against her waist as a wicked gleam illuminated his blue eyes. His thumb drew a lazy circle in her wrist as he held her, and Liliah's heart pounded an excited rhythm. She pulled her lips into her teeth, silencing a slight mew of pleasure.

"Dear Lord, Liliah, I won't be held responsible for my actions should you continue that exceedingly pleased expression. And indeed, your reputation won't survive such an event."

Liliah released her lips and nodded, but grasped his hand tightly, and with the slightest of movements, twisted her hip just enough for him to discern the movement.

"Minx."

"Are you surprised?" Liliah asked softly, losing herself in his gaze.

"No, not at all," he murmured as his gaze seared down her jawline and dipped lower, as if undressing her with his eyes.

Liliah's skin flushed with heat, her body pulsing with something she couldn't name but had certainly experienced before.

"When are you shopping next?" Luc asked covertly, his gaze lazily traveling upward to her eyes.

"Not nearly soon enough," Liliah answered honestly.

"Then am I to understand that your experience was satisfactory?" He grinned a seductive and secretive smile.

Liliah tilted her chin, regarding him coyly. "I'm not certain *once* has given me enough experience to give an educated reply."

Luc chuckled, shaking his head in amusement. His crystal-blue eyes danced with merriment and seduction, making her wish they were in a more private venue—my, how rapidly she had become a wicked wanton!

"Then I must find a way to remedy that, for educational purposes, you understand."

"It pleases me that you're concerned with enriching my mind."

"I've been told I'm an excellent teacher."

It was Liliah's turn to giggle. "I've been told I'm a horrid student."

Luc's grip on her waist tightened as he murmured low, his gaze fixed upon hers. "I'm a persistent educator—thorough in every way." His expression was pure seduction, and Liliah's knees weakened, but she squared her shoulders.

"Then I look forward to my education," she replied bravely, then glanced away from the heat of his gaze, lest she do something utterly impulsive and kiss him on the dance floor. She'd never recover, and it would destroy Luc as well, for he wouldn't be brought up to scratch, which would only tarnish his honor.

It was a dangerous line she flirted with, yet she couldn't muster up enough will to consider any other option.

It was simple.

She wanted him, desperately.

And by some miracle, he wanted her as well.

She wasn't going to ignore such a golden opportunity—rather she'd run headlong into the folly, delighted.

Be it her ruin or her sanity.

"You've gone quite pensive," Luc commented, regarding her.

"Simply reminding myself to act the lady," she replied with a saucy tone.

"Propriety requires it . . . here."

Liliah shook her head in amusement, then paused as Luc's expression sobered.

"I learned a bit of information that might be of use to you, if you wish to hear it."

"Of course," Liliah answered, both curious and touched that he'd consider revealing it to her.

"It would seem that several men, including Lord Greywick, have placed large bets on your betrothal to Meyer." He watched her intently.

Liliah frowned. "It seems an odd thing on which to bet."

"Believe me, there have been more foolish ones. Yet it struck me as odd for Meyer's father to bet a large sum. I know not what it implies, yet it might mean something to your friend." He glanced over her shoulder and Liliah followed his gaze to see Meyer and Rebecca dancing.

"I see. I'll certainly try to uncover more details." Liliah turned back to him. "I, I sincerely appreciate your taking note of this, and relaying the information to me. You didn't need to, yet you did. For that, I'm thankful." Liliah's heart swelled with appreciation.

"It was of no consequence." Luc shrugged.

"It was to me," Liliah answered shyly as the music came to an end.

"Until later." Luc pulled her wrist up to his lips and kissed her gloved hand slowly, then kissed it a second time before releasing it.

"How much later?" Liliah asked under her breath.

"Not nearly soon enough." His gaze traveled up her person, setting her nerves to tingling with desire. After bowing smartly, he strode away.

Liliah watched his broad back retreat into the crowd that studied him unabashedly. As she walked to the edge of the ballroom, she noted the determined stride of her father, heading toward her. Her heart pinched in fear, yet before her father could cross the distance, her attention was sought out by Viscount Kilpatrick. "Ah, my lady, honor me?" He held out his hand.

Liliah took it quickly and escaped back to the dance floor as the quadrille music began to play.

"Thank you," Liliah replied heartily as he led them into the square formation with three other couples.

"Think nothing of it," he replied in his smoky brogue.

Liliah took position and curtseyed to Lord Kilpatrick, then turned to curtsey to the other couples. Soon she was trading partners with Lady Lessman, and grasping the hand of Lord Lessman for a turn, then returning to Viscount Kilpatrick. It was a delightful dance, but not one that allowed for conversation. However, the joyful music lifted her spirits from the trepidation of her father's ire, and she danced with abandon.

As she performed the final turns, the music ended as the dancers clapped in appreciation. Liliah joined in, even has her gaze searched for her father.

He was nowhere to be readily seen, and she exhaled a sigh of relief as Lord Kilpatrick offered his arm.

"Thank you."

"My pleasure, it is not every day that I get the opportunity to dance with such a lovely lady."

"You flatter me, sir."

"Yes. I do," he teased, leading them to the refreshment table.

"I must say, I was quite surprised to see you in attendance," Liliah hedged.

Lord Kilpatrick offered her a glass of madeira, which she accepted thankfully, even as she braced herself to sip of the overly sweet concoction.

"Believe me when I say no one is more surprised than myself—except perhaps Heightfield." He chuckled and took a long drink of the orgeat he procured for himself.

Liliah regarded him. "How so?"

"Ah, but that is for me to know, and for you . . . to discover." He winked, then bowed, taking his leave.

Liliah took another sip of her beverage, her mind wandering—so much so that she startled when a cold hand gripped her elbow.

"We are leaving," her father commanded, sending a shiver up her back.

"But the last waltz . . ." Liliah said, even as he tugged on her elbow demandingly.

"Isn't important. Come," he asserted and steered her toward the exit.

He moved slowly, deliberately, clearly not wishing to cause a scene. There were a few whispers, but Liliah noted that he forced a smile to each of the people who dared glance their direction, as if deflecting attention.

It was brilliant.

It was calculating.

It truly shouldn't surprise her.

As the carriage was pulled around front, Liliah took her seat and waited.

Because while her father smiled at the world, it was only a mask that hid the truly black heart within.

Chapter Twenty-two

"Where is Liliah?" Lucas asked in a tight tone. Heathcliff shrugged, glancing about as if curious as well. "I left her by the refreshment table not a half hour ago. Where were you?"

Lucas studied his friend's glass of orgeat. His stomach turned at the idea of it. He'd much prefer brandy at the moment—hell, even water was better than the overly sweet, almond-flavored syrup they called a beverage. "I was conversing with an acquaintance."

Heathcliff arched a brow. "Who in the hell were you talking to here?"

Lucas sighed. "Meyer, if you must know. Greywick's son, the idiot who's found himself betrothed to Liliah."

"Ah, that actually makes sense. You had me concerned, thought maybe you were losing not just your heart, but your sanity. The ton, bah!" Heathcliff shuddered.

"Those same people line your pockets, and mine," Lucas reminded him.

"All the more reason to pity them," Heathcliff added with a chuckle. "What did you speak of with Meyer?"

"I simply informed him of his father's substantial bet. The poor chap about choked when I named the amount. Makes me wonder if the earldom is in some sort of financial difficulty."

"Ramsey said he was good for it, did he not?"

"He did, but he's been wrong before."

"True." Heathcliff nodded. "Anything else of note?"

"Not in particular. The final waltz will come up later, and I was simply making arrangements."

"Ah, never thought I'd see the day when you'd play coy with a lass."

"I'm doing nothing of the sort," Lucas replied in an offended tone.

"You are indeed. Pussyfooting around, making *plans*. Why, if you want something . . . someone—take it! Be a man about it, Lucas." Heathcliff nodded empathically.

"This isn't the Highlands."

Heathcliff huffed. "You needn't remind me of that. I'm quite painfully aware."

"There's protocol, and if I were to misstep, then—"

"Then what, exactly? You're sounding more and more like Ramsey."

"That's because you're a brute, and I sound nothing like Ramsey."

"I've been called worse." Heathcliff shrugged.

"By me, no doubt."

His friend grinned.

"Why go about like a bull in a china shop, when one

can be far more stealthy and gain more information and . . . privacy?" Lucas asked, grinning.

"Ah, diabolical. I like it. Carry on." Heathcliff gave a dismissive wave.

"I would, could I find the woman in question."

"Perhaps you should find her father first, to make sure they didn't take their leave."

Lucas's blood ran cold. He hadn't considered that Chatterwood would spirit his daughter away so quickly. Yet now, in hindsight, he could see its potential quite clearly. "Damn and blast."

"Try the faro table," Heathcliff encouraged.

But Lucas was already heading in that direction.

His fears were confirmed when he couldn't find the duke at the gaming tables, or milling about in the ballroom, nor could he find Liliah.

They had most certainly left.

His memory flashed back to Liliah's father's grip on her arm, the way he controlled her, held her tightly.

Hurt her.

Rage smoldered within, yet he was powerless to do anything save charge to the estate—which would only serve to have him thrown into the street on his ear.

He needed a different plan.

And he knew exactly whom he needed to ask for assistance.

He only hoped she hadn't left as well.

Lucas searched the ballroom for Lady Rebecca. It wasn't difficult to find her, for she was ever within earshot and eyesight of Meyer. At his approach, she cocked her head curiously.

"My lady." Lucas bowed.

"My lord," Lady Rebecca returned politely, her head still tilted, her eyes illuminated with curiosity.

"I find myself in need of your assistance. Would you mind taking a turn about the room with me?"

Lady Rebecca nodded once, placing her hand on his offered arm. "I find myself exceedingly curious as to why you'd need assistance from me, given our short acquaintance."

"It is in efforts to assist a mutual . . . friend." The word tasted bitter in his mouth.

"I see. And would this friend be the daughter of a duke?" Lady Rebecca asked.

"Quite astute."

"Thank you. What assistance do you require?"

Lucas studied Lady Rebecca, debating which approach to take with her. "Would you mind inviting your friend over to your estate on the morrow?"

Lady Rebecca nodded once. "Yes, but I highly doubt her father will allow it. He's been quite overbearing, and I've not received my friend in several weeks."

"Blast," Lucas swore, then glanced at Lady Rebecca and apologized.

"It is of no consequence." She waved off his offensive word.

"I still beg your pardon," Lucas continued. "Perhaps you could send a missive? Would she meet you in the park, perhaps?"

Lady Rebecca nodded once, hesitantly. "It is possible, yet I wouldn't expect her father to allow a missive to reach her without his approving of its contents first."

"Is there anything the man leaves sacred?" Lucas asked with tight frustration as he led them around the perimeter of the ballroom.

"Not of which I'm aware, I'm afraid," Lady Rebecca replied, then she gasped slightly. "Except . . ."

"Yes?" Lucas asked with unabashed interest.

"Meyer." Lady Rebecca breathed his name reverently.

Lucas wasn't surprised at her overly familiar use of his name. "Ah! Brilliant, my lady."

"I do have my moments. Since the banns are to be read this weekend, it's quite . . ." She swallowed and Lucas paused in their progress to give her time to collect her emotions. "Decided," she finished. "Their betrothal, I mean." She sighed deeply.

Lucas nodded, waiting.

"I'd be surprised if the duke didn't even encourage correspondence between the two."

"I see. Then I shall heed your excellent advice and speak with Meyer." Lucas added. "And I thank you for your kind assistance." He nodded gratefully.

Lady Rebecca squeezed his arm, as if unwilling yet fully expecting him to dart away. "Wait, I do have a few questions of my own."

Lucas paused. "Of course." He started their sedate walk once again and waited, tamping down the impatient desire to track down Meyer and set a plan in motion.

"What are your intentions toward my friend?" Lady Rebecca asked with stark honesty.

Lucas cut a glance to her. "Of a variety," he answered cryptically, not certain how much information Liliah had imparted.

"Spoken like a rogue," Lady Rebecca replied, but a grin softened the accusation. "I feel the need to impress, in the strongest fashion, that my friend is not one to be trifled with, Lord Heightfield." She arched a delicate brow and awaited his response.

"How well you champion your friend, and well she deserves it," he said by way of answer, neatly dodging the question.

"Yes, well . . . that wasn't exactly a vow of your honor," Lady Rebecca responded.

Lucas lowered his chin slightly, leveling her with his most intense gaze. "I'm not exactly a man known for honor, Lady Rebecca. But I can assure you that I wish no harm or assault on your friend's character."

Lady Rebecca looked as if she wished to question him further, but paused, then after a moment, nodded. "Then I cannot ask for more. I can see I will not gain any more from you."

"Wise and lovely," Lucas answered, lifting her wrist and kissing her hand to take his leave. "I thank you again for your assistance."

Lady Rebecca simply nodded, and Lucas took his leave in search of Meyer.

He found his target conversing with the Earl of Lisness. Lucas had only met the chap once, and had disregarded him as a rather boring fellow with his overly curly hair and stodgy personality. So he rather considered himself doing a good deed in saving Meyer from the conversation. He nodded to the gentlemen, and waited till he had Meyer's attention. "If you wouldn't mind?" He gestured to the side.

Meyer agreed quickly and excused himself from the conversation rapidly.

"You're quite welcome." Lucas smirked as Meyer fell into step beside him. Meyer shot him a curious glance that shifted slightly into chagrin. "It would appear you are acquainted with Lord Lisness."

"Barely, which is more than is necessary to develop an opinion," Lucas replied honestly. "Now then, I've an inquiry."

"After the information you've disclosed this eve, I find myself quite in your debt. How may I assist?" Meyer inquired with a sincere gaze.

"Lady Rebecca seemed to be of the mind that if you were to attempt corresponding with Lady Liliah, it would be a permissible avenue of contact," Lucas explained neatly, making sure to drop Lady Rebecca's name, hoping to smooth over the slightly scandalous edge to his request.

Meyer's brow pinched. "It is indeed likely."

"Brilliant." Lucas nodded. "Would you mind requesting she take a stroll in Hyde Park, around four tomorrow?"

Meyer studied Lucas. "Why?" he asked suspiciously.

"Because if I were to come and call upon her, her father would not only disapprove, but the tyrant would likely blame Liliah, creating worse problems," Lucas articulated, frustrated that he should have to spell out his thoughts so plainly. Damn, it was difficult to persuade people to go along with a plan. It was so much easier to work with Heathcliff, or even Ramsey—at least they were usually of the same mind in situations.

He tamped back his impatient nature and waited for Meyer.

"And your intentions?" Meyer asked quietly, glancing about to make sure their conversation was private.

"Are private, and none of your concern. But I assure you, the same way I assured your lady friend, I have no desire to bring about harm to the lady in question or her reputation."

Meyer twisted his lips as if considering Lucas's words, weighing them. "I hesitate, I must admit. This goes against my moral obligations."

Lucas swallowed his frustration. He wanted to hang both Meyer and his bloody moral obligations, but it wouldn't help his case, so he held his peace. "But?" he encouraged, waiting.

"But I see Liliah's delight when she is with you, so for her sake, I'll do it," he answered.

Lucas nodded, then held out his hand to Meyer. After a firm shake, he grinned. "Thank you."

Meyer acknowledged his words with a curt nod, and with a slight bow, took his leave.

Lucas strode away in search of Heathcliff. Since Liliah was no longer in attendance, he had no reason to tolerate the rest of the ton's company. Furthermore, he found last night's lack of sleep was catching up with him. Tomorrow promised to be a delightful day.

Four in the afternoon couldn't come quickly enough.

Chapter Twenty-three

Liliah pulled her knees to her chest as she sat on her bed. She should be angry, she should be utterly distraught after the conversation with her father last night—yet she found she was none of those things.

Perhaps it was that she was simply too numb to care any longer. Or, maybe, she was finally realizing that her father's words only held weight if she let them.

And she was determined to not let them sink into her heart.

Become truth.

Become anything other than hot, hate-filled air.

She determined that the pity she felt was not for herself, but for her father.

It was all the same words as before.

And while they were significantly more accurate—after all, she was quite thoroughly ruined—the words were simply that: words.

Her father had blustered, threatened to forbid her friendship with Lady Rebecca Grace, and even to hold her prisoner in her own home—yet she found it didn't concern her as much.

Worse came to worst, she would marry Meyer, and then divorce quietly.

She'd made up her mind, and surely Meyer would understand and be willing to accept the scandal associated with such an act. Divorce wasn't impossible, just uncommon. And while she certainly enjoyed her active social life, it was an acceptable sacrifice to simply be free.

Dear Lord, how beautiful that word sounded, just in thought.

She almost dared not whisper it.

Reluctantly, she stood from her bed and rang for her maid. It would serve no good for her to mill about all day. Rather, she found the idea of escaping all too enticing, and she set about to uncover her father's plans for the day, and when would be the perfect time to steal away.

After she was readied for the day, she requested tea be served in the library, where she was certain she'd find Samantha. Since today wasn't a usual day to accept callers, her sister would certainly be enjoying the view of Hyde Park while immersing herself in some sort of novel.

Liliah left the confines of her room, nodding knowingly to the footman placed opposite her door—no doubt assigned with notifying her father of her whereabouts. That would complicate her escape later, but not make it impossible, or so she hoped.

As expected, she found her sister in the library, and the sight of her warmed Liliah's heart from its numb state. "Good"—Liliah glanced at the large grandfather clock in the corner—"afternoon."

"Look who decided to leave her exile," Samantha replied with a warm smile. "I was worried for you, but expected you'd emerge when you were ready."

"How empathetic of you," Liliah replied with feeling. "But I am much stronger than he thinks," she added in a hushed whisper.

Samantha nodded, then adjusted her posture as Liliah took a seat beside her on the brocade couch.

"Are you going to tell me the story, or am I left to my own imagination?" Samantha asked, setting her book neatly on her lap.

"I'm afraid I created quite the scandal—danced with someone other than Meyer." Liliah rolled her eyes with effect, but didn't add details about the scandalous reputation of the man who requested that dance.

"Ah, I see." Samantha didn't inquire further, yet her expression was curious and expectant.

"What are you reading?" Liliah asked, shifting the focus.

"Romeo and Juliet." Samantha blushed.

"Ever the romantic," Liliah teased. "That is a good thing."

Samantha nodded once, then frowned. "Do—"

The knock on the library door interrupted Samantha's words, and Liliah looked up expectantly.

A maid brought in the tea service, followed by their butler. As the maid curtseyed and set out the service, Liliah's attention was directed to the butler, who carried a card on a silver platter.

It had been weeks since Liliah had received a missive that wasn't an invitation—she suspected her father had some sort of involvement in it. So it was with a suspicious heart that she took the heavy envelope from the tray. Immediately her eyes fell to the navy-colored seal on the fold.

Greywick.

Her heart pounded with trepidation before she assured herself that it was probably simply Meyer.

Though why he'd send a missive confused her.

After all, only betrothed couples could send correspondence, and his taking advantage of that liberty only strengthened their betrothal. It was curious indeed.

"Thank you." Liliah nodded to the butler as he took his leave. Apparently there was no servant awaiting a response.

She lifted the seal and then twisted her lips in frustration.

Open.

The missive had clearly already been opened, as the wax seal was broken. Her suspicion that her father was reading her correspondence was confirmed.

"Who sent it?" Samantha asked, serving herself tea.

"Meyer," Liliah remarked, showing her sister the letter's already broken seal. "Which is why it made it to my person. Is nothing sacred?" Liliah asked in a frustrated whisper.

"Oh my." Samantha's brow pinched in empathy and she shook her head.

Liliah sighed, then lifted the letter from its envelope.

> *Four o'clock at the Serpentine, if you wish.*
> *H. Regards—M*

Liliah reread the words, studying the 'H' before the closing of the letter.

It was quite odd, and she was sure that Meyer wished to communicate something only she would catch, just in case her father read her correspondence.

Belatedly she wondered if Meyer's father did the same.

Life had turned into quite a muddy soup of a mess.

She reread the letter.

"Is something wrong?" Samantha asked, taking a sip of her tea.

Liliah glanced at her. "No, just curious."

"Because?" Samantha prodded.

"It's probably nothing, yet it seems as if Meyer is wishing to meet me—which I find strange. Unless his father is behind the idea, in which case I wouldn't find it surprising at all."

Samantha tilted her head, then whispered quietly, "What if he wishes to speak to you about something he knows is of a sensitive nature?"

Liliah nodded. "Perhaps. Regardless, such a meeting will get me out of the house, and with the approval of our father as well." Liliah set the letter aside and reached for a delicate blue-flowered teacup. The steam swirled around her cup as she poured the liquid, then disappeared as she added a generous amount of cream.

"How do you ever enjoy the flavor of the tea with that much cream?" Samantha asked, not for the first time.

Liliah smiled in response. "What makes you think I wish to enjoy the flavor of the tea? Maybe I simply enjoy the cream," she teased.

"How positively uncouth," Samantha replied in her best nasal tone, clearly attempting to imitate an overly proper dowager.

Liliah giggled in response.

Samantha set down her tea and turned her body to face her sister fully. Liliah sobered and studied her sister. "Yes?"

Samantha took a steady breath and lowered her gaze. "Do you think . . . that perhaps Father has designs for my future, as he has for yours?"

Liliah bit her lip, thankful Samantha wasn't studying her expression. Hadn't that been on her heart for over a year? The idea that her father would oppress Samantha's already quiet spirit to the point of extinguishing it?

Samantha glanced up, meeting her sister's gaze with a forthright one of her own.

Liliah studied her sister. Her impulse to protect her from everything unpleasant and dangerous welled up within her, yet as she met Samantha's gaze, she noted the resolve deep within that gave Liliah the courage to be fully honest.

Because while Samantha was quiet, that didn't mean she was weak.

And just because she obeyed, didn't mean she didn't have her own opinions.

"Yes. I'm utterly terrified of it," Liliah answered, then reached out with her free hand and grasped her sister's hand. "And I wish I knew how to save you from it. I'm already working on a few ideas, and if I must marry Meyer—and it certainly is looking like that is what will happen—then he and I will be your refuge, and you will have nothing to worry about," Liliah promised, hoping she could make good on it when the time came.

"I see." Samantha nodded. "I suspected as much, but hoped that maybe as the second daughter—"

"You're just as worthy as me, but you're worthy of

love, Samantha, and if I have anything to say about it, Father won't strip that from you as well." Liliah blinked back fierce, protective tears.

"Thank you." Samantha nodded, causing a tear to slide down her cheek and into her lap.

Liliah gave a slow nod of affirmation.

"Thankfully I still have time before my season." Samantha gave her sister's hand a slight squeeze, then released it so that she might pick up her tea.

"At least a year," Liliah confirmed.

"There is much that can happen in a year," Samantha murmured, then took a sip of tea.

"Truer words have never been spoken," Liliah replied and took a sip of her tea as well.

Samantha's gaze flickered to the letter. "Will you meet him?"

Liliah set her teacup in the saucer with a slight clank. "Yes. If for no other reason than to escape this house."

Samantha gave a gentle chuckle. "You've always had a restless heart."

"And you've always had a contented one."

"True enough."

Liliah finished her tea and passed the next hour in quiet company with her sister. As the afternoon waned, she excused herself to don a walking gown for her meeting with Meyer. After Sarah had assisted her with readying herself, Liliah bid her join her on the walk. It was a nuisance to have a chaperone, but on the occasions when she didn't sneak from the manor, it was required in order to pass through the door.

As she took the stairs to the foyer, she wasn't surprised to find her father by the door, waiting, his cold gaze studying her as if determining the risk in letting her leave the premises. A footman, one she didn't recognize, stood beside him stiffly.

Irritation flared within her as she approached her father, yet she held her tongue in check. She didn't want to jeopardize the opportunity to escape for a while.

"I see you've accepted the invitation." Her father spoke in a clipped tone as he placed his hands behind his back.

"Indeed," Liliah replied, watching him warily.

He took a step toward her. "You will be on your best behavior. Your reputation is currently questionable, based on the company you've been keeping." He bit out the last words as he slowly circled her. "To accompany you, I'm sending along Fredrick. He's to be of any . . . assistance."

Liliah bit her tongue, using all her will to resist giving a scathing retort, and rather than reply and risk her control, she simply nodded.

"Very good." He met her gaze, then strode away.

Liliah closed her eyes for a moment, collecting herself from the searing anger, then took a deep breath. "Come along, Sarah." She turned to the footman. "And Fredrick." She practically sneered. As if she believed he was simply a footman. She'd never seen him before, and she was quite certain she'd at least recognize all the hired footmen in her home.

As soon as she stepped from the manor, her heart started to calm. The sky was a pale blue with only a slight smattering of clouds, and for once it looked as if it might not rain. The air danced with a slight breeze, and Liliah relaxed into the embrace of the open space. A smile teased her lips as she made her way to the park. It wasn't a far walk, and she could have easily readied a carriage, but she found she wanted—no, needed—the time to unwind. Plus, ladies were to walk at a sedate pace, so surely that would be the perfect excuse to take her sweet time in returning home.

She grinned at her devious thoughts. Yet they were tempered with the sound of the two sets of footsteps that lagged behind.

Freedom, but not solitude.

At least not today.

Chapter Twenty-four

Lucas tapped his knee impatiently as he watched from his carriage window. Truly it was a rare spectacular day, and as such he could have taken his curricle, yet he wished for privacy.

Craved it.

He studied the gentry as they strolled around the park. The sound of horses' hooves pounding the earth drew his attention to Rotten Row, where two dandies tested their horseflesh. The park was teeming with activity, everyone set on enjoying the break in the weather.

Bloody rotten luck.

He wondered just how Meyer had invited Liliah to the park. All he knew was that she would arrive near the Serpentine by four. He lifted his gold pocket watch and noted that he was still early.

Thankfully, Meyer wasn't planning to make good on his invitation, which left only one maid to evade to have Liliah to himself. Or so was the plan. Yet as he studied the path that wound toward the Serpentine from the roadway, he spotted Liliah, along with two chaperones.

One of whom wasn't of the feminine variety.

And was likely her father's hired guardian.

The lovely day took a dark turn.

Irritated at this complication, Lucas debated how best to proceed. He opened the carriage door and stepped down, nodding to the driver. He strode toward Liliah. Her pace was sedate, as if savoring each moment in the park. A gentle grin tipped her lips as she glanced up at the sky, then traced her gaze down the tall trees, unaware of Lucas's intense study of her person.

The maid behind her seemed ill at ease as she glanced at the footman, and Lucas grew suspicious himself. The footman's nose was slightly crooked, not overly obvious, but anyone who had engaged in fisticuffs would notice. He wondered where the duke had found the man.

Disregarding him, Lucas wound his way around the path so that he would catch Liliah's eye in a more natural way, rather than have it appear as if he was intentionally seeking her out.

He walked around a hedge and took the path she was already on, slowing his pace to appear unhurried. He lifted his gaze upward to study the foliage on the tall oak and beech trees. The breeze rustled the leaves and he forced a calm that replaced the air of excited expectation that lingered in his blood.

He purposely kept his gaze from the trio in front of him, instead shifting his regard from the trees to the Serpentine. A small gasp made his lips twitch in amusement before he flicked his gaze forward, meeting Liliah's wide blue eyes. Her expression was surprised, then shifted to a knowing amusement.

Whatever Meyer had said was cryptic enough that she clearly hadn't expected to see Lucas.

Her approval of his presence, however, was evident by the grin that spread across her beautiful features.

"Why, if it isn't Lady Liliah." Lucas bowed, then reached for her hand.

A soft blush illuminated her features as he grasped her offered hand and kissed it.

"Lord Heightfield," she replied, her gaze amused. "What a surprise and delight."

"You stole my very thoughts, my lady," he answered, studying her features. "It's quite a lovely day, is it not?"

"Quite. The fresh air is a welcome . . . distraction." Liliah spoke with a wry expression, and Lucas's memory shifted to her hasty exit from the ball last night.

"I trust you're doing well." He spoke softly, studying her eyes for the answer her lips couldn't give.

"Well enough, my lord. Thank you for asking." She gave a brave nod, and Lucas wondered just how often she'd chosen to see the joy in life, when it was a difficult task. And how often he'd chosen to do the opposite.

"Of course."

"And how are you?" Liliah asked, tilting her head, her gaze flickering to his hand grasping hers.

"My day is improving by the moment," he answered with a flirtatious wink, not releasing her. "Would you care to join me for a stroll?" He shifted her hand to his arm, anticipating her acceptance.

Liliah grinned knowingly at his actions and fell into

step beside him, even as the footman and maid silently followed. "Interesting company you're keeping," Lucas commented, glancing behind them.

"Ah, yes. It's quite frustrating, and I'm quite certain that my every move will be reported with alacrity, yet I'll face that problem when it comes." Liliah spoke with an irritated tone.

"I see." And Lucas did, all too well. Anger simmered under his skin as he considered just how Chatterwood treated his daughter like a prisoner under house arrest. And he was quite certain Liliah didn't disclose the full extent of her father's control.

And if there was one aspect of her father he understood all too well, it was the desire for control.

For how it made one feel powerful, sovereign, capable.

How often had he used his love of control as an excuse?

It shamed him to think he had that character flaw in common with the Duke of Chatterwood.

"You're quite pensive, my lord," Liliah commented, pulling his thoughts back into line.

"Just reflective," Lucas replied quickly, offering her a warm smile, hoping to alleviate whatever tension his silence may have created. He made the effort to enjoy each stolen moment.

For that is exactly what their time was—stolen.

"Did you enjoy the party last eve?" Liliah asked.

Lucas nodded. "I had quite a brilliant dance partner."

"Truly? I did as well," she teased. "My toes were stepped on only once or twice, quite the improvement."

"Foul," he responded, earning a saucy grin. "I did

nothing of the sort. I'm quite capable on the dance floor, even if I say so myself."

"Who's to say I was referring to my dances with you?" Liliah asked tauntingly.

"And here I fell for the trap." Lucas chuckled. "I see my folly."

Liliah grinned at him, her eyes sparkling with intelligence and mischief. "I would never abuse your dancing to your face, sir. Merely behind your back."

Lucas gave a low chuckle. He played at offence. "Ah, so that is how the game is played. I understood you to have a more frank character than this."

"I jest," Liliah replied with a soft laugh. "Honesty is something I prize, so how could I neglect to use it myself? It would be hypocrisy of the worst sort. No, I'm much too honest and forthright for any sort of deception—in conversation," she added belatedly.

Lucas shook his head, immediately reminded of her grand deception that had led to their acquaintance.

Who would have imagined?

Either the Fates were cruel or brilliant. He wasn't quite certain which.

"So what brings you out and about today?" Liliah asked as they took the path that circled the Serpentine. She nodded gently to a passing person, someone Lucas faintly recognized, then dismissed.

"I'm simply taking the air. And what of you? What brings you out of doors?" Lucas flickered his gaze behind them, arching a brow.

"I was to meet a friend, but I don't think he was able to make the arrangement," Liliah answered neatly, her eyes sparkling with understanding. "However, in retrospect, I should have expected as much, since he was less than forthright in his correspondence."

"I'm more than happy to take your friend's place and enjoy your lovely company."

"How fortuitous," Liliah replied.

They walked on in silence for a few moments, and Lucas took the opportunity to ponder several plans for extricating Liliah from her chaperones.

Yet with each plan he devised, he couldn't help but reflect on the resulting punishment that Liliah could face at the end of their folly. In short, he decided he had no other option but to enjoy her chaperoned company and find another way to steal private moments at a different time. His body agonized at the delay in gratification, yet he could see no other option.

Not without resulting in punishment or pain for the lady in question.

And damn it all, that was enough to alter his plans.

He tried not to consider what that could mean, so he pushed the dark thought into the back of his mind and instead focused on the beauty on his arm.

"Will you attend the Morrison ball tomorrow night?" he asked.

Liliah colored softly, her cheeks taking on a rosy hue that was reminiscent of when she'd gazed at him after their entanglement. His body hardened at the thought, his blood pumping with a persuasive demand for an immediate repeat performance. He sucked in a fortifying breath as he waited for her answer.

"Indeed I am planning to attend. Will you be there as well?" she asked.

"And miss an opportunity to step on your toes? I think not," he teased.

"Ha! Then I shall look forward to seeing you then. And will your friend attend as well? Viscount Kilpatrick?"

"If I can talk him into it."

"I doubt it is so very difficult. He seems to enjoy society."

Lucas gave a scoffing laugh. "In part," he answered cryptically.

They came back to the point in the path where they had begun their loop, and he sensed the hesitancy, the expectation of saying adieu. In response, he placed his hand over her arm. "I'm truly enjoying the fresh air. Would you care to find a spot under the trees to observe nature?" He almost rolled his eyes at his request. Surely he could have come up with a more intelligent option. He reflected back to when Heathcliff asked if he even knew how to make love anymore. While that skill was in top performance, his art of flirtation was lacking, he decided.

But why practice flirtation when there was no need for innuendo? Flirtation was an art, one that used manipulations, hidden meanings, and veiled seduction— all things for which he had no use and, clearly, didn't know how to use well.

Yet Liliah took pity on his sad efforts and readily accepted. He selected a bench below a beech tree that overlooked the Serpentine and a length of path that would supply them with fresh faces about which to converse and reflect. As he took a seat beside Liliah, he noted the steadfast surveillance of the footman and the apparent unease of the maid who chaperoned. Liliah followed his gaze and he noted that her shoulders straightened as she turned her focus to the footman.

"Fredrick, please give me a greater span of space. I'm not going to run away from you, and I dare say if I tried you could easily catch up—or are you so frail that you think me able to best you?" she added with just a slight taunt to her tone.

It worked, and Fredrick reluctantly took several steps back. The maid's body lost its rigid posture and she clasped her hands before her, relaxing.

"There, much better," Liliah replied, turning to Lucas. "It's quite irksome."

"I can't imagine," he replied, then asked the question that was on the forefront of his mind, grateful for a measure of privacy. In a low tone, he whispered, "I was quite . . . surprised at your hasty departure last night. I'm quite certain it wasn't your expectation to leave so suddenly?" He studied her expression for any clues.

Liliah's smile faltered and turned into a pinched expression, and he readily noticed her irritation.

"It was indeed unexpected," she answered. "Yet in hindsight I can see that it should not have been wholly surprising."

Lucas hesitated, not sure how to frame the question without being overly direct. He decided to hang the propriety, and asked in frank honesty, "Was he harsh with you?"

Liliah's gaze fell to her lap. "Angry, yes. Yet I found that his words only hold power if I allow them to, which I've chosen to not tolerate."

"I see. And it was in direct response to my dancing with you."

She gave a slight nod. "But should I stand up with anyone save Meyer, he would have the same reaction. Therefore, it is of no consequence. I've already made my decision on the matter and am allowing myself the freedom of that decision."

Lucas frowned slightly. "What have you decided?"

He suspected several things, yet he found his curious nature held him firmly in hand as he waited for confirmation—even as his stomach clenched in frustration, and dare he admit it?—Dread.

Liliah glanced to where Fredrick waited several paces away, intently staring at their shared bench. When she turned her gaze back to Lucas, she simply shrugged. "Perhaps another time."

Lucas nodded once, accepting her response, yet he vowed that soon he would uncover the truth of the matter.

"I'd best head home, as much as I am loath to admit it," Liliah remarked with a mournful edge to her tone. "But I must say, it has been an utter delight to . . . run into you. Fate is kind indeed." She stood and gave a soft smile.

Lucas stood as well, also loath to lose her company yet understanding the wisdom of her ending the assignation. "The pleasure was all mine." He reached for her hand and kissed her wrist ever so delicately, inhaling the fresh scent of her, conjuring up all sorts of other memories he'd rather repeat than simply remember.

"Until tomorrow," Liliah whispered, as if afraid her guardian would hear.

"Far too long," Lucas whispered seductively, allowing his gaze to rake over her body, greedily savoring each delicious curve.

When his gaze returned to her face, he grinned at the blush his hungry perusal of her figure had enticed, and he gave a wink.

Liliah shook her head and he released her hand.

"Come along." She glanced back to her maid and footman, and Lucas had the fleeting vision of her calling her dog to follow—and it was probably closer to the truth than was humorous.

As she walked away, he tucked his hands behind his body and watched her till she was out of sight; not missing the footman's suspicious glances as he accompanied her. Lucas only hoped that her father didn't suspect that Meyer had helped create the ruse.

With a reluctant sigh, he decided to look forward to tomorrow, and a renewed opportunity to steal Liliah away.

Even if it was for only a few moments.

Pleasure was the greatest temptation of all—and time seemed always at war with it.

Chapter Twenty-five

The duke had asked for his daughter to join him the moment she arrived home, and so Liliah was quickly escorted to his study.

"You were away quite long for your intended to be unable to accompany you," he said by way of greeting.

Liliah took a deep breath and finished walking into the study, noting that the footman no longer lingered behind and had closed the door, leaving her alone with her father.

Delight of all delights.

"It is a beautiful day. I'm not going to squander it just because Meyer had different plans."

"This arrived only a quarter hour after you departed." Her father lifted a missive from his broad desk, studying her with his cool eyes. She had the impression that it was how men at the war office studied people accused of espionage.

"And what excuse did my friend give?" she asked innocently.

Her father's eyes narrowed. "Your *betrothed* stated that business came up and he had to attend to it."

Liliah nodded once, unsure as to the problem her father seemed to see in the situation. Yet suspicion was always in the back of his mind, so she resolved to wait it out, offer no information and await his questions, or dismissal.

"Have you nothing to say?" he asked, standing and setting the missive back on the wooden desktop.

Liliah tilted her head slightly. "What do you wish me to discourse?"

She met his gaze, trying to keep her expression innocent when she truly wanted to engage in a verbal spar—hang the fact she knew she'd lose.

Her father tapped the desk impatiently with one hand. "Fredrick!" he called out. The door opened almost immediately, as if dear Fredrick had been awaiting his summons.

Liliah grew more wary as Fredrick walked in and stood before her father with a gracious bow.

"What did you observe this afternoon?" the duke asked, arching a gray brow of inquiry.

Fredrick straightened, as if addressing some officer in the ranks. His tone was clipped and precise, his understanding far more shrewd than Liliah had anticipated.

"The lady took the path beside the Serpentine just as the letter requested, but upon her arrival there was no sign of the Baron of Scoffield, only the Earl of Heightfield, who appeared to be awaiting her arrival." Fredrick paused.

The duke's gaze narrowed. "And how are you sure that Heightfield was awaiting her arrival?"

"He alighted from his carriage the moment we came

into view, then took a circumspect route that would intersect with the lady's."

"I see." The duke nodded, his steely gaze sliding over to Liliah, then back to Fredrick. "Did my daughter engage in conversation with the earl?"

"Yes."

"And how long did they continue their interlude?" her father asked, casting an accusing glare at Liliah.

"The majority of the time we were in the park, Your Grace," Fredrick answered.

"And were they ever out of your sight?" the duke asked, taking several steps toward his footman.

"No, Your Grace. They were always within a few steps."

"Very good, you've done your job well, Fredrick. You're dismissed."

Fredrick didn't even spare a glance to Liliah as he quickly quit the room, shutting the door behind him.

Liliah watched her father, curious as to what line of offense he'd take. It was a public park, and while Fredrick suspected a planned meeting, it could have been by chance. Suspicions didn't prove points; however, she wasn't certain her father would feel the same way.

"Liliah." Her father spoke forcefully.

She tipped her head slightly, acknowledging his address.

"It would seem that you're either stubborn beyond rational intelligence, or you were the prey in a grand scheme to ruin your reputation." He took a deep breath, then slowly shook his head. "I'm afraid I'll have to address this incident with the Earl of Greywick. It would seem his son is of the rather vulgar variety, and trying to dissolve the betrothal by sullying your reputation. It cannot be borne, and as such I will see that the earl deals heavily with his wayward son." He spoke as if it caused him great pain.

Liliah froze, processing his words. She was certain he knew it was her stubborn nature that created the ripe opportunity for such a meeting, yet for him to mark Meyer as the villain, even suggesting that he receive punishment, it was a twist she hadn't expected.

She wanted to claim responsibility, yet she held her tongue. She found herself at an impasse, because she knew enough of her father's character—or lack thereof— to suspect that such a reaction on her part was exactly the goal he had in mind. It was a quandary, so she simply waited, even though it went against every fiber of her being.

After a moment, her father addressed her. "Have you nothing to say? Is your betrothed deserving of the blame . . . or are you?" The force of his regard was so powerful it nearly made her blurt out the answer.

Yet she held fast.

"You may believe that which you wish to believe. I've learned that it is not for me to involve myself in your affairs," she answered submissively, trying to play the game.

But the problem with playing any game was that usually those who made them up were also the only ones aware of the rules.

It was a risk, yet she took it willingly. She resisted the urge to hold her breath, and waited.

"I don't know if you're actually learning some discretion or if you're simply a conniving woman. Regardless, I'll find out the truth of the matter. You're dismissed."

Liliah curtseyed low, and forced herself to take sedate steps from the room and down the hall. It wasn't until she reached her room that she finally relaxed and sighed a deep breath of relief. She wasn't sure what avenue her father would take, but she was certain that he was just as confused.

Hopefully.

Only time would tell.

And time was always the enemy.

Chapter Twenty-six

Lucas wasn't sure if he was surprised by the summons, or if he was subconsciously expecting it. Regardless, his curiosity must be satisfied, and to see the inside of Liliah's estate was an opportunity he couldn't miss. It was the day of the Morrison ball, and as such he eagerly anticipated seeing Liliah once again.

Bloody hell, he was becoming everything he swore he'd never be again. It was humbling and irritating to think that he was so weak to fall for a woman's charms once again.

Yet he assured himself that Liliah wasn't just a woman, she was far more, and in that lay the danger.

But like a moth drawn to the flickering flame, he was helpless to resist the draw toward her, and he found he wasn't exactly inclined to struggle against the temptation either.

With a tug on his shirt cuffs, he strode from his room to his awaiting carriage in front of his home.

Hopefully it would be a short meeting, since he was scheduled to speak with Heathcliff before the ball. There was some pressing business with the club. With their annual silver masquerade event coming up within the week, one of their larger events, several details needed attending to.

He stepped into his black carriage and the driver snapped the ribbons, causing the four blood bays to spring into action. Lucas adjusted his seat at the movement, and watched the stately homes as the carriage passed by.

It wasn't a long journey to the duke's residence at Whitefield House, but it was enough time to give him the opportunity to think about which topics the man might wish to discourse. He was certain that Liliah was the primary topic of interest, yet what avenue did he wish to explore? Certainly he knew that any warnings against Lucas's interest in his daughter wouldn't hold any weight. But could the arrogant nature of a man such as the Duke of Chatterwood truly be questioned? No. He decided that the man probably was accustomed to using his title and power to contrive whatever result served him best. He certainly had acted that way in the past, and Lucas had no reason to believe the man had changed at all.

As they approached the estate, he wondered fleetingly if Liliah knew of this meeting, or if she had been kept in the dark about it. As he stepped from the carriage he studied the stately house. Built of white stone, the estate looked royal and bespoke of the wealth of the owner. Red and blue decorated the entrance, the colors of Chatterwood's dukedom, and Lucas smirked at the ostentatious décor. The butler allowed him entrance, merely stating that the duke was awaiting his arrival, and as Lucas followed him down the wide hall, he scanned his surroundings and dismissed them as just as overstated as their owner.

When they approached a large wooden door that was slightly ajar, Lucas waited while the butler reached for the brass handle. As it swung open slowly, Lucas took a deep breath and suppressed a grin of eager anticipation. For this was one arena where, while the duke surely felt he was in control, Lucas knew he was anything but. Rather, Lucas expected to toy a little with the man, but he was also resolved to hold his tongue before he provoked him to the point of taking out any anger on his daughter. Lucas was all too aware of the man's temper, and he wasn't willing to gamble with that temper being unleashed on Liliah. So it was with eager and cautious energy that he strode into the room as he was announced.

"Heightfield." The duke nodded once as he stood beside his desk, one hand splayed against the wood as he leaned against it.

"Your Grace." Lucas bowed slightly. "To what do I owe the honor?" He kept a careless manner as he walked into the room. It was quite amusing to see the tick start in Chatterwood's eye as he watched his approach.

"There is nothing pleasurable about this meeting," Chatterwood said.

"Ah, and here I thought we were burying the hatchet and all that." Lucas shrugged, then placed his hands on the back of a chair, facing the duke.

"Not likely," the duke replied, scoffing.

"Hope springs eternal." Lucas gave a dismissive wave. "What then did you have in mind? I daresay that there's such a long list of grievances you and I could both name, that we might be here for a week."

The duke's frown deepened. "What aspect of my integrity or character do you wish to malign this time? A week's worth? To outline your faults we would need the rest of our natural lives. Yet, thankfully, I'm not inclined to wax poetic on all the ways you're a menace to society. Rather, I'm going to keep this short and direct. Stay the hell away from my daughter."

Lucas bit his lip to keep from grinning too wide. "Don't hold anything back, Your Grace." He made a sweeping gesture with his hand.

"Rest assured that I'm in no jovial mood, Heightfield. This is not a veiled threat, this is an outright demand." The duke underlined his statement with a chilly gaze.

Lucas tucked his hands behind his back and nodded once. "Why?"

The duke's jaw ticked as he seemingly ground his teeth together. "Because she is none of your concern."

Lucas lifted a shoulder. "I beg to differ. I rather find her intriguing and I'm not inclined to quit her acquaintance just yet. Things are ever becoming . . . interesting." He gave a wicked grin, enjoying the flush of red that reflected the duke's apparent ire.

"Now see here—" The duke took a few menacing steps toward him. "She is betrothed to the Earl of Greywick's son. It's a union that we have long planned and eagerly anticipate! There is nothing that you have to offer that would tempt such a lady."

Lucas couldn't restrain a chuckle. He had more than succeeded in tempting Liliah; he'd had the pleasure of thoroughly ruining her.

But one could never be too certain, so he was damned determined to make sure he repeated the process just to ensure a job well done.

"What in heaven's name are you smirking about?" the duke demanded, a look of disgust marring his face.

"It would seem I'm more informed about your family than you, Your Grace. I find that interesting. Either you are lying to me, or you have no idea. I'm not quite certain, but I will say that it truly is in your best interest for Greywick to win your daughter's hand." He arched a brow.

"How dare you impugn my integrity!" the duke bellowed.

"Do you wish for pistols at dawn? I'm more of a rapier man myself, but I'm quite certain that neither would give you an advantage. Besides . . ." He inched closer to the duke. "When I best you, who would ensure the betrothal would continue? Why . . . there would be a mourning period and"—he shrugged his shoulder—"I suppose then you could take your sordid secrets to hell with you."

"Damn you to hell, Heightfield."

"Is that a yes?" Lucas challenged.

The duke narrowed his eyes, then shook his head. "I'm not as foolish as you think."

"Such a pity."

Luke ignored the vein pulsing in the duke's forehead, instead studying his adversary's posture. Rigid shoulders, cold expression. He tried to think of a time he'd seen the duke even grin.

He couldn't think of one.

How was it possible that Liliah was his blood?

"Stay away from her," the duke reiterated.

"No," Lucas answered carelessly. "And why do you

even care? Anyone with eyes in their head can see that it's a reluctant match. What do you gain, Your Grace, that you don't already possess?"

The duke didn't answer, simply kept a cold silence.

"If you do not wish to discourse, then it would seem that I'll be left to the devices of my own imagination." Lucas stepped back and walked around a chair before lazily sitting down. He toyed with the idea of telling the duke about Greywick's bet, then decided on a different route. "If I had any kindness in my heart, I'd simply assume you were a protective father—however, we both know that true kindness is in short supply within this room, so I must devise an alternative reason." He paused. "Maybe money, maybe secrets . . ."

The duke gave an irritated grunt.

"But since I'm quite certain you're not about to visit debtors' prison, it must be Greywick applying the pressure. And that must mean that Greywick knows something . . . that you wish to remain in the dark." Lucas shrugged.

"That's preposterous," the duke ground out. "Take your leave, I have nothing more to say to you, and you have made your position quite clear."

"But we're just now starting to have an interesting conversation," Lucas admonished as he stood.

"You always were a bastard."

"Ah, and here we bring up that nasty little secret."

The duke lost his color and glanced away.

"Remembering that which you wish to forget. Hmm . . . I wonder if that is the secret that Greywick hides," Lucas whispered softly, watching loathing fill the duke's expression.

"Out." The duke swore the word.

Lucas gave a slow bow. "It was a lovely time.

Quite . . . educational, I'd say." Lucas turned to the door.

The duke didn't make a sound as Lucas quit the room, his mind spinning in several different directions.

He wasn't sure why he hadn't seen it before, but it was becoming clearer by the minute.

He'd have to dig a little deeper.

How in the hell had he gone from no strings attached with Liliah, to scrounging through her father's past?

Hell hadn't just frozen over, it had imploded from the chill.

Chapter Twenty-seven

Liliah was leaving the library when she caught sight of a familiar gaze. Heart stopping, then pounding as realization hit with full force, she glanced about for servants. When she assured herself that the hall was vacant, she lifted a hand to her lips to signal silence, and pointed back to the recently vacated library. As she held the door open, she kept an eye on the hall as Luc hastily made his way to the open door. He kissed her quickly on the lips before tugging her inside the library and closing the door firmly.

"Tell me it locks," he whispered against her lips as he pulled her into his embrace. Liliah's senses were overcome with the scent of him, the familiar hint of mint that clung to his clothes, and the spicy flavor of his kiss, all vying for her attention. Molding herself to his person wantonly, she gave herself fully to the kiss, delighting in each sensation as it rocketed through her.

When Luc released her lips, her eyes slowly opened

and focused on his questioning expression. Belatedly she remembered the inquiry. "Yes." She turned back and twisted the mechanism, securing the door.

"Delightful." He leaned in, capturing her lips once more as his hands caressed down her shoulders to the swell of her hips, tucking them in tight against his in a not-so-subtle hint of desire.

Reason was forgotten, but curiosity wasn't as easily dismissed, and Liliah reluctantly leaned out of the kiss, studying his handsome face. "How are you here?"

His blue eyes danced excitedly as they roamed her face. "A little tête-à-tête with your father." He shrugged dismissively, and Liliah's curiosity burned hotter.

"Why in heaven's name—"

"I was invited," Lucas answered, grinning mischievously.

"That's . . . surprising." She frowned slightly as she tried to imagine what would possess her father to invite someone so despised over for a private conversation.

"It was intriguing. He's quite controlling and severe, which is no surprise to either you or me. But it was different to see him display such character traits in relation to his own family versus in the House of Lords."

Liliah gave a wry grin. "I assure you his character is universally displayed, regardless of person or place."

"I can see that," Lucas answered, squeezing her hips as his gaze lowered to her lips.

A cautious thought entered Liliah's mind. "Were you shown out?"

Lucas shook his head, then leaned down and kissed along the curve of her neck. Liliah's eyes drifted closed as she fought for coherent thought.

"So, they expect you to still be on the premises?" Liliah asked in a breathless tone.

"I expect so," Lucas murmured against her skin, the warm air from his breath causing a shiver of pleasure to vibrate down her back. "Do you want me to leave?" He leaned back as if withholding his attentions.

"Heaven's no," Liliah replied, reaching up to hold his shoulders, pulling him in close. He chuckled in response and teased her skin with more kisses.

"That's the right answer. However . . ." He nipped at her earlobe, then licked it teasingly. "I will have to disappear soon. After all, my carriage is in front, waiting."

"Damn," Liliah breathed.

"Such language from a lady," Lucas scolded jokingly, then placed several quick kisses to her lips, fleeting ones that were merely a taste of the passion withheld.

"Wicked," Liliah remarked, following his retreating mouth with her own, desperate for more.

"Indeed you are," Lucas said, then kissed her hungrily, his breath coming in short gasps as he pressed himself against her, making his insistent arousal apparent.

Lucas suddenly withdrew from the kiss and studied her, his gaze calculating as if trying to make some sort of decision.

"What?" Liliah asked artlessly, tilting her head slightly with curiosity.

Lucas glanced to the door, then back, resolve hardening in his expression. "Are you willing?" He slowly traced his hand from her shoulder down to her breast, covering her curves seductively, then tracing his touch down her belly to the heated part between her legs. The fire in his expression made her burn.

"Yes."

"Thank God," he swore, then kissed her deeply but quickly and lifted her in his arms. In short order she was reclining on the sofa that she had so often sat upon while reading, with his delicious weight pressing into her. The memories of their one night came back in full force and Liliah arched her back, needing to feel more.

Lucas's movements were hurried, desperate and needy as he slipped his hands up her skirt and navigated her underthings. She aided by tugging at his breeches, and with a low oath, he assisted her in removing all barriers. With one hot stroke, he buried himself within her, kissing her deeply with each movement. Liliah's body shook with the violent need of it, arching her back, her hips, allowing her hands their hungry need to roam his person as he savagely loved her.

It was everything she remembered but so much more. Her senses were just as heightened, yet there was this powerful expectation that built her body's need into a fever as she settled her hands on his lower back and pressed him deeper within, feeling the edge of her release coming closer—knowing its power and expecting its pleasure. Luc's body shook with raw power, adding to her already aroused senses and he silenced her cries of pleasure with his kiss, devouring her passion as he released his own with a muffled groan.

Liliah's body pulsed, the afterglow almost as poignant as the climax as she forced time to slow down so that she could memorize every nuance. The weight of Luc as he completed her with his own body was erotic in its own right, but add to it the familiar scent of him, the warmth of his body melting through her clothes, the warm expression in his eyes as he met her surely awed gaze.

His blue eyes were clear, the cynical and hard edge absent. His shoulders were rounded with sheathed muscle as he supported his position, and his body still sang within hers. With a slight wince of displeasure, he slowly withdrew himself and sat upright, his hair disheveled just enough to hint at scandal. Liliah yearned to run her fingers through its thick texture, yet she understood the necessity in remaining undiscovered.

Not for her sake.

But for his.

Her heart ached with the knowledge that while these moments were precious, they were fleeting and of no lasting consequence. She pushed such melancholy thoughts to the back of her mind and chose to bask in the glow of being thoroughly loved—at least physically. For while it was certainly the act of the marriage bed, it was only an act of passion for them—and could never be more.

Her heart threatened to fracture at the thought, yet she breathed deep and slowly sat up, righting herself as much as she was able.

While she collected herself, she kept her gaze away from Luc, lest he suspect her deeper feelings that she had been warned against. She almost missed the low oath he muttered. Startled by the shift in emotional atmosphere, she glanced at him, immediately noting displeasure on his face.

Unexpectedly, her heart pounded with suspicion that it was some sort of lack on her part. Insecurity crept into her heart. "What is the matter?" she asked hesitantly.

His tousled hair became more disheveled as he ran a

hand through its dark texture before wiping down his face in a regretful gesture.

Liliah's heart pounded harder.

"I—that is—" Luc began, then froze as a knock sounded at the door.

Liliah's gaze shot to the locked door, her heart pounding a new rhythm born of fear. "Yes?" she asked, then belatedly wondered if she should have kept her peace.

"Oh, my lady!" Sarah's relieved tone had Liliah rising up on her feet, casting a wary and frantic glance to Lucas.

Lucas held a finger to his lips, then glanced about the room. He silently strode to a row of low bookcases and slipped behind them in a crouch.

Liliah took measured steps to the door, adjusting her hair and dress as she walked, formulating a believable lie.

Or so she hoped.

She paused before the lock, then a smile tipped her lips. Tugging the door, she shook it meaningfully, then tried again. "Oh my, it seems to be locked, Sarah. Wait just a moment." She unlatched the lock in an exaggerated motion, then opened the door to her maid.

"My lady!" Sarah sighed in relief, then tilted her head in bewilderment.

"I confess I fell asleep. The door must have locked when I shut it. Have you been looking for me for very long?" Liliah asked, yawning for good measure.

"Oh, my lady! Your father had a guest who has refused to leave. Just now he has sent the staff after you, but I'll report directly that you're quite well," Sarah added, curtseying.

"Thank you, I assure you, I'm quite well." Liliah gave a small smile while her mind worked on a plan to get Lucas out of the house unnoticed.

"Very good, my lady. Your father wished me to remind you of the ball tonight, he intends to leave slightly early."

"I shall be ready," Liliah replied, hoping that Sarah would be on her way quickly. She'd have requested it if she didn't think it would raise suspicion, but she elected to simply wait.

"Very good." Sarah curtseyed once more, then begged her leave.

Liliah granted it, and closed the door, releasing a pent-up breath.

Her gaze wandered to the bookcase, a grin teasing her lips as she approached.

"Hide-and-seek?" Liliah teased, watching a grin spread across Luc's face as he stood.

"I win," he replied. "After all, I wasn't found."

"I found you."

"No." He leaned down and kissed her softly. "I found you."

"Details," she murmured.

Lucas chuckled against her lips, then withdrew, his expression clouding.

"Yes?" Liliah asked, fisting her hand lest she reach up and caress his pinched brow in efforts to soothe it. But she wasn't sure if such a gesture was welcome.

"I—that is . . ." He swore again. "I did not control myself as I should have."

Liliah frowned in confusion, her mind flipping through the last twenty minutes.

He tenderly grasped her chin, forcing her to meet his expression. "I did not pull out as I did the first time. Liliah, do you understand what I'm saying?" He narrowed his eyes curiously.

Liliah shook her head with some effort, since his grasp was still upon her chin.

Lucas swallowed. "It means that there could be consequences . . . Dear Lord, what have I done?" Lucas ground out, releasing her. "In this you see exactly who I am, Liliah." He shook his head angrily. "I not only willingly ruined you, but selfishly I took you as well, and even now as I should be loathing myself for such a deplorable act as giving seed to your womb, I have no shame; rather, in my selfishness, I only pray I don't get caught with such a consequence, though it would certainly be my due." He twisted his neck, tugged on his shirtsleeves, and smoothed back his hair, all the while holding her gaze as if unable to release her.

Liliah wasn't certain how to respond. Fear and anxiety washed over her first before the wonder and hope of the idea of a carrying Lucas's child—of never having to let go of that part of him.

The wonder melted into shame, and she suspected that his anger wasn't only aimed at himself, but her as well. It wasn't a rational thought, but she was finding that the more she emotionally responded to Lucas, the more jumbled her thoughts became.

"Have you anything to say?" Lucas stood up straight, as if expecting a blow.

"What would you have me say? Or do, for that matter?" Liliah asked, her brow pinching.

Lucas took a breath, then paused as if thinking better of whatever he was going to say. Finally, he simply shook his head. "Nothing." And with a long look, he strode to the door and peeked out. Without a backward glance, he was gone.

Liliah sighed deeply, then walked aimlessly to the center of the library. Reaching out, she caressed the back of the sofa as her mind wandered back to the stolen moments.

This clear idea had become more distorted by the moment. What had started as simply experience, had grown into something far less tangible and far more deep. Unable to fully understand, she had the sensation of treading water and failing to reach the surface. Her heart constricted each time she flickered her thoughts to Luc, and she forced herself to consider the option that had no future.

That maybe, just maybe, she was falling in love.

All the powerful sensations aligned with every account of love, yet the sinking feeling was ever present—and she wondered if that was because deep in her heart, she knew.

Love was impossible.

Lords of temptation were surely immune—and Lucas was certainly the king of their ranks.

Chapter Twenty-eight

Lucas called himself every loathsome name in his extensive repertoire. He had easily evaded the servants in the duke's household, at least to the front door, where the butler simply arched a brow as he passed by. He forced a calm walk to his awaiting carriage and instructed the driver to head to the club. He needed time to think, but mostly, he needed someone who would beat some sense into him.

Heathcliff was always up for a challenge, and today he was going to get a fresh one.

Of all the stupid, misbegotten, and utterly reckless things to do. He had been so careful, only to have every coherent thought filter out of his mind as soon as her hands encouraged his instincts to claim her irrevocably. He'd had every intention of withdrawing, but as she called his name, his body sang in return and he lost control before he even realized, and then it was too good, too erotically enticing to regret. Even now as he called himself utterly deserving of his scoundrel status, he gloried in the idea that he had christened her body with his seed, that even now she carried some piece of himself with her. It was the baseness of his nature, yet undeniable.

And just as dangerous.

Because he didn't want to simply walk away.

And if she allowed him to bed her again—for after his actions this afternoon, that was uncertain—it would be too easy to reason that he'd already allowed himself the pleasure once, what would it matter if he didn't withdraw? Wasn't the damage likely done?

He was wicked to his core, and still couldn't find a shred of regret.

Perhaps this was why Catherine had acted the way she did. His body clenched and cooled to a frigid degree as he thought her name. He might be a scoundrel and rogue of every sort, but Catherine was the devil in a dress. Of course she was also put in a difficult position, but that position was one of her own choosing, of her own manipulations, and of her own deceit. While married, he fully expected loyalty from her till death did them part. That misunderstanding was utterly communicated not long into the marriage. And after spending the afternoon in Chatterwood's study, he wondered anew what had tempted Catherine to make the choices she had. Perhaps the duke was just as calculating and opportunistic as Catherine. Maybe that was how the duke had won the hand of Liliah's mother. Or it maybe it could have simply been a worthy alliance. Heaven only knew, but it was unfortunate nonetheless for the poor woman.

Much like it had been unfortunate for Lucas.

But while Liliah's mother had surely been powerless against her husband, Lucas had been anything but powerless against his wife, Catherine.

Rather, he learned the game.

Played it well.

Then when the chessboard was situated perfectly: checkmate. After all, a woman without a protector is not only ruined, she is in constant peril. Lucas knew that the duke didn't value her enough to create the scandal that would surely follow should he claim the child. So the duke waited, and at the perfect moment, he took away her future, the one she had so callously calculated.

It was the fatal mistake that had sealed Catherine's demise and secured Lucas's future.

Alone.

Very few people knew the truth of it—the duke being one of those people. It was easier to let the stories circulate, even when the evidence was quickly noted and dismissed by the authorities. Suspicions lingered, and Lucas was happy to allow those suspicions latitude and the privacy and solitude it afforded.

As the carriage pulled up to Lord Barrot's house, he quickly stepped down and left his morbid thoughts in the carriage. The butler swung open the door without a word, and Lucas saw staff bustling about as they decorated for tomorrow's party. It was to be another masquerade, but it was to be of the silver variety. Everything would be chilled, cold, icy, and every patron would wear a silver mask to hide their identity—if they wished. The courtesans were all outfitted with silver gowns—at least the ones that the club employed—and the guest list was overflowing.

It would be a night for the dark ton to remember.

Lucas passed Lord Barrot's office door, and took the next right, seeking out his own office. As he pushed open the door, he both welcomed and grew frustrated at the sight of Heathcliff behind the desk.

"Comfortable?" Lucas asked, arching a brow.

"No. I bloody hate it here, but you're off chasing a duke's daughter and leaving the damn work to me," Heathcliff replied with a smirk.

Lucas glared for a moment, then closed the door.

"What? No reply? My, I do believe you're losing your edge, Lucas," Heathcliff remarked, chuckling.

"Shut up." Lucas strode to the desk and studied the papers spread across it. "What is this?"

Heathcliff sighed. "Orders for the kitchens, special requests by the selected guests, and here"—he gestured to a large drawing—"is the proposed arrangement of the ballroom. It was suggested to have more faro tables on the right side, which meant we needed to shift the design. I had no complaint since—"

"The house wins." Lucas chuckled.

Heathcliff nodded sagely. "Fairly."

"Always. And you'll be happy to know that after my appointment with the duke there are no pistols at dawn . . . at least tomorrow."

"Am I to guess at your meaning?" Heathcliff asked, shuffling several stacks of papers and then folding his hands, regarding his friend.

"Yes and no. I . . . am in a bit of a quandary," Lucas hedged.

"What did you do now?" Heathcliff chuckled lewdly, assuming much and yet still probably not enough.

"First, what do you know of Greywick's alliance with the duke?"

Heathcliff narrowed his eyes a moment, then gave a shrug, accepting his friend's change in subject matter. "I'm simply aware of Greywick's bet on the books, and that he is a long-standing ally in the House of Lords. Same as what you know."

Lucas nodded. "Greywick, is he any relation to Catherine?"

Heathcliff blinked, his brows raised in surprise. "Do I need to offer some sort of blood sacrifice after you mentioned her name?" he asked in a thick brogue. "Ye canna speak of the devil so lightly." He shuddered.

"I wasn't speaking lightly. I was speaking directly." Lucas shook his head, but understood his friend's sentiment. After all, Heathcliff had heard of it, Lucas had survived it.

"It's been an age since you've even spoke her name. Are ye dying?" Heathcliff frowned.

"No, and will you just answer the damn question?"

Heathcliff studied him a moment more, then replied, "I'm not sure. But I can find out. Why?"

"Because I have some suspicions. Also, I haven't been keeping up on the new proceedings in the House of Lords. Are you more knowledgeable than I?"

"You're talking to the wrong friend. You need to ask Ramsey that question. He'd be able to tell you far quicker than I," Heathcliff answered.

"True, true." Lucas nodded.

"Now back to the first question . . ." Heathcliff leaned over his elbows as he glanced up at Lucas expectantly. "What kind of 'situation' did you create?" He waggled his eyebrows.

"I'm not sure I wish to tell you any more." Lucas strode away from the desk to the sideboard to pour a liberal portion of brandy.

"Drinking will only loosen your tongue," Heathcliff called after him.

Lucas chuckled. "My tongue is by far the least dangerous part of my body."

A moment passed before Heathcliff burst into laughter. "Pour me a glass, I expect I'll need it after this story."

"I don't find it quite as humorous as you, my friend," Lucas replied and poured a second glass of the amber liquid.

He carried the glasses back to Heathcliff and lifted his in a toast. Heathcliff took his glass and lifted it too. Lucas grinned devilishly, clinked his friend's glass, then waited till Heathcliff was taking a sip. "Hell has frozen over. I may not end up being the last of my line."

As expected, Heathcliff choked, sputtered, and smacked the desk with his hand as brandy trickled down his nose and into his beard. Lucas chuckled at the sight and took a celebratory sip of his brandy.

"Say wha' now?" Heathcliff spoke after he recovered.

Lucas shrugged. "Which part has you confused?"

Heathcliff studied him. "All o' it. I tho' she simply wanted a tumble, not an heir and spare." Heathcliff tossed his hand in a bewildered gesture.

Lucas shook his head. "I said nothing of a spare, and that wasn't in the agreement." He took another sip of brandy.

"You simply tossed that in? Like an extra roll from the bakery?" Heathcliff all but shouted, his expression bewildered.

Lucas narrowed his eyes. "I wasn't exactly pondering that at the time."

Heathcliff chuckled lightly. "I expect not. So this . . . event . . . wasn't planned? I tho' you were careful the first time."

"I was. I'm referring to a more recent event, and I'm not aware if it will be fruitful or . . . not." Lucas frowned slightly, then took another sip thoughtfully.

"You're taking this remarkably well. You are dying, aren't you?" Heathcliff asked.

"No. I'm afraid you'll have to suffer my presence for many years more."

"Your presence and a smaller version, likely as not." Heathcliff took a tentative sip. "Does the lady know?"

That was the rub that made Lucas rather uncomfortable. He wasn't sure how Liliah took the news. He surely hadn't lingered, and he was regretting his hasty retreat now, even if it was prudent for him to leave as quickly as he did. Her expression had given nothing away, rather he had the impression that she wasn't fully aware of the implications, even after his swift explanation.

"Lucas?" Heathcliff reminded him.

Lucas gave a curt nod. "As much as I was able to explain under the circumstances."

Heathcliff gave him a reproving frown. "So you were able to sow the seed, but not be bothered to explain the deed, eh? I would expect more, Lucas. Yet . . ." Heathcliff's expression was thoughtful. "I do not think you to be in danger."

"Danger?" Lucas repeated, confused. He had been expecting his friend to give him a solid set-down, not alleviate the guilt.

"Yes, of the lass trying to bring you up to scratch. After all, this actually works out neatly for her, should she care to use it well." Heathcliff nodded once, as if impressed with his own brilliance.

Lucas decided he must be having an off day, since he wasn't following the trajectory of Heathcliff's thoughts—amongst other mishaps.

"You had mentioned the details of her betrothal . . ." Heathcliff let the words linger.

Understanding bolted through Lucas's mind, and he was surprised he hadn't seen it from the start.

He had been rather distracted at the time, and as such he gave liberal license to the inner workings of his mind. Yet now, it had become quite clear.

He wasn't sure how he felt about it.

And he suspected that it could as easily work against him, as for him.

"Finally catching on?" Heathcliff asked, raising his glass in a toast.

"Yes, it's an intriguing idea," Lucas replied, mulling it over in his mind.

"True enough, and, you scoundrel, it leaves you quite free and unattached," Heathcliff added.

"It would seem so."

"Yet you don't seem as encouraged by the prospect as I anticipated," Heathcliff noted.

Lucas shifted his weight and glanced down to his almost empty glass. "I'm contemplating it."

"You should be bloody celebrating it!" Heathcliff remarked, his tone frustrated.

"But you're forgetting that this grand idea can also be used in another way, and I'm trying to ascertain if that is likely." Lucas speared Heathcliff with a glance.

Heathcliff shook his head. "As I see it, should the world be inflicted with one of your progeny, it is much better for the lady in question to allow others to believe it is the heir of Greywick. You said yourself that they are to be married soon, and even I am aware that the timelines match up enough to give the babe credit as Meyer's child—all without having to bed the lass when he's enamored with another. It quite sews up the problem neatly, if I say so myself. And it gives Lady Liliah relief from the pressure to produce an heir. Heaven knows Lord Greywick will be a pain in the arse concerning a probable heir to his title; this creates a solution to every problem—you lucky dog. And you haven't the need to own up to any action. You'll be free to continue on in your merry debauchery of ruining ladies of quality."

"Lady," Lucas amended, glaring at his friend. "Singular."

"Ah, that's right, you're quite the monk. Though I do find it splendidly funny that the one time you decide to engage in congress with a woman, you find the one who makes you forget reason. It's amusing, I tell you."

"I'm laughing . . . on the inside," Lucas remarked. Yet he considered Heathcliff's explanation of the situation. Honestly, he couldn't have solved more problems if he tried, yet something about it rubbed wrong.

He couldn't quite place it, and as he examined it he saw more merit in the idea. If Liliah wished to continue their tryst after her marriage to Meyer, it would be simple, and he need not become entangled.

"Cheers!" Heathcliff strode toward Lucas with the decanter of brandy and splashed a generous amount into his cup. "Let us celebrate! You've neatly dodged every obstacle, and that deserves a commendation!" Heathcliff lifted his own glass and took a long sip.

Lucas followed suit, not quite celebratory—but warming up to the idea of having no consequences for his actions.

After all, for one who appreciated control, it was a delightful relief to find out that his lack of it would produce no unforeseen consequences.

He simply had to make sure that Liliah and Meyer married when they had planned.

Yet where did that leave the situation with the duke? Was Greywick still planning on blackmailing him to keep the information concerning Catherine a secret? Was that even worth looking into anymore?

He refused to answer the probing questions of his heart and instead celebrated his good fortune with his friend.

His thoughts would catch up with him soon enough.

And he suspected it would happen the moment he saw Liliah tonight at the ball.

He took another long drink of brandy, pushing the thoughts further away from his mind.

He'd deal with them—and her—later.

Yet even as he resolved to do just that, he knew that the lie he was telling was to no one—but himself.

Chapter Twenty-nine

Liliah paced her room, her thoughts a jumbled mess of confusion, hurt, elation, and fear—all warring within her. It was a fruitless battle, since each emotion was equally intense. It was a blessing her father hadn't summoned her, and as Sarah had readied her for the Morrison rout, she had allowed her thoughts to wander and grow till they became their own creature. After she dismissed Sarah, she had begun pacing and hadn't stopped.

Thirty minutes before they were to depart, and she hadn't sorted even one minute detail from the mess of emotions swelling within. She had to pull it together.

She glanced to the mirror and paused.

How was it that she didn't recognize the woman in the reflection? A month ago, she had been so certain of who she was, what she wanted, and how she was going to go about it. Now, she saw the confusion swirling in her gaze, and she wondered if others would notice as well.

What had started as an experiment in pleasure had resulted in a consequence of substance, and she wondered how long she'd need to wait to find out if Lucas's warnings had validity?

Not enough time.

Yet, even if she had enough time, would that change anything?

No. She thought not.

She hated the weakness she felt, but she straightened her shoulders, knowing deep within, regardless with how difficult it would be, she would rise to the occasion. It was a stretch, uncomfortable and risky, yet what choice did she have?

Her hand involuntarily caressed her flat stomach, and she both marveled and feared the implications it could create.

Lucas was not going to want her simply because of a child.

He had made his position abundantly clear, and rightfully so. She hadn't asked for his heart, nor expected it.

Nor had she expected to lose hers, yet that is exactly what happened. Was this how Meyer and Rebecca experienced every day? To love and know it could never come to fruition? What torture! Yet at least in Liliah's case, she knew her feelings were one-sided. Luc surely enjoyed her company, her body, and even her mind, but she didn't delude herself into expecting him to create a firm attachment.

That would be folly of the worst sort.

Of the most painful variety, since expectation on that front would only lead to disappointment.

Liliah resumed pacing, fortifying her heart with determination and the stubborn will her father so often had tried to break. There had to be some sort of silver lining.

She froze as she considered an idea.

And as she considered the facets of such a plan, she realized its merit.

It was the only solution.

Oddly enough, their indiscretion could prove to benefit them all.

As long as her father never suspected, and she had the inclination that he already did.

For it to work, she'd have to end the tryst with Luc. Even the thought of good-bye created a deep ache in her heart, but continuing in the same manner as they were would only lead to more pain in the future. And, if she were to pass off any potential child of Luc's as Meyer's, then she had to commit fully to the idea.

As did Meyer.

It was a plan contingent on a great many things, but it could work.

Resolute, Liliah squared her shoulders and studied herself in the mirror once more, recognizing the light in her eyes as a fierceness that faded when she let fear control her heart.

No more.

Growing into the woman she'd become meant putting folly behind her once and for all.

Whereas before she was fearful of potentially carrying Luc's child, she now prayed she did.

Forever she'd have a piece of him, even though she would never have his heart.

And that would be enough.

It had to be.

Liliah strode to the door and took the stairs to the

foyer, giving a curtsey to her father as he strode into the hall.

He barely gave her a nod before striding to the waiting carriage.

Liliah followed, wearing her determination like armor, daring her father to manipulate her.

He was silent for the first half of the carriage ride, then he shifted slightly, the movement causing her to take note. "You will not dance with Lord Heightfield tonight."

Liliah tilted her head. "Is he planning to attend?"

"I care not," her father replied hastily.

Liliah nodded, hoping her father would drop the subject.

"You will dance with Meyer, however," he added.

She paused but a moment. "Yes, I will." It was of utmost importance that she portray a solid engagement now, lest people suspect should she conceive.

"Good," her father replied, then turned his attention to the passing scenery.

Liliah planned out the evening. At first opportunity, she would seek out Rebecca and suggest they meet during the week at the park, that she might notify her of the plan. Then, at the first waltz she would whisper it to Meyer, praying for his approval. It would be better to Rebecca once she had gained Meyer's cooperation. Surely the plan would be in all their best interests?

As the carriage pulled up to Morrison Hall, the duke stepped out and all but abandoned Liliah as he sought out several other gentlemen, and then certainly would find the faro table. As she walked into the manor, she traveled down the hall and into the ballroom. A tingle skated up her spine and she turned to an Ace of Spades, the dowager widow Lady Markson, watching her closely. Apparently her father made previous arrangements for her to be chaperoned.

Liliah grasped the hand of a footman as she stepped out of the carriage and into the torchlight. Her soft yellow dress captured the firelight and made the fabric shimmer slightly. Her cap sleeves didn't ward off any of the evening chill, but she had elected to keep her pelisse at home, expecting the ballroom to be overly warm with the sea of humanity within. Her slippered feet were silent as she took the stairs with several others. She nodded to those who welcomed her, and she found her way into the Morrisons' grand ballroom. English lavender dotted the tables, lending a sweet fragrance to the room along with a muted splash of color. The room wasn't well populated yet, as they had arrived just as the party began, and she didn't see any sign of Meyer or Rebecca—*or Luc*, she thought.

She lifted a glass of lemonade from the table and took a sip of the sweet and tart liquid. While awaiting the arrival of her friends, she thanked Lady Morrison for the invitation, and conversed about a potential whist party for a few select friends. As she was finishing up the dialogue, she noted the entrance of Lord and Lady Grace, without their daughter.

Liliah tilted her head as she watched their entrance to the ballroom and then excused herself from Lady Morrison with a gentle curtsey. As she made her way to the door, she still didn't see Rebecca. She approached Rebecca's parents. After the formalities, she directed her attention to Lady Grace, who was standing quite regally in her pale blue gown with a peacock feather in her golden hair. "Is Rebecca well?" Liliah asked.

She didn't miss the quick exchange of glances between the two, and awaited Lady Grace's response. "She's well enough, simply out of spirits for the day. I'm sure she will attend the Reimers' rout next week," Lady Grace replied, then made her excuses. Lord Grace offered his arm to his wife and they continued into the room, leaving Liliah perplexed and suspicious as to why Rebecca was out of spirits, though she likely knew the cause.

Yet she had hoped they had made some sort of tenuous peace.

But truly, how was Liliah to expect it to last? She needed to speak with her friend, and made a mental note to ask Lady Grace to convey a message to her daughter.

Liliah took another sip of her lemonade and watched as her father skirted the ballroom, shaking hands with several peers before entering one of the many gaming rooms. Thankfully she was more than aware of her father's shrewd and miserly opinion of gambling, lest she be concerned he waste their fortune on faro. The man never bet more than a few guineas, though he had much more to spare.

It was a mystery, as much of her father was, yet she expected it was one of the few things he actually enjoyed in life—odd as it was.

The music began and several couples lined the dance floor in a reel formation. Lord Jaymeson approached her and requested a dance, which she readily accepted. He was a kind sort of fellow, one of the older bachelors and quite forthright about his search for a wife, but Liliah didn't expect that he had turned an eye toward her as a prospect, not with her betrothal to Meyer being public knowledge. It was a carefree dance and a delightful and worry-free partner she found in Lord Jaymeson, who smiled encouragingly and easily continued light conversation when they happened to turn about together. All in all it was a delightful beginning to an otherwise unproductive evening.

Lord Greywick and Meyer arrived during the reel, and Liliah kept a mental awareness of Meyer's position within the ballroom so that she might meet him after the dance. As the music came to an end, she clapped gratefully and nodded a kind smile to her partner as she took her leave of the dance floor.

The ballroom had grown considerably more crowded in the span of the dance, and it took some time to wind around the congregated London elite. The strains of the cotillion started, and Liliah neatly dodged a potential dance partner and intercepted Meyer.

"Good evening, Meyer." She gave a friendly smile as her gaze flickered to the thwarted partner.

Meyer gave a crisp bow and nodded warmly. "Good evening to you."

"Take a turn with me?" Liliah asked, offering a cheeky grin.

"Delighted to," Meyer replied, offering his arm. Liliah saw Meyer dart a quick glance toward his father, Lord Greywick. No doubt being seen together would please both of their fathers.

As they gained some distance from Lord Greywick, Meyer started the conversation. "I know you well enough to anticipate that you have some specific topic of conversation on your mind. But I must first ask, how was your trip to the park? I trust you had little difficulty finding a suitable replacement for my company," he said with a mischievous expression.

Liliah had quite forgotten about the park escapade.

"Oh! You were quite clever indeed! I must admit my ineptitude to discover your intent, but I did suspect something, I just wasn't certain what," Liliah replied with a wide smile. "Clever man."

Meyer chuckled. "I wish I had thought of it on my own, but I did have ample encouragement."

Liliah's face heated with a blush at the implication. Had Luc sought out Meyer simply to create a rendezvous? It was a delightful thought, and hinted at maybe some deeper attachment, but she pushed it aside lest she create the most dangerous creature—hope.

"It was a lovely afternoon," Liliah replied calmly, even as her heart raced at the mere thought of Luc.

"I'll bet." Meyer chuckled. "So, what is it on your mind, minx?"

Liliah took a deep breath, fine-tuning the way she'd start the conversation, especially with potential eavesdroppers surrounding them. As she opened her mouth to speak, she met Luc's searing blue gaze from a few paces away. She had not seen his approach. The air left her lungs and her body grew warm all over. A slow smile started in his gaze, then tipped up the edges of his full lips, illuminating his face in a seductive grin that made her belly flutter.

"Liliah?" Meyer's voice broke through the spell, and before she could answer, Luc approached and bowed.

"Good evening, Meyer." Even as he spoke to Meyer, his gaze never left Liliah, and she was quite content with it.

"Heightfield," Meyer replied. "I'll . . . leave you to it then." Meyer released Liliah's arm and gave a smart bow, a smirk on his lips as he walked away.

Liliah cast a teasing grin to her departing friend and turned back to Luc, feeling the power of his regard like a touch that awakened all the senses. "Good evening," she said, rather unremarkably.

"It is now."

Liliah couldn't restrain her laughter. "I'm not sure whether to be insulted or flattered at such a comment," she teased.

"Foul, why would you say such a thing?" Luc asked, offering his arm.

Liliah gladly took it, his warmth seeping deep into her bones at the touch, her body relaxing as if finally feeling safe.

She resisted the temptation to remember her prior resolution.

Surely a few stolen moments couldn't hurt?

"I say it because I'm quite certain your imagination could have come up with a more clever answer. That phrase has been used many a time before."

"That doesn't malign its distinct honestly, however."

"I must concede that fact."

"Ah, humility and beauty," Luc replied.

"Ah, flattery and a silver tongue," Liliah said cheekily.

Lucas chuckled warmly. "And well you know it." He regarded her tenderly and leaned down slightly. "Are you well?" he asked just above a whisper.

Not certain of their privacy, she simply nodded.

She met his gaze, and watched as several emotions flickered across his face: curiosity, regret, resolve. Before he could continue, Liliah interrupted. Knowing that if she didn't do this now, she would likely never have the strength to do it at all. She had wanted to just forget for a few moments, yet it was too perfect an opportunity to let it go to waste. With a trembling heart, she forced a strength she didn't feel.

"I think, under the circumstances . . ." She let the phrase linger, and she kept her gaze downward for the duration of her resolution. "That we should give our respective regards to one another. I do not expect anything more from you than what was previously discussed, and I do not wish you to be burdened by the expectation that I may." Liliah took a slow breath, feeling the tension of Luc's arm beneath her hand. "And, from the bottom of my heart"—she hazarded a glance up to him, allowing the shield she'd put around her heart to retreat as her attachment was surely recognizable in her gaze—"I thank you. Because no matter what, I'll always keep a piece of you in my heart, Luc." She whispered his name, ignoring the hundreds of people around them, wishing they were alone, hoping he understood.

His gaze searched hers, as if testing to see if her words were authentic, or if they were a choice she'd been forced to make. "And you're certain?" he replied, his grin at war with the tension in his body. How had she come to know his nuances so well?

"I'm certain that you will evaluate the circumstances and see things the very same way, that this is your certain way to freedom . . . and maybe mine too," Liliah answered.

Luc nodded. "Then this is farewell."

Liliah forced the lump in her throat to go away as she swallowed. "I believe so." She didn't trust herself to say more.

"Then"—he paused and lifted her hand, kissing her knuckles so softly it was only a whisper of a touch—

"may I just say that it was a pleasure, Lady Liliah. In absolutely every nuance of the word." He slowly bowed, released her hand, and without a backward glance, melted into the crowd.

Taking her heart with him.

Yet she didn't regret her decision.

She only hoped that it wasn't in vain.

As she watched Luc's retreating back, she closed her eyes for a moment, allowing herself to have a moment of self-pity, of longing, and then she turned to seek out Meyer once more.

The hardest part was over; all that was left was convincing her friend of the plan's ideal merit. Meyer wasn't difficult to locate, and his confusion was evident in his expression when she approached. Surely he expected her to spend her time with Luc.

The first waltz began, and Meyer extended his hand by way of greeting. Liliah took it readily, her heart pounding with anticipation for the conversation that needed to take place, and that she wished were already completed.

As Meyer led her to the dance floor, he whispered, "Is something the matter?"

Liliah offered a weak smile. "It doesn't have to be," she answered honestly.

He didn't reply, simply held her in the frame of the waltz and started to blend among the other dancers. "Care to elaborate?" he asked after a few moments.

"Yes. But it's going to be difficult to explain. And you'll surely need to consider it, but I have faith that you'll see the promise of such a plan readily enough."

Meyer nodded. "This sounds serious."

"It is, my friend," Liliah answered. "You see, because neither of us has been able to disengage from the betrothal, I've somewhat resigned myself to the marriage. But because our friendship will never be more than friendship, regardless of the marriage contract, and there will certainly be expectations your father, and mine, will wish to see fulfilled as a result of our marriage . . ."

Meyer frowned, then closed his eyes. "An heir."

"Which would be betrayal of the worst sort to our sweet Rebecca. Fate has potentially offered us another alternative." Liliah hedged, hoping she wasn't being too forward. It would be months before she knew if she carried Luc's child, yet they didn't have time to figure out the details.

"And what is that alternative?" Meyer asked, his eyes narrowing, suspicion deeply evident.

"It would seem that I could already be carrying an heir for us," Liliah whispered so low she wasn't sure Meyer heard.

"Dear God, Liliah," Meyer whispered, his gaze flickering from her face to her belly, then back. "What a bast—"

"I'm not certain, mind you," she finished. "And while I could demand he make amends, the question I have is if we were to publicize the information, would your father or mine believe it, act on it, and null the betrothal?"

Meyer's wide-eyed gaze was cast downward as he frowned, as if deep in thought. "As much as I wish to say yes, I'm afraid that they would simply put forth the lie that it was my doing, and the wedding would be hastily completed. They've both been beyond reason, so why would they see it now? Especially when this could be the opportunity they need to hurry things along. Besides, they would then know the heir wasn't mine, and would await another." He shook his head.

"That is what I suspected as well. And I've had no luck in discovering why there is such a push. It's beyond reason," Liliah answered.

"Indeed it is." Meyer sighed, his gaze kind as he regarded her. "I see no other option either, my friend. And I must say that as much of a trial and heartbreak this is for you, it certainly does solve several problems, loath as I am to admit it."

Liliah nodded once.

"Liliah," Meyer said gently.

She glanced up at him questioningly.

"Do you love him?"

Liliah glanced at the floor, then to the side, before meeting her friend's gaze. "Yes. But I also realize that my loving him wouldn't make trapping him in an unsavory position the right thing to do. It wasn't intended, not that it makes it right, but it is far more forgivable. And I do believe he intended to at least keep some sort of attachment to me, but I said my good-byes earlier this evening."

Meyer frowned. "You ended it?"

"Yes. It was really the only way. If you agreed to move forward, then our attachment needs to appear solid so others don't suspect, including our fathers."

"And I thought I was the one to give up much." He shook his head. "Liliah, you are giving up far more. And my heart breaks for you." He spun her in a graceful twirl and held her in the perfect frame as they continued their waltz.

"So what now?" he asked.

"Now . . . we wait. And I'll try to communicate the circumstances to Rebecca. At least she will be aware of the situation, lest she doubt our resolution to remain as we are," Liliah added delicately.

"I thank you," Meyer replied. "I do not know how I could ask more."

"I do not know how I could offer it," Liliah answered.

As the waltz ended, Liliah found a quiet corner and sat in one of the few vacant chairs, collecting her thoughts. As another partner requested a dance, she willingly obliged. What she needed was distraction.

Distraction from realizing just what sort of future she had sealed.

Distraction from seeking out a pair of crystal-blue eyes that may or may not still be in attendance.

Distraction from running back into the only arms that ever felt safe.

Chapter Thirty

Lucas spent the night replaying the miserable scene from last night. His mind wouldn't let him forget it, as much as he wished he could. By three in the morning he was in his study swirling brandy before the low fire. The amber liquid offered no respite, and by six, he was marching toward the breakfast table.

He walked to his place setting and took a seat in the comfortable chair. His glass was filled with water, his teacup with tea—two sugars, no milk—and a silver spoon rested upon his saucer. He lifted it and stirred the tea. The familiar routine didn't give him a sense of control, which he sorely missed. He turned to his coddled eggs and three rashers of bacon as they sat upon a single piece of buttered toast, like every morning. He draped his napkin over his lap and proceeded to break his fast, but the peace of the familiar was broken. Agitated, he abruptly stood from the table before he had taken more than two sips of tea and two bites of toast, and quit the room.

His usual rhythm was off like a wobbly carriage wheel that resisted improvement. Restless and haunted, he stalked back to his study. The scent of brandy made his stomach sour and he simply grabbed several stacks of papers and left for one of the parlors. As he selected a chair in the green room, he noted that even the sunshine from the windows seemed diluted and less brilliant.

What in the bloody hell was wrong with him? He should be thrilled! Life had no inclination to trap him in any entanglement, his life was perfectly organized and controlled, and he had no threat of well . . . anything! He should be carefree and delighted; instead he found he was restless, irritated, and angry.

He decided that life simply didn't make sense.

"There you are." Ramsey paused in the hall and welcomed himself into the parlor, much like he welcomed himself into the house. Lord only knew the servants were used to such behavior.

"What do you want?" Lucas asked with little finesse.

Ramsey paused, then shook his head and continued into the room. "What fell into your tea this morning?"

"Nothing." Lucas waved dismissively.

"Right," Ramsey enunciated. "Well then, I'm assuming from your stack of paperwork that you're starting in on the guest list for the evening. The security men have been outfitted in their footmen attire, lest we give the appearance of being overprotective, and the kitchens have made a promising start to the fare for the eve."

"You've been busy this morning," Lucas replied, his tone slightly sarcastic.

"I'll choose to take your words as a compliment."

Ramsey arched a dark brow and continued. "The betting books have been updated and I have kept an eye on the particular wager we discussed. It would seem there is a slight discrepancy that I think we need to address." Ramsey seated himself without invitation and leaned forward.

Lucas followed suit, leaning forward to hear Ramsey's update. "What discrepancy?"

Ramsey took a deep breath. "Greywick's estate is not as solid as we had anticipated. Because of your inquiry, I asked an investigator to dig around and find out if the money was readily available."

"Legally, of course." Lucas chuckled.

"Enough." Ramsey echoed his amusement, then continued. "It would seem that Greywick isn't as heavy in the purse as he wishes people to assume. In fact, his estate is actually in arrears. We have it from a credible source that the help is quietly being let go at intervals, and new help is being hired, only to receive little to no pay." Ramsey lifted both brows.

"No." Lucas gave his head a shake.

"Yes. Indeed. So you can see that this leaves us in a quandary. Do we call the bet, or do we allow the gentleman to . . . tie his own noose . . . should he lose?"

Lucas twisted his lips. "He's not going to lose," he answered, then thought it over. So many sensations filtered through him as he spoke the words out loud. The words seemed innocuous enough, yet they threatened to shake him to his core.

The bet on Meyer and Lady Liliah's marriage would certainly be won because, inadvertently, Lucas had played an instrumental role in ensuring the marriage took place.

Greywick would win.

Would clean up.

And the house would lose.

Rather, Lucas would lose.

"How much would it cost us?" Lucas asked, not caring but unable to resist the curiosity.

"The odds are for the event happening, so the payoff wouldn't be overly substantial, but those betting against the event would lose mightily," Ramsey answered in a calculating tone.

"I see. And . . . what would happen if the marriage didn't take place?" Lucas asked, his body warming at the very thought.

"With the amount that Greywick bet, he would face ruin."

Lucas nodded. "I see. And this knowledge that he is in financial trouble, this is not well known, yes?"

"It took quite a lot of digging to uncover. He's hidden it well."

Lucas leaned back on the sofa, thinking. His instincts told him he was on the cusp of something larger.

But was it his battle? No. Liliah had released him from the need to uncover any further information when she made her choice. But while he was able to rationally grasp the concept that he didn't need to act on the knowledge—let the chips fall where they may—he found he couldn't let it go.

"That's quite an odd expression on your face, Lucas. Are you quite all right?" Ramsey asked, his tone dubious.

"I think . . . I'm about to do something quite foolish," Lucas answered honestly.

Ramsey paused, his eyes narrowing. "Is it something I need to not be aware of, should I be questioned later?" he asked in a wary tone, always looking out for his reputation.

"I think not, but to preserve my reputation, I think I'll keep my plans to myself."

"Your reputation," Ramsey said wryly. "Because it's quite pristine," he added with heavy sarcasm as he stood.

"You misunderstand my implication. Rather, my tarnished reputation is indeed the reputation I wish to keep."

"So you're going to be valiant, is that it?" Ramsey chuckled. "Then I commend you in your insanity, and I hope it is not folly that follows you, but courage. I dare say you'll need it," he joked, then took his leave.

Lucas's brow pinched as he considered his next step. As he rose from the sofa, he noted the soft dust floating about in the air, dancing like sparkling light. It was oddly lovely.

His stomach growled with hunger as he considered his abandoned breakfast.

Odd how one decision could change everything.

From darkness to light.

From anger to determination.

He didn't want to consider the reasons behind his abrupt change in outlook. They certainly would be quite damning to his bachelor status.

Yet he found he cared not a fig.

Rather, for the first time since waking up at two this morning, he was at peace with himself.

And maybe, just maybe, he no longer was the man he was a few weeks ago.

Maybe he was better.

Temptation had many forms, and who would have

imagined that one of them would be both his demise and rebirth. But wasn't love known for miracles?

Lucas dismissed his fanciful thoughts and quickly broke his fast. While he was finishing his tea, he hastily sent a note to Heathcliff, requesting he come by that morning. After that missive was dispatched, he sent off another to Meyer, knowing Greywick would likely intercept it, yet he didn't care if the man read the contents.

Hyde Park, Grosvenor Gate, noon.

It was a simple message, one he hoped Meyer would heed. The plan Lucas was concocting was quickly brewing, and he knew that time was of the essence. He only hoped that Meyer would be amenable to meeting him. The scene that had haunted Lucas's dreams was Meyer's dance with Liliah the night before. Anyone else would have simply disregarded the soft whispers and the inclined heads as betrothed lovers conversing, but Lucas was far too aware of Liliah's facial expressions to be fooled. She was telling him of her plan, the one that she hadn't needed any of his help in concocting, the one that he wasn't sure he could have executed.

As wise as it would have been to save his skin, he had gone to the ball with every intention of hinting at the solution of Meyer accepting Lucas's by-blow, but when he'd seen her, all he could think was *mine.* To his astonishment, she had broached the topic and had had the will to walk away.

When he wasn't sure he would have had the strength to do the same.

It was bloody humbling.

And damned infuriating to see her in Meyer's arms.

Yet now he suspected that Meyer, knowing much, would be less inclined to have a rational conversation. Lucas only hoped he himself was restrained enough to be the wiser of the two.

It never had been his strong point.

Lucas left the breakfast table and took the stairs two at a time as he rang for his valet. In short order he was tugging on his cuffs and descending the stairs, only to find Heathcliff just entering the foyer.

"What's all this bloody business about meeting you so abruptly?" Heathcliff had the appearance of a man who had not slept, and Lucas pulled up short.

"Bee in your bonnet, lass?" He teased his friend with a crisp English accent, just to irritate him.

"Ach, I hate it when you do that. And yes, but clearly I'm not the only one. Ramsey stopped by and warned me about some harebrained scheme and that you were in a foul disposition. Well, that makes two of us."

"Ramsey has been a busy fellow."

"One of us has to be." Heathcliff ran a hand through his hair. "What are you needing that's so damn important?"

Lucas gestured to the study on the left and Heathcliff all but stalked in. Lucas followed and closed the door softly. "Now, I do believe that my information will be a much longer story, so why don't we start with why you look like Master Death?" Lucas rubbed his hands together and took a seat by the low fire.

"It's a bloody mess, I tell you." Heathcliff didn't even hint at subtlety. It never was his strong point; it was refreshing, since the large man was as transparent as glass when it came to his motives.

"Enlighten me." Lucas arched a brow and waited.

Heathcliff rubbed his hand down his face, again, as if in disbelief. "I'm to have a ward, and oversee her come-out. She's almost of age, which means I'll be rid of her soon, but from my understanding, she has had little training from a governess." He shook his head and collapsed onto the sofa. "As if I'm a proper guardian."

"Well." Lucas blinked, absorbing the news. "That's indeed interesting. How did this all come about?"

Heathcliff shrugged. "Her parents were off gallivanting in the Indies and caught the fever. They never returned, and she had been living with her grandmother, who also passed. I was the last and very distant relation." He blew out a sigh.

"That's an odd turn of events. But the girl cannot be without fortune, or is she destitute as well?"

"Not destitute, she's actually quite well situated, but without proper guardianship and not of legal age to oversee her fortune. I just learned all this yesterday, and already I'm having a headache trying to organize all the different needs for the lass."

"A governess, of course," Lucas added helpfully.

"That's first on the list. I already put an ad in the *Times*, but I've asked several acquaintances for references as well. I don't want some old crow." Heathcliff shuddered.

"Already turning your eye to the help," Lucas teased.

"Heavens no, I just do na' want to subject the poor lass to a mean biddy. Life's been hard enough on her."

"Listen to you, being kindhearted to the girl."

"Pain in the arse," Heathcliff retorted.

Lucas chuckled. "Where is the girl going to stay? Not in London."

"No." Heathcliff shook his head. "I'll set her up in the county seat while the governess gives her some polish, then will bring her to London for a proper season, and pray the Good Lord gets her matched up real quick."

Lucas arched a brow. "Never thought I'd see the day when you'd join the ranks of the matchmaking mamas of the ton."

"Desperate times call for desperate measures, my friend."

"Clearly," Lucas replied.

After a moment of reflection, Heathcliff said, "So, what is your news, and if it's more startling than mine, I may have to start drinking now and pray I get drunk rapidly."

Lucas gave a little shake of his head. "Pour a glass, my friend. Your world is about to turn on its ear."

"Not again." Heathcliff groaned. "My heart can take only so much shock in a day's span. What the hell did you do this time?"

"Would it shock you to hear that I may have a tendre for Lady Liliah Durary?"

"No. I'd say you'd been bloody denying it for a while though," Heathcliff replied suspiciously.

"Well, then what if I told you I was finally taking my head from my arse and doing something about it?"

"Then I'd say it was about time for you to grow a pair of bollocks and be a man about it. Took you long enough." Heathcliff shrugged. "What are you planning to do?"

Lucas grinned, then explained what Ramsey had shared earlier that morning concerning the current state of Greywick's estate.

"You don't say! The blackguard!" Heathcliff all but shouted. "I knew something was suspicious."

"Very suspicious."

"Ramsey didn't give me that information, bastard."

"I'm sure he was more than inclined to allow me the honors, based on your current fit of pique."

"I'm not pitching a fit," Heathcliff grumbled.

"Close enough, but back to the subject at hand. I have an idea as to how to address the situation, but I'm going to need some help digging around."

Heathcliff sat up straight. "I love digging."

"I know. Of the three of us, you're the one who enjoys getting his hands dirty." Lucas gave a low chuckle.

"What do you need to find out?" Heathcliff's gaze narrowed, his expression one of intense concentration.

"Several things. First, I need tangible evidence of Greywick's estate's financial status."

Heathcliff nodded once. "Done. Next."

"I need to know if there's any possible way Greywick would be aware of the truth of Catherine's . . . situation," Lucas added in a strained tone.

"Very good. Anything else?"

"I need to know if anyone else is involved, or if it's simply a . . . transaction of sorts between Greywick and Chatterwood."

"Understood. This will be a welcome distraction from all the irritation of making accommodations for the new ward. Good Lord, I need a drink." Heathcliff stood and marched over to the decanter and poured a liberal splash, then raised it. "To us, may we survive the challenges we face!" He took a long drink.

"Well said, even if it is too early in the morning for such things." Lucas chuckled; it was a well-placed toast.

Heathcliff gave a swift nod and set down his now empty glass. "I'll send word when I have the information."

"Very good. I thank you, my friend." Lucas nodded.

"Well, it wasn't a total damn waste of time. Till later." Heathcliff gave a curt nod and quit the room.

Lucas sighed and thought over what was needed in order for his plans to fall into place. So far, so good.

But the day was young . . . enough.

He rang for his butler, ordered his carriage readied. It was close enough to noon that he could depart and arrive a little early, giving him time to collect his thoughts.

He only hoped Meyer dared meet him at all.

Only time would tell.

Chapter Thirty-one

Lucas selected a spot opposite the Grosvenor Gate. It was a warm day that had the scent of rain lingering in the air from earlier that morning. Being noon, it wasn't the fashionable hour and the park was sparsely populated, which served Lucas's purposes quite well. The trees gave unnecessary shade along the path and several squirrels ran from one tree trunk to the next.

But no sign of Meyer.

Lucas took the path that would wind toward Rotten Row, but turned back before he went more than thirty paces, wanting to remain near the gate should Meyer make an appearance.

Sure enough, just after Lucas checked his gold pocket watch for the third time, he noted a black carriage of quality roll up the street, pausing before the gate. Meyer stepped from the conveyance, and immediately spotted him. Lucas took measured steps to meet up with his intended guest. Suspicion, anger, and cool distance all reflected in Meyer's expression. It was a warranted and deserved reception.

As Meyer closed the distance, Lucas offered a nod, only to be given a cut as Meyer refused to acknowledge the greeting. Lucas slowed his approach, then halted completely as he noted the increase in Meyer's pace. Before he could ascertain his motive, Meyer reached out and gave a solid roundhouse to Lucas's left eye.

Lucas took the hit with practiced calm—it was not the first, nor probably the last time he'd engaged in fisticuffs—but rather than beat Meyer to the ground, he simply shook off the hit and regarded the man. "Are you finished or would you like another shot?"

Meyer worked his jaw, irritation and anger evident in his gaze. "I could bloody well beat you and it wouldn't be justice enough for the likes of you, Heightfield. And you're a blackguard of the worst sort if you think you're not deserving of it." Meyer almost spat the words.

Lucas glanced around, thankful for their lack of audience. This wasn't exactly the best way to start out an alliance. "I'm fully aware, thus why I didn't defend myself, or knock you out in return," Lucas answered calmly, his eye swelling as he regarded the man before him.

Meyer's expression gave nothing away.

"I was rather hoping we could have a calm and rational conversation, one that I hope you will find to be in the lady in question's best interest."

"Believe me, I think you've done quite enough to the lady in question," Meyer retorted.

Lucas breathed out a frustrated sigh. "No one is more aware of this than I. May I continue?" he asked, trying to keep the exasperation from his tone.

Meyer paused, then nodded once.

It was enough, Lucas decided.

"What do you know of your estate's situation?" Lucas asked quietly, gesturing for them to take a slow stroll. If they walked, it would look less suspicious should anyone happen by.

Meyer fell into step beside him, his gaze confused. "And why is it of your concern?"

"Do you remember when I mentioned your father's substantial bet?"

Meyer's face lost some of the color it had carried from the altercation.

"I'm assuming that is a yes." Lucas nodded. "It would seem that your father doesn't have the collateral to back up his bet."

Meyer met Lucas's gaze. "That simply cannot be the case. He does nothing but hire more servants and speak of his grand plans for his estate. If there is nothing in the coffers, then how—"

"Because he's spending money he's expecting to gain." Lucas was even more convinced that Greywick was blackmailing Chatterwood, and placing a bet on the side to tidy up another large sum. As underhanded as it was, Lucas gave credit to the man for being resourceful.

"I'm not certain how this pertains to our mutual friend." Meyer's expression shuttered, and Lucas forced the patience he certainly didn't feel after such a long night of no sleep.

"Because I have reason to believe your father . . . has created some circumstances that will once again inflate the earldom's wealth. I'm not in a position to mention exactly what those circumstances are, but I do have a few additional questions. The answers to those questions just might allow you the freedom to break the betrothal," he added quietly.

Meyer's gaze sharpened. "Then by all means, continue."

"How long has your father been pushing the alliance between the lady and yourself?" Lucas was careful to never mention Liliah's name, for insurance against eavesdroppers.

Meyer gave a shrug. "About a year. But I do remember him mentioning it once before, maybe four years ago? It wasn't a large push, just a suggestion. In the past year it became far more insistent."

Lucas nodded. It was near five years ago that the situation with Catherine happened, so the timelines almost coincided, at least enough. "Would you consider your father a confidant of the duke?"

Meyer frowned. "They have had several closed-door meetings. Once there was shouting, but I wouldn't say they confide in one another."

Lucas turned his gaze to the path before them. "Are you aware of any reservations your father has toward Lord and Lady Grace?"

Meyer didn't answer for a moment, and Lucas turned his inquiring gaze to him.

"If what you're saying is true about the current state of the my father's affairs, then an alliance with the Graces is one he wouldn't entertain," he answered cryptically.

Lucas paused in his steps, waiting for Meyer to elaborate.

"What I am about to tell you is of the strictest confidence." Meyer started.

Lucas nodded.

"Lady Rebecca confided in me about two months

ago. Her father's investment in the West Indies faced a huge loss after a storm. Their estate is not as endowed as it was earlier. There's hope it will once again thrive after the next year's investment returns, but for the time being, there isn't much to spare."

Lucas closed his eyes. "I see." He met Meyer's anguished expression.

"So, that would make a union unhelpful for either family."

"Yes."

"But a duke's daughter . . ." Lucas let the words linger.

"Would be a huge asset to a poor estate," Meyer murmured. "I see."

"Don't we all." Lucas sighed. "I need to ask a favor of you."

Meyer gave a curt nod.

"If your father, or if the duke suspects that we are aware of what is going on, they will likely move forward the wedding. I need time to collect evidence and play my hand if this is going to work. Can you play along for the time being?"

Meyer agreed. "It isn't as if I have a choice either way."

"Let's see if we can give you some more options, shall we?" Lucas offered a smile.

Meyer didn't return it, rather he frowned. His expression bespoke of a myriad of questions, but he continued with the one of most importance. "Then what of Lady Liliah?" he asked in a hushed whisper.

Lucas's brow pinched, then he realized that he hadn't made his intentions clear. "We'll see about regularizing the situation posthaste." He offered a slight grin.

Meyer gave a disbelieving look. "Truly?"

"It seems that we are not all immune to her charms, like you," Lucas admitted.

Meyer gave a small smile. "Well then, I can most certainly get behind this plan."

"I didn't think you'd object," Lucas added.

"No, no indeed. Rather I find it a quite fantastic solution, except for the fact that I might soon be penniless." Meyer shook his head. "I'm not certain how to solve that problem, but one disaster at a time, eh?"

Lucas had renewed respect for the man. It wasn't many men of the ton who wouldn't fall to their knees in worship of their wealth, and here was a man who faced his potential bankruptcy in a forthright manner. "I might be able to assist in that matter as well. We shall see." Lucas gave a quick bow, and took his leave.

He had a masquerade to oversee tonight.

And a blackguard to take down on the morrow.

There was, indeed, no rest for the wicked.

Chapter Thirty-two

Liliah had chosen to be at peace.

And it was quite certainly a choice.

Because if left to her own devices, she would be having the largest pity party of all. Yet she refused, and focused her attention on her sister. It had been a relaxing afternoon and was one of the few nights when they were not engaged for some sort of theater production or ballroom party, out and about. After dinner, Liliah retired to the library to spend the remainder of the evening with her sister and a favorite novel.

Unbidden, sorrow flowed over her soul with the realization that these evenings with her sister were numbered. Samantha was sitting in the chair, her softly curled hair was styled in a simple chignon, and the firelight gave her an angelic glow.

Yet her brow was pinched and her lip was pulled between her teeth as she read. Liliah sat up straighter. "Are you well? What are you reading that has you so concerned?" she asked, a slight teasing tone in her voice.

Samantha met her gaze, then set the book down gently on her lap. "Actually . . . may we speak of something?" she asked.

Liliah nodded, setting her own book to the side and awaiting her sister's leisure.

"Today . . . father called me into his study. I expected us to speak of my come-out next season, but it would appear that I'm not to have one. He's already secured my match." Samantha's words were spoken slowly, as if being pulled from her unwillingly.

Liliah's first reaction was anger, then pain for her sister, then all the emotions melted into fear.

What possible reason would their father have for keeping Samantha from having a season? She had been looking forward to her come-out for several years, and they had already selected a modiste to make the gowns. It didn't make sense.

"I'm so very sorry." Liliah scooted over on the sofa so that she could reach her sister's hand and hold it. "Who is the man our father has selected? Do we know of him?"

"I confess I do not remember the name, I was in such shock I don't remember much more of the conversation. It was something like Mayson? Father dismissed me shortly after, not wishing to hear my reaction, and—"

"And you've been mulling about it ever since. That is just terrible! Why would he do such a thing? It makes no sense!" Liliah was growing increasingly angry by the moment. Why destroy Samantha's chances at finding a suitable match? Why take it into his own hands? And if it was Lord Mayson, he was an older gentleman at least twice her age, and known for his penchant for brandy. Surely her father wouldn't do that to his daughter!

"I'll figure this out, and we will see how we can prevent it," Liliah added with feeling.

"I'm afraid he won't listen to reason, much like he has been with your betrothal to Meyer. He did say something about being done with the whole . . . er . . . situation, with no longer having daughters to oversee. I rather think he simply finds the errand of securing our matches tiresome."

"What a terrible thing to think!" Yet Liliah saw the truth in her sister's statement. During her own come-out, her father had resented each action he'd had to make to secure a marriage—that was, until the situation with Meyer came into play. The duke wasn't a man who suffered the needs of others well, or tolerated their interference with his own plans. He would likely be thrilled to be rid of the baggage of two unmarried daughters—after all, there was no heir for him to consider, and as long as Liliah and Samantha were married off, they could see about producing heirs. It truly did make sense, in a distorted way.

"What are you thinking?" Samantha asked, her tone worried.

Liliah gave her sister a gentle smile. "Just that our father doesn't deserve us."

Samantha returned the smile, but it faded quickly. "Thank you, I actually needed to hear that. It's difficult to think of myself as a burden to him. I've always tried to be what he wanted me to be, and for me to consider that it was all for naught, it . . . hurts."

"Of course it does. Well, what I will do is this. I

shall speak to Father about overseeing your come-out, since as a married lady I'll be a proper chaperone, and then perhaps that will change his mind." Liliah gave a squeeze to her sister's hand.

Samantha squeezed back. "Thank you. You always know what to do."

Liliah giggled. "No, but I usually react, and that's sometimes good, and sometimes . . . not good."

"I wish I had your courage."

"I wish I had your sweet and kind heart, my love." Liliah released her sister's hand and patted her knee. "Now, since we have a plan, let us leave it to rest and talk about something much more diverting."

"What do you wish to speak about?" Samantha asked, her smile returning.

"Anything but Father! How about we discuss that delicious new gown that you ordered the last time we shopped on Bond Street!" Yet as soon as Liliah mentioned it, she regretted her words. Memories flooded back to her of her secret tryst with Lucas, and she missed him all the more. Her body carried around a dull ache that never truly subsided. Love was truly the most beautiful and wretched thing she'd ever experienced.

Samantha didn't seem to notice her shift in mood. "Oh, it will be so very lovely!" She continued to expound on the detail of the gown, and Liliah tried to follow her words, but the dull ache throbbed, and she wished that she could simply see him again. But she knew the foolishness of such a hope, and tried to extinguish its frail flame.

But hope was nearly as stubborn as love, and refused to subside.

Her heart was a traitorous thing, and refused to listen to reason.

No matter how many times she called herself a fool.

She still clung to the hope that maybe, just maybe . . . what she knew must be the end, would somehow become a beginning.

Chapter Thirty-three

"Do I want to know?" Heathcliff asked as he strode down the Barrots' hall toward Lucas.

Lucas chuckled. "I'd like to say that the chap is in a worse state, but I actually took the hit and didn't give recompense."

Heathcliff nodded, his gaze skeptical. "You're bloody lucky it's a masquerade; that shiner of yours is quite impressive."

Lucas winced as he grinned. The swelling had increased and his eye boasted grand hues of purple and blue, but the silver mask would indeed help in hiding his current injury. It would also help with the swelling; the cool metal would be a welcome relief to his tender flesh. "Was there anything of import that you wished to notify me of, or are we done here?" Lucas asked dryly.

Heathcliff arched a brow and paused in the foyer just before Lucas. "I was going to confirm that the guest list has been set up at the side entrance. The carriages will deposit the guests in the front and they will follow the torchlit path to the correct entrance so that we can double-check for invitations. It was the only way we could make sure that no one unsavory crept in."

"Very good. I'm sure we'll have a few complaints about having to take the footpath, but the side entrance is much easier to manage for security, plus it's almost a direct entrance into the ballroom, so fewer people to, er, get lost." Lucas chuckled.

"That does happen quite often." Heathcliff nodded his agreement, his grin wide against his dark beard. "Just last week I found Lord Jaymeson passed out on one of Lady Barrot's fainting couches."

"How poetic," Lucas remarked.

"Lady Barrot didn't feel that way about the situation. She poked him with her cane till he roused."

"And what did you do while the poor man was being assaulted?" Lucas asked, chuckling.

Heathcliff hitched a shoulder. "I observed."

"How noble of you."

"I do what I can." Heathcliff gave a curt nod. "Needless to say, Lord Jaymeson rolled off the couch and quickly make his departure. I'm not certain as to how he made his exit from the estate, but I'm assuming he made it home."

"Good, good. He's a confirmed guest tonight, so he's obviously no worse for wear."

"Lady Barrot no doubt appreciates our additional safety measures."

"For the sake of her furniture, I'm sure," Lucas added.

Heathcliff grinned in response. "I'm assuming your altercation was with Meyer?" he asked, changing the topic of conversation.

"You assume correctly," Lucas said in an irked tone. He didn't wish to converse about Meyer, because then his mind would certainly wander to Liliah, and he was already fighting the temptation to think of her constantly. It really was becoming exasperating to be so obsessed with a skirt.

"Your face bears an odd expression," Heathcliff remarked.

Lucas sighed. "It was an odd afternoon. Were you able to gain any progress in the matter we discussed earlier?" Lucas glanced about for listening ears. Lord and Lady Barrot's staff were notoriously discreet, practically invisible, which only meant they could easily overhear. Lucas would take no risks, even if they were probably trustworthy.

Which gave Lucas an idea, but he waited to hear Heathcliff's news before he expounded on his newfound thoughts.

"Just confirmation of your suspicions, and the amounts. I'm still awaiting news on the possible . . . awareness said person could have of past circumstances," Heathcliff answered cryptically.

Lucas nodded. "Have you interviewed the Barrots' staff?"

Heathcliff frowned. "No, but that's a good idea. I hadn't thought of it."

"I hadn't either until just now," Lucas admitted.

"I'd wager they have at least some insight. While the one person in question isn't a member, the other is quite loose lipped when brandy is involved. I'd suspect someone has heard something of note."

Lucas nodded. "I agree. We have several hours before the hordes arrive. Why don't you take a few of the staff aside and question them? It might make the night easier if we have more information to use."

Heathcliff scolded his friend. "The staff are already overworked preparing for the event tonight; I'll not add to their workload by taking up their time. This is too important an event, and they need time to do their jobs."

Lucas twisted his lips. "You're quite the compassionate soul."

"I'm nothing of the sort, I'm simply more practical than you. I'm thinking with my mind, you're thinking with your willy." Heathcliff chuckled.

Lucas gave a lewd gesture to his friend, but grinned. "Be that as it may, I'm anxious to end this whole sordid mess."

"I'm anxious for it to end as well, just to get you off my back and onto . . . someone else who would appreciate it."

"Are you quite finished?" Lucas asked in an exasperated tone.

"No, I'm sure if you give me time, I'll come up with another inappropriate remark."

"Lucky me."

"That's what—"

Lucas interrupted. "Enough. Aside from the side entrance, what other information do you have?"

"Be sure to wear the mask, you look like hell."

"Thank you, you're so entirely helpful. Anything I'm not already aware of?"

"One thing . . ." Heathcliff stepped a little closer to Lucas. "We had a late request for membership. One of which you'd like to take note."

Lucas nodded. Membership was by invitation only,

and the invitations were always sent out at night, returned by the next night via their private courier. Only
after your membership was approved could you attend
and become acquainted with the other members—provided it wasn't a masquerade, which it usually was.
People were so much more comfortable when they had
privacy on their side. "Who?"

Heathcliff whispered the name. "Chatterwood."

Lucas frowned, meeting his friend's sober gaze.
"Why in heaven's name does he reply now? We sent
the invitation over a year ago, and he never replied, so
we assumed he refused." They had welcomed his re-
jection; they felt obliged to extend an invitation to one
as powerful as a duke, but didn't truly wish he'd attend.

"Apparently he had a change of heart," Heathcliff
said.

"He kept the invitation for a year, and then submit-
ted it? Bloody hell, how?"

Heathcliff twisted his lip. "Apparently the duke had
it sent by private courier. It was left with the butler and
then Lord Barrot opened the missive. It wasn't in the
usual envelope."

"Interesting. So he will be attending tonight?" Lucas
asked, thankful that the event would be a masquerade. It
would be helpful to be less recognizable.

"That is my assumption."

"And Greywick?"

"Yes."

Lucas blew out a tense breath. "Who needs Vauxhall fireworks when you have this intrigue afoot? It's
far more explosive."

"At least has the potential to be."

Lucas narrowed his gaze as he studied the floor, his mind racing. "There has to be a reason."

"I'm assuming that, but it would be wise for us to uncover that tonight."

"Agreed. Please communicate that to Ramsey."

"Done." Heathcliff nodded, then strode down the hall, presumably to speak with Ramsey.

Lucas's brow pinched with confusion and frustration as he tried to figure out how attending the party would benefit the duke. Lucas knew he was missing a vital piece of information, he just didn't know what.

And not knowing could be the most dangerous thing of all.

Chapter Thirty-four

Lucas studied the ballroom from the balcony that overlooked the main level. His hands gripped the highly polished banister with a force that had his knuckles turning white. The glitter of silver masks twinkled against the candlelight that they had chosen as the sole illumination for the evening. The air was scented with the rose petals that were crushed under the dark ton's feet as they walked into the room from the hall. The dull roar of conversation and the music from stringed instruments blended together as Lucas oversaw the evening, searching the crowd for the men of note.

He knew they had arrived, for Ramsey had been ever vigilant while overseeing the guest list as each gentleman presented his invitation in order to gain entrance to the event. Ramsey had taken pains to study each man's attire so that he could give a report to Lucas. However, above it all, on the balcony, it was a bloody blur of people and Lucas couldn't distinguish one man from another. For once he wasn't a supporter of the masquerade idea and the anonymity it created.

Irritated with his inability to narrow down his search, he pushed away from the banister, his fists aching from the release of tension. He reached beside him and lifted the cold metal of his silver mask. He set it over his face, the metal an icy chill against his skin, and he secured it behind his head. It was a new mask, one he had never donned before, in hopes that it would lend him additional privacy. His hands ceased their ache as he squeezed his hands open and closed several times. He then pulled out his gold pocket watch, checking the time. It had been over two hours since the party started, so surely now the men would be well into their cups, causing lips and information to flow freely.

Lucas strode toward the back stairwell, adjusting his mask slightly as he took the stairs. The dark hall was lit by a few sputtering candles, only the amount necessary to illuminate the path, but not light enough to encourage exploration by any straggling club members. To clarify, they always made a distinguished path for the members for entry and exit from the main ballroom, for at times they already arrived foxed and only became more so as the evening progressed.

He skirted the ballroom via the hall and entered through one of the side entrances that was the least populated. The last thing he wanted was to gain attention. He passed a table of whist and a table of faro on the left before lifting a glass of champagne from a passing footman. He took a tiny sip, more to simply appear at ease rather than from thirst. He scanned the gentlemen before him, searching for the details that

Ramsey had described to him: Chatterwood was wearing a thick, solid silver mask with little adornment. He was also wearing a sapphire cravat pin. Greywick's mask was far more ornate than most, and the jewels embellishing the nose piece would make him easy to spot. Lucas suspected that once he found one gentleman, he would find the other in close proximity.

The scent of rose petals was far more fragrant below than when he was observing from above, and as he breathed in the scent, his mind wandered to Liliah. The scent was deeply sensual, and anything along that vein always led back to her. He didn't even try to fight the overwhelming desire to have her, rather he used it to add fresh strength to his search.

He walked among several men speaking about horseflesh and an upcoming race. He noted Lark milling about another gambling table and he assumed that Lord Kribe was nearby, even possibly Lord Warrington. It was well circulated that Kribe had found a new mistress after Lark had shifted protectors. Lark gave him a seductive smile, then turned back to the table. Lucas read nothing into it, she was a woman always on the lookout for another green pasture to graze, and he did not fault her. It was also a boon to realize that she hadn't recognized him, for if she had she would have given him an amused grin rather than a seductive look. She had learned long ago he wasn't interested—at least in her.

Truth be told, he was quite convinced he had sworn off the fairer sex altogether, yet here he was, going to war over one.

War and women, how did they so often go hand in hand?

Bloody mess, the lot of it.

Yet none of it had him retracing his steps or questioning his motives; rather he simply acknowledged his accursed state of falling for Liliah, and moved forward.

A reflection shimmered in the corner of his eye and he halted his steps and pretended to study a gambling table. After a moment, he turned to study from where the bright reflection had come. Sure enough, a very smooth and reflective mask was seen in a congregation of several men in close conversation. The mask was thick, not dainty and thin in design like most, and Lucas suspected it to be Chatterwood. He studied the men in conversation. One was wearing a rather common mask, the other he was unable to see because the gentleman's back was to Lucas. Yet Lucas could see the silver color of the man's hair, and he suspected it to be Greywick.

Lucas glanced to the table, then feigned disinterest. He then made a wide arc around the conversing gentlemen and selected another point of view to study the men. The man whose back had been to Lucas, was now in full view. The line of gems down the bridge of the nose of the mask confirmed it was Greywick, and Lucas bit back a grin of victory. Sipping his champagne, he slowly ambled toward the men, closing the distance enough to overhear their conversation. Blessedly, a faro table was nearby, and Lucas stood behind a few of the gentlemen playing, his gaze on the table but his attention focused on the men speaking a few paces behind him. Their tone was low, and amidst the ambient noise of the ballroom, the conversation was hard to decipher, but Lucas listened intently, recognizing Chatterwood's voice and Greywick's as well. Once he caught their tones, it was easier to listen.

"I'm assuming you've drawn up the settlement for the betrothal?" Greywick asked, and Lucas clenched his teeth. To ask such a thing wasn't abnormal but wasn't in good taste either.

"Just yesterday, as we discussed," Chatterwood remarked. "And I'm assuming you've addressed the other matters we discussed?"

Lucas listened carefully, wishing they would give more detail on the *other matters* . . .

"If everything goes according to plan, you need not worry," Greywick answered.

"I was under the assumption that it was already taken care of." Chatterwood's tone was clipped, irritated, and cold.

Lucas shifted his feet to try to appear less tense as he listened.

"And lay all my cards on the table? I think not, there's no rush. And as long as everything goes to plan, there's no reason for concern . . . unless you foresee some sort of . . . problem?" Greywick replied with the tone of a man assured of winning a gamble.

Chatterwood didn't reply right away, and Lucas resisted the urge to turn and see if the duke stalked off. "There will be no problems," he finally ground out.

"Good, good. Then see, ol' chap! There's nothing to be concerned over! This is why I knew you simply must accept the invitation. Let us celebrate and be merry together!" Greywick was clearly at ease, judging by his jubilant tone. Lucas doubted Chatterwood had the same enthusiasm.

"I rather hate it here, and I don't understand why I let you drag me into such a situation. I know Heightfield is here, and while I damn the man to hell, a gambling hell isn't exactly the place I had in mind for him." Chatterwood gave a small chuckle, likely impressed at his turn of phrase.

Lucas rolled his eyes.

"I've not seen him here often, he rather keeps to himself."

"Unless he's chasing after my daughter," Chatterwood remarked bitterly.

Greywick's tone was inquiring. "I thought you addressed that particular problem?"

"I did. But that doesn't mean I trust him to leave her alone as he should."

"Do . . . we need to make arrangements to move up the event?" Greywick asked significantly.

Lucas awaited Chatterwood's response with great anticipation. His heart pounded loudly in his ears as he listened.

"It will appear rushed."

"I care not, and neither should you . . . I'm of the persuasion that there are more important matters that we don't wish to be widely circulated. A hasty wedding isn't the most scandalous thing, is it?" Greywick's tone was taunting.

"Indeed it is not," Chatterwood answered after a moment's pause. "Very well, the more rapidly I'm rid of her, the sooner I can be rid of the next daughter." He paused for a moment. "I've already secured her a match, so I'm done with both of them. A bloody miserable business, not having an heir and having to marry off daughters. I rather regret—" He didn't complete his thought.

Greywick chuckled. "My, how the brandy has loosened your tongue, Chatterwood. But it is all of no consequence. Let us drink to a swift alliance, and a swifter conclusion to our situations. It shouldn't take more than three days."

Lucas turned to leave, but did so in an unhurried manner so that he could allow his gaze to rake over the men speaking. As expected, Greywick was rather joyful, his lips spread in a winning grin. The Duke of Chatterwood's expression was far more sober, his eyes narrowed behind his mask.

Lucas ambled away, listening as he went, just to ensure that they didn't harbor suspicions of his eavesdropping.

To the random passerby, their conversation wouldn't hold any interest. But to Lucas, it had been a wealth of information.

Especially the plan to secure a special license, which meant that Lucas had to secure one first. Good thing he had a favor he could call in at Doctors' Commons.

Three days.

He had three bloody days.

As he quit the room, he signaled for a footman. He sent the man off to fetch his carriage.

Because if Chatterwood was here . . .

His blood burned with the anticipation of sneaking into the duke's residence to find Liliah.

It was likely a foolish errand, since she was of the persuasion that their tryst had concluded.

But things change.

People change.

And she deserved to know that she was no longer fighting for her future alone.

Rather, her future had a new name.

His.

Chapter Thirty-five

Liliah was just saying good night to her sister when a prickling sensation traveled up her spine. As she closed her sister's door, she glanced down the hall at the flickering candlelight. Nothing seemed amiss, yet the sensation lingered. With silent steps, she started down the hall toward her room, glancing back after every few steps. The highly polished wood floor creaked as she passed over the threshold of her chamber, casting one more furtive glance up and down the hall before closing the door. On a whim, she locked it. Sarah had already helped her ready herself for bed, and she was looking forward to a sedate few moments reading in bed. She slipped between the covers, the slightly chilly sheets a contrast to her cozy room heated by the fire, and a grin teased her lips as she snuggled deep. She reached over to the nightstand to pick up her book when the doorknob rattled softly.

Gasping, she held her breath and watched the handle start to turn, even though she'd locked it! In a moment, she was out of bed and lifting the fire poker from its place beside the fire, arming herself against whoever dared to interrupt her peace.

She released her tight breath and willed strength to her fearful heart, assuring herself that it was simply Samantha, yet unable to convince herself.

The door swung open and Liliah lifted the poker behind her to increase the power of her swing, then she froze.

Her jaw dropped, and she sincerely thought that she was hallucinating.

It was impossible.

It was improbable.

It was a sure sign she had lost her mind.

She had heard that love made people crazy, but she had never expected it to be such a literal application. Good Lord.

Her hallucination offered a cautious smile as his familiar blue eyes shifted from her to the weapon in her hand, then back. "Liliah, love. Would you mind putting that down?" He closed the door silently, tucking something into his coat pocket.

Liliah's brows pinched in confusion.

"The fire poker, unless . . . unless you wish me to leave?" he asked, his tone immediately sobering as if never having thought of that option before.

This shook her from her confusion, and she set the poker beside the fire. Was it truly Lucas, then? How the devil had he gotten past the footmen?

"Thank you." He tugged on his shirt cuffs, something that she'd seen him do several times when he was slightly uncomfortable. The sight made a smile tip her lips, and she decided that she didn't care of if she was hallucinating—it was still Luc.

And he was here with her.

But that begged the question—rather, many questions. But of first importance—"Why?" she asked, so much longing, pain, and hurt crushed into her chest at once. The bitterness of missing him, the sweetness of seeing him again, turned over and over in her heart a hundred different ways.

"It's quite simple, actually." He took a few tentative steps into the room, his warm gaze lingering over every part of her.

"I'm waiting," Liliah replied, forcing a brave calm.

At her words, he chuckled softly, shaking his head. "Who would have thought that of the two of us, you would be more stubborn? Not I."

Liliah's brow pinched again as she wondered at his words.

"No, rather, of the two of us, you were willing to say good-bye, end everything—no strings attached." He circled around her and reaching up, placed a warm hand at her neck, moving it downward to her hand before releasing her and moving to caress her shoulders as he passed behind her.

Liliah closed her eyes at the extreme pleasure of his touch, simple as it was. "Oh?" she said unremarkably.

"Yes. It was rather humbling to realize that it wasn't that you needed me, rather . . . that I needed you. I, who had convinced myself that I needed nothing, or no one, was utterly held prisoner by a person who was willing to set me free." He came to stand before her, his hands at his sides as he met her gaze. He gave a small, woeful smile. "And I find that being set free doesn't suit me."

Liliah's breath caught as she considered the implications of his words, refusing to think about the repercussions that they could create.

"So, I suppose the most important question is one only you can answer." He reached out and brushed his fingertips against her lips as he cupped her cheek tenderly.

"And what is that?" she asked, her tone braver than she felt.

He visibly swallowed, revealing the weight of the question before it was ever voiced. "Do you want me?"

Liliah's lips widened into an uncontainable grin as she nodded, utterly beyond words. Luc didn't hesitate a moment before he met her lips in a searing kiss that settled deep within her bones, sealing the bond between them. His lips branded her, his hands mapped every curve, and she allowed herself the luxury of lacing her fingers through his dark mane, the texture delightful, sensual, and erotic all at once. Her breathing came in gasps and she was disappointed when he didn't initiate more; instead he gentled the kisses and then leaned his forehead against hers, his hands at her shoulders, his breath coming in the same excited gasps as her own.

"I was hoping you'd say that," he murmured.

Liliah couldn't resist the invitation. "Actually, I didn't say anything . . ."

"Minx." He chuckled and leaned back, tracing his hands from her shoulders to her waist and holding her. "So, it would seem we need to make a plan, since the only person you'll be marrying is me."

Liliah arched a brow. "Again with assuming my answers."

"I'm not above kidnapping," Lucas replied with a teasing tone.

"Is that a threat?" Liliah asked, giggling.

Lucas leaned forward, kissing her all too willing lips ever so softly. "It's more of a promise."

"Then how could I refuse?" she murmured in reply between kisses. "Provided you ask rather than assume."

Lucas gave a soft laugh and leaned back. "Life will ever be interesting, will it not? Very well." He took both of her hands within his and knelt. "Lady Liliah Durary, make me the happiest of men and consent to be my wife?"

Liliah nodded, tears prickling her eyes.

Lucas moved to stand, then paused, tilting his head in a teasing manner. "I need to hear the words."

Liliah laughed, keeping her tone soft so as to not create curiosity should a servant walk by her door. "Yes."

"Ah, she speaks!" he teased, then stood and pulled her into his arms as he kissed her with a fierce passion.

Liliah pulled back, studying his almost drunken expression. "What made you change? I had quite given up on you before I even dared hope, and now I find I'm quite frustrated to have endured such heartache. I missed you, Luc."

"Forgive me, love. Just as you are stubborn, so am I, and it took a while for me to come to grips with what had transpired. I'm sure it's not easily forgivable, but I'm willing to work off my debt." He leaned forward and nipped playfully at her earlobe.

"I'm sure we can make some sort of arrangement." Yet as she spoke the words, her emotions sobered as she considered the mountain still to climb that was before them both. "How are we to move forward?"

Lucas leaned back, his expression sober as well, having likely sensed the change in her mood. "There is much to discuss. I trust we will not be interrupted as you are ready for bed?"

Liliah nodded. "Which begs an altogether different question—"

"One question at a time, love." He nodded and took a seat at her writing desk, quite far away from her.

"Why the distance?" Liliah asked as she moved to take a seat by the fire, her body chilled from the emotional rush and the subsequent absence of her lover's embrace.

"Because you're entirely too tempting to my senses and I need to be thinking clearly as we converse about plans," he replied honestly.

Liliah's lips tipped in a crooked grin, but she didn't reply.

"Now, I have some information, and am missing a bit more, but before we dive into that, I need to tell you about my past."

Liliah frowned. "I've heard the titter about . . . Catherine, was it? I don't fault you for anything, Luc."

"I thank you, but I rather need to tell you the information that the public doesn't know." He took a deep breath.

"Are you afraid it will change how I feel, or my decision?" she asked cautiously.

Lucas chuckled, but it held no mirth. "No, but that could simply be my arrogant pride speaking. The tale has more to do with your father . . . than I."

Liliah tipped her head, her mind spinning with the various implications, and she leaned forward in her seat.

"Around six years ago I was married to Lady Catherine Blymont. She was a ward of Lord and Lady Barrot, with whom I've had a longstanding relationship. The marriage was a suitable arrangement for both of us financially, and I expected us to get along quite well. I realize now how blind I was, but it is of no consequence now." He took a deep breath.

Liliah shivered, premonition stealing her warmth. Even the nearby fire wasn't enough to ward off the chill.

"I was quite happy with Catherine as my wife. But she was far more social than I, and grew increasingly spiteful of her station as an antisocial earl's wife, so began attending parties alone. To make a longer story shorter, she commenced an affair that led to a pregnancy. She was quite convinced of the gentleman's affection, and was quite forthright about her intentions to divorce me and find her happiness with another— damn the consequences to her social status. This blatant disregard for her social standing is what never made sense, till later." He leaned forward, folding his hands on his knees.

Liliah waited, the sound of the crackling fire overly loud in the anticipation-filled room. Yet a moment later, her thoughts filtered into place, creating a startling realization. "A woman who cherished social standing so deeply wouldn't risk the grievance of a divorce unless the reward was more than ample recompense."

"Exactly." Lucas nodded, approval glowing in his eyes. "The man in question was already married, with two daughters within a few years of a come-out. Turns out the man was sorely out of spirits with his current wife for never producing a son, and the thought of marrying off daughters was made even less palatable by the fact that he would be unable to marry them off if his indiscretion was known."

"Dear Lord," Liliah remarked. "It makes so much sense." She flipped through the memories of the events to just before her mother's death. She had never understood why her father had been so hard-hearted, almost incensed at her mother's death. "My mother died four years ago." She blinked back tears.

"It was less than a year after your father ended his relationship with Catherine. She died in a rather freak carriage accident not three weeks after the abrupt end."

Liliah shook her head. "He likely harbors some misbegotten anger toward my mother for not dying sooner. It explains much. But does not excuse any of it."

"Your mother's death would have rectified the mess he had created, had it been earlier, yes. But I rather think he resents not only your mother, but you two daughters as well."

"I've known that for some time. Mother protected us from it till she caught pneumonia." Liliah sighed, then her thoughts turned to Samantha. "My sister! My father already spoke of an arrangement for her marriage and—"

"Yes, I know. I learned of it tonight. And I've been thinking on that front . . . and have an idea." Lucas arched a brow. "But it would require the utmost secrecy. But let us finish this vein of thought first before we move on to the next. I have reason to believe that Lord Greywick knows something of Catherine's indiscretion and perhaps even the carriage accident. With that, I think he is blackmailing your father to secure your dowry for his estate."

Liliah frowned. "My dowry? I didn't take Greywick as a fortune hunter for his son."

"Desperate times call for desperate measures. And Greywick's estate is bordering on poverty. He used his information to secure the best source of income available, and the most legal. A duke's daughter."

Liliah's eyes widened, then she frowned. "But why then, would he not allow Meyer to seek Rebecca's hand? They are quite secure—"

"Her family suffered a large loss recently."

"Dear Lord. Am I nothing but a pawn?" Liliah's chest heaved in anger and she pushed off from her chair and paced about the room, fuming. "How dare he, how dare Lord Greywick! Damn them all!" She all but shouted, then covered her mouth and glanced toward the door. Her heart pounded fiercely for several moments at her loud outburst, and then she flickered her gaze to Lucas.

"Well, how do we stop this?"

Lucas bit back an amused grin. "You're quite fetching when angry, my love."

"Focus, Luc," Liliah ground out.

He chuckled, then sobered as he continued. "They are going to secure a special license to make the . . . transaction quicker. Greywick is anxious to get ahold of your dowry, and your father is anxious to destroy any damning evidence."

"So . . . how do we eliminate the problem?"

Lucas grinned, then withdrew a piece of paper from his coat pocket and unfolded it. "We beat them at their own game."

Liliah walked toward it, her eyes slowly taking in the script across the top.

Doctors' Common.

It was a special license.

"I suppose you'll say that I didn't specify when you'd marry me . . ." he teased.

Liliah grinned, caressing lightly the important document that would both set her free and secure her future. "Yes, but under the circumstances, I'm willing to make an exception."

"Brilliant." He folded up the document and tucked it away. "For this to work, I need to make several arrangements, one of which is for your sister. Can you convince her to write something for me? I need a letter, something that mentions her running away to . . . the Americas. That should be difficult enough. Have you any connections there?"

Liliah nodded slowly. "My mother has a cousin who lives in Boston."

"Then fabricate a story. We need your father thinking that Savannah is on her way to Boston, and I shall take care of the rest." He stood. "Do you trust me?"

Liliah nodded. "Yes."

"Then all will be well. Bring the letter tomorrow to Bond Street. Do you think you can make that happen?"

Liliah nodded. "Yes, I have to check on the progress of my wedding dress. I have a fitting."

"Seems we have all the luck then, my dear. I'll find you. Be sure to take your sister," he added.

"I will." Liliah closed the distance between them. "Thank you. You were able to do what I thought was impossible." She met his earnest gaze.

"It seems that love truly does make all things possible." He hitched a shoulder.

"So . . ." She glanced down and intertwined her hands with his, his warmth creating a cocoon of peace over her soul. "You're saying you love me?"

Luc chuckled. "I'm saying I really never had a choice. But yes, I love you, Liliah." He sealed the words with a kiss, tender, sweet, and lingering. He pulled back as Liliah leaned in for more. His affectionate chuckle met her ears and she blinked her eyes open.

"If I engage in kissing you longer, I won't have the strength to leave, and I must if I'm going to arrange everything by tomorrow. What time is your appointment?"

Liliah pouted, but answered, "One."

"Brilliant. We should have sufficient time. And you're of age, so it shouldn't be a problem."

"So you won't stay?" Liliah asked brazenly, wanting to feel the security that she'd found in his arms.

"Not tonight, but every other night henceforth? Yes. Always yes." He kissed her nose, then headed to the door.

"Good-bye." Liliah offered a small wave.

"No, just see you in a few hours," Lucas corrected and opened the door a crack. After a moment he slipped into the hallway, closing it once more.

As Liliah listened for any sounds, she shook her head, realizing she'd never asked him how he'd been able to sneak in.

And really, it didn't matter how.

It only mattered that he had.

Chapter Thirty-six

Lucas knocked on the door of Heathcliff's residence at what surely his friend would call an ungodly hour, but there was no time to waste. The butler answered with cool reservation, and with the long established friendship between the men, didn't inquire as to why Lucas was calling. His friend was less than amicable, but received Lucas nonetheless.

"Please tell me you have something of life-or-death importance, or please see yourself to the door," Heathcliff muttered from his position behind his desk in his study. He had dark circles around his eyes and his beard was less than tidy. Never more had Heathcliff appeared more beast than man, save one time. Lucas thought of a previous time, and shuddered.

"I'm getting married today and I thought you'd wish to know."

Heathcliff spit out the tea he'd just sipped and coughed.

"Good morning to you too." Lucas withdrew a handkerchief from his coat pocket and dabbed his sleeves where some tea had landed. He took a cautious step back from his glaring friend.

"Say wha' now?" Heathcliff coughed a few more times and muttered a curse as he dabbed the papers on his desk with a linen napkin.

"Liliah and I are to be married today, I've a special license and all."

"Well, if that doesn't beat the day." Heathcliff wiped down his beard with the same napkin. "Congratulations, you old dog!"

"Thank you." Lucas nodded. "I've come hoping you can give me additional information on the situation with the duke and Catherine?" Lucas asked hopefully.

Heathcliff nodded. "It seems the lad who had, er, arranged the mishap with the carriage sang like a canary when one of Greywick's hired men cornered him. Seems Greywick had suspicions of his own, and he filed away the information for use later. He knew of his precarious financial position a while ago, it would seem."

"Interesting. He was quite patient," Lucas added.

"And it almost paid off."

"So he does have evidence."

Heathcliff seesawed his hand. "Not the kind that would hold up in court, not against a duke. Truly the worst it could do would be to harm his reputation or create suspicion."

Lucas nodded. "But with two daughters of an age to marry off, it was an easy way to rid himself of one daughter, and also eliminate any evidence against him."

"Tidy it up all around. The lady's dowry wouldn't be missed from his coffers since it had been designated long ago, and he'd be killing two birds with one stone. Bastard," Heathcliff swore.

"Indeed. Very well."

"You're quite nonsensical over this chit, aren't you? Can't say I envy you. Rotten mess, all of it," Heathcliff replied cynically.

"Ah, yes, your sour grapes. How is the young ward you are so generously taking in?" Lucas asked, winding up for his next part of the plan—unbeknownst to his friend.

"A bloody nightmare. Do you have any idea how difficult it is to find a governess who doesn't make me want to claw my eyes out? I'm not expecting to be around either her or the girl much, but I don't want to slit my wrists when I am, if you catch my meaning."

Lucas chuckled. "Then I bring you some great news."

"You've found a way to remove me from guardianship?" Heathcliff asked hopefully.

"No. I found you a governess. She's knowledgeable, well educated, and beautiful. But I need your word that you will not touch her . . . this is not the sort of help you take a tumble with, am I understood?"

"Look who is becoming all honorable!" Heathcliff chuckled. "Where is this untouchable governess?"

"I can't tell you. But I can deliver her to your estate in Scotland within a week," Lucas added quietly, as if imparting a secret.

"Why the secrecy?" Heathcliff asked suspiciously. "She some battered wife and I'll be challenged to a duel for taking her in?"

"No, just a lady whose situation has recently changed, and she needs employment—proper employment," Lucas added significantly.

Heathcliff nodded. "I see. She has experience?"

"Yes, of the best variety," Lucas replied.

"Very well. What's this mysterious governess's name?" he asked.

Lucas paused, his mind going into overdrive. He hadn't thought of an alias for Liliah's sister.

"She has a name, hasn't she?" Heathcliff asked.

"Miranda," Lucas replied. "Miranda Smythe."

Heathcliff arched a brow, surely questioning Lucas's honesty, but he simply nodded. "I don't want any more details. The less I know, the better. Just have the girl there so the ward is under some direction."

"Very good." Lucas nodded, rocking back on his heels. "And, one more matter of business."

"Bloody hell, how much can one man do in a day?" Heathcliff grumbled.

"I need you to task Ramsey with overseeing the end-of-the-season masquerade. We often close for the duration of the winter, but I doubt I'll be around for the last event—as I'll be celebrating in a quite enthusiastic way with my wife." He grinned wildly.

"Dear Lord. Very well. Anything else? A kingdom?"

"No, that will be all today." Lucas nodded.

"I wish you luck, my friend. And keep in touch, if I don't see you till the next season," Heathcliff said with an earnest smile.

"Upon my word," Lucas replied, then quit the room with a wide smile.

His to-do list had just grown significantly smaller.

He only hoped that Liliah could get her sister to write the letter.

And agree to the plan.

Only time would answer all the questions.

Chapter Thirty-seven

Liliah wiped her damp hands on her gown before tugging on her soft kid gloves. So far everything had gone according to plan. Her gaze flickered to the reticule she planned to carry to the modiste's, and tucked inside was the letter her sister had written according to Luc's specifications.

Samantha hadn't been overly enthusiastic at the prospect of leaving her future to a man she didn't know, but she had said that she trusted Liliah's judgment. It was enough for her to agree to write the letter, all the while remarking that Samantha could easily choose to return home if need be.

Liliah didn't believe her sister to have that option, but she was trusting Lucas to help Samantha understand. Liliah had explained their father's plans and betrayals to Samantha. Samantha had been affronted, hurt, and yet at the same time, much like Liliah, she had seen how they all made sense in light of his current behavior.

It was nearing one, and Liliah stood from her vanity, lifted her reticule, and tucked it under her arm. She walked to the door and turned, facing her room, her sanctuary. It hurt to think that she would never see it again, yet the pain was minimal compared to the joy of having Lucas. She had tucked several small keepsakes and trinkets into her reticule as well, her pieces of home to take with her on her next adventure in life. With a curt nod, she opened the door and strode down the hall toward Samantha's room. This was the rather difficult aspect of their escape. While Liliah was certain she could easily acquire all the things she might need, she wasn't as sure about Samantha. Therefore, they had the logistical problem of packing some necessities in a small carpetbag. Liliah had taken the bag and set it under a bush behind the servants' entrance of the estate, and hopefully would be able to grab it if they were slightly early to the carriage and decided to walk to the carriage house, rather than wait. It wasn't a foolproof plan, but it was the best she had. She was taking no risks. Should someone come upon them, she didn't want to have to explain what she was doing.

As she knocked on Samantha's door, she met her sister's wide gaze. Both resolution and fear shone from within, but she was ready with her small reticule, also packed with small trinkets from her room, tucked under her arm.

Liliah grasped her hand and squeezed. "Ready?"

Samantha gave a weak smile. "As I'll ever be."

As they started down the hall, a footman intercepted them, bowing smartly. "My ladies, His Grace wishes to speak with you in his study."

Liliah's heart picked up speed like a hummingbird's

wings, but she nodded sedately and squeezed Samantha's hand.

They took the stairs and walked to the often visited study of their father, the duke. Liliah stepped forward and curtseyed. "Your Grace?"

"At last." He grumbled impatiently. He glanced up from behind his desk and the missive he was writing. "I've spoken to Greywick and it seems Meyer is ever anxious to make you his bride—why I cannot imagine. However, it follows that you will be married by special license tomorrow, as long as Greywick is able to secure the license today. I assume by your reticule that you are going out?" He studied them suspiciously.

Liliah nodded, thankful she had the only excuse he would likely accept. "Yes, I have the final fitting for my wedding dress, and if it is all as it should be, it will be delivered later today."

"Very good." He dismissed Liliah.

"And you." He turned his steely gaze to Samantha. "You will meet Lord Mayson tonight. He's coming over for supper and will make you an offer you shall accept."

Liliah bit her tongue, tasting the salty flavor of blood, but she kept her face impassive even in her extreme anger. He was the man she had assumed! How dare her father take away the opportunity for Samantha to experience a season, to know the joy of an offer from a man she could come to love, or at least respect? Lord Mayson was simply an easy arrangement for her father to make with as little effort as possible. It was horrid in every way.

"Of course," Samantha replied, curtseying deeply. Liliah could see the slight tremble in her movements, but didn't think their father would notice.

"Very good, you're dismissed." The duke turned back to his work and ignored the daughters he resented.

Liliah and Samantha quit the room, then took the hall to the front entrance of the manor. Liliah prayed the carriage was late in arriving so they could grab the carpet bag, but it was a futile hope. As they took the stairs outside, the carriage rolled up and dashed their expectations. Liliah turned an inquiring eye to Samantha, but her sister gave a small shake of her head.

As they entered the carriage, Liliah held her breath as the carriage rolled forward down the drive, past the gate. "I'm sorry," she murmured, still afraid to speak loudly.

Samantha wiped a tear from her face. "I had wanted to believe that maybe, just maybe, there was some hope that he'd change his mind. It was a foolish thing to do, to hope. I remember meeting that man last year. It was just a quick introduction, I nearly forgot, but upon hearing his name again I remembered. I cannot marry him!"

Liliah reached out and grasped her sister's hand. "It is never a foolish thing to hope. Ever. I'm just thankful that we are about our business today, rather than tomorrow," Liliah remarked.

"Indeed," Samantha replied.

Liliah was quickly lost in her own thoughts as they traveled through the London streets to the modiste's shop. As they pulled up, Liliah wondered at the fact that her father hadn't sent additional footmen to ensure their obedience.

She was thankful her father's arrogant nature knew no bounds.

He didn't expect them to have any will of their own, and in that, she knew that Samantha couldn't return. She prayed that Luc had secured a safe place for his future sister-in-law.

As the carriage halted, Liliah alighted first, then waited for her sister. Her gaze darted up and down the street, but she wasn't able to locate Lucas. With a shaky breath, she led Samantha to the modiste's stop, the familiar bell tinkling as they walked in. Several ladies were milling about, and one gentleman—odd. Liliah studied him as he turned and offered a familiar grin. She reached for her sister's hand. Lucas flickered his gaze toward the back, then disappeared around the dark corner of the back of the shop.

The clerk welcomed them. "Good afternoon, my lady, and my lady. Are you ready for your fitting?"

Liliah replied. "Almost, I wish to look about for a few minutes. I see you've some new material?" she lied, hoping it was true.

"Ah, yes! Of course! Simply let me know when you are ready," the clerk replied kindly and took her leave to address another patron who had just walked into the store.

Liliah tugged on her sister's hand and nodded toward the back where Lucas had disappeared. She kept her steps slow and measured, caressing bolts of cloth here and there, pausing to study one pattern or another to keep up the appearance of being interested, and as soon as she was close, she ducked around the corner with Samantha, where Lucas was waving toward a back exit. They escaped into a back alley filled with discarded material and trash, with one exit where a hired hack waited.

They quickly made their way to the hack and Lucas helped each of them into the carriage, then tapped the roof. In short order they were traveling down the streets of London as they passed from the shopping district into the residential community of Mayfair. Liliah sucked in a breath as they neared her home, only to turn left down a different street. She cut a glance to Lucas as she started to recognize her surroundings. "Brilliant," she remarked.

Lucas chuckled. "I thought you'd appreciate my idea. I rather thought it was a wise selection. While St. George's would be preferable, there was not an appointment available for several months, and since I had to call in a substantial favor with the archbishop's representative at Doctors' Common, I didn't want to wait to use the license, you understand." He nodded.

"That must have been some favor," Liliah replied, reaching over and grasping her silent sister's hand encouragingly.

"Let's just say the man has long wished for an invitation . . . somewhere." Lucas flickered a glance to Samantha, then frowned slightly. "I'm afraid we haven't been properly introduced."

Samantha's dark hazel eyes met his and she gave her head a slight shake.

"I'm Lucas Mayfield, the eighth Earl of Heightfield, at your service." He smiled broadly, the warmth in his gaze tender and kind.

Liliah glanced at her sister. "And this is Lady Samantha Durary, my dear sister."

Samantha chimed in cautiously, "Pleased to meet you, sir. I've heard much about you."

Lucas chuckled. "I'm quite certain you have. Now,

I'm assuming that your sister gave you the generalities of the plan we discussed?"

Samantha nodded. "Yes, my lord."

"She's much more biddable than you." Lucas gave Liliah a teasing wink.

"You wouldn't know what to do with me if I were biddable," Liliah teased back. "And you love me as I am."

"This is true," Lucas replied with deep feeling, then seemed to collect himself and turned back to Samantha. "Now then, I have arranged for your departure this evening. You'll have a very respectable chaperone to accompany you to Edinburgh, Scotland, where you'll be employed as a young lady's governess."

Samantha's eyes widened. "Scotland?"

Liliah studied her sister, watching as hesitation and uncertainty melted into a hardened resolve.

"That may be far enough away," Samantha replied, startling Liliah with her bold statement.

"Perhaps she isn't so biddable," Lucas remarked, grinning at her. "You'll be in excellent care. Liliah knows the gentleman who will be your employer."

Liliah frowned and waited for him to explain.

"Viscount Kilpatrick," Lucas supplied.

Liliah grinned as she remembered the mountain of a man with the kind eyes. "That will work splendidly." She turned to her sister. "I've met the man in question and you'll be quite safe with him. He's kind, Samantha, and you'll appreciate his dry wit."

"Very well." Samantha nodded sagely.

Liliah was impressed by her sister's determination to make a change for her future, to take the opportunity and run. She was essentially becoming a bluestocking—her sweet, demure, and polished sister was changing her spots.

Liliah was all too familiar with the siren call of freedom.

It would seem that Samantha had the same drive, and she was so very thankful.

The carriage pulled over beside a carriage house, and Liliah watched as Lucas's smile broadened. "Any second thoughts?"

"No," she answered quickly.

He chuckled softly and poked his head out of the carriage before stepping down. After checking to the left and right, he waved his hand for the ladies to step down.

Liliah grinned to herself as Lucas led them to the back of the manor where she had snuck in so long ago, meeting him and somehow changing her future. They took the servants' entrance, now empty, and filed down the same hall where Liliah had stumbled into the changing room to meet one of the demimonde, Lark. Her face ached from the wide grin that was a result of the very literal walk down memory lane that had them filing past the ballroom and toward the larger foyer. "We're almost there." Lucas spoke softly, invitingly.

Liliah reached out and grasped Samantha's hand, squeezing it encouragingly.

They turned down another hall and Lucas paused before a double wooden door with stained glass windows casting a glow on the floor.

Liliah glanced at Lucas, who turned to meet her gaze. "Ironic, I know."

"Usually an . . . establishment such as this doesn't have a chapel," Liliah remarked.

"It is true irony, yet I'm quite thankful for its privacy." Lucas opened the door.

A vicar was waiting, seated on the wooden pew, and at the sound of the door opening, he moved to stand and cast an impatient glare toward them. "Are you ready, then?" he asked in a gravelly tone.

"Another favor?" Liliah asked Lucas, suppressing an amused giggle.

"It helps to know everyone's secrets," Lucas said. "It makes it so much easier to arrange important events."

Liliah shook her head, bemused. "Shall we?" She offered him her hand as she released her sister's.

"One moment." He ducked his head back out into the hall and grinned. "Just in time."

Another gentleman whom Liliah hadn't met before entered the room. He wore spectacles and had an intelligent air about him. He met her curious gaze and bowed with expert precision. "Ah, it's lovely to meet you, Lady Liliah. I'm Ramsey Scott, Marquess of Sterling. It is a pleasure to meet the woman behind the fall of the devil himself." He gave a wink to Lucas, then reached out and kissed Liliah's outstretched hand. As he released her, he gave a slight bow to Samantha, but didn't wait to be introduced. He simply moved to take a seat at the front of the small chapel.

Liliah put the pieces together. A second witness.

She turned to her sister. "I love you," she murmured, pulling her into a tight hug as tears stung her eyes. It wasn't the wedding day she had always planned in her mind, but the most important people in all the world were there to see it: her sister and her love. How could she ask for more?

Lucas reached out for her hand and she willingly gave it, feeling Samantha follow them as they made their way up the short aisle. The vicar impatiently fumbled through a small black book and began to read from First Corinthians, chapter thirteen. He finished with, "'But the greatest of these is love.'"

Liliah met Lucas's gaze as they held hands before the vicar, following his directions, reciting the words and vowing them with all her heart. It was a blur, a beautiful blur of tears, joy, and completion that she had never expected to experience. How different was this wedding than the one her father had planned for her to experience with Meyer! With her friend, it would have simply been a transaction, forced at best, to appease the greed and indiscretion of others. All the fanfare, frills, and show would have been for others, not for her, or Meyer.

But this, this wedding was small in guests, but large in love. And she didn't know how anything could ever compare with its beauty, its earnestness.

The honesty of the love she had for Lucas.

The love he had for her.

As the vicar finished the final words, he gave them permission to kiss, and a warm blush crept up her neck to her face at the thought of kissing Lucas in front of her little sister. As if sensing her discomfort, Lucas reached up and cupped her cheek. During the entire ceremony, his gaze had scarcely left hers, all the love and promise of his words echoing in his expressions. His warm hand calmed her slight embarrassment, and narrowed the world down to just him. His blue eyes were glowing from the inside out with a passionate love that resonated deep in her soul. Ever so slowly, he lowered his head to meet her lips in the most delicate, chaste kiss. He lingered just a moment before leaning back and murmuring his love.

"I love you more," Liliah replied, feeling her eyes well with joyful tears that this man was hers alone, forever.

The vicar snapped his book shut, startling Liliah. Lucas shot a dark look to the vicar, who sobered and took a hesitant step back.

Their witnesses clapped as Lucas lifted her hand in the air as if pronouncing victory, and Liliah laughed joyfully. Lucas tugged on her hand as he lowered it and gave her another solid kiss, then led her back down the aisle.

"Come, dear sister. We still have work to do," he called over his shoulder to Samantha and awaited her as he headed back down the hall. He paused before a door and knocked once.

"Enter."

Lucas walked in, leading his party into the warm and richly furnished study. A man of about seventy sat behind his desk, his dark eyes immediately glowing with approval when he saw Lucas. He stood on slightly unsteady legs, reaching for his cane, which leaned against the desk. "May I be the first to offer my sincerest congratulations!" He stepped forward toward Lucas, his grin wide and accepting. His gaze flickered to Liliah. "My, well aren't you a pretty little thing? You did well, my boy." He nodded to Lucas.

Liliah flushed at the forward compliment, but smiled her thanks. Lucas bowed to the older man. "Lord Barrot, allow me to introduce you to my wife, Lady Liliah Mayfield." His tone held a ring of triumph.

Liliah curtseyed prettily, inclining her head. "A pleasure, Lord Barrot."

"Believe me, the pleasure is all mine. It's been a delight to see how the mighty have fallen." He winked at Lucas.

Lucas rolled his eyes as Liliah cut him an amused glance.

"Now, I'm assuming you're the sister?" Lord Barrot nodded to Samantha.

"Yes," Lucas answered.

"Let the poor girl speak for herself," Lord Barrot scolded kindly. "Tell me your name, ducky."

Liliah bit back a grin at the endearment reserved for children and waited for her sister to reply.

"Lady Samantha Durary, my lord." Samantha curtseyed as well.

"A lovely name for a lovely lady." Lord Barrot gave her a kind smile. "Are we sticking with that name, Luc?" He turned to Lucas.

Lucas took a breath, then paused before answering. "I thought it best to modify the name slightly, just to protect her from . . . others," he added delicately.

Lord Barrot nodded. "What were you thinking?"

"Miranda," Lucas replied.

"And are you at peace with that, my dear?" Lord Barrot turned to Samantha, who gave a single curt nod.

Liliah was consistently surprised at her sister's resilience and resolve to move forward. She had been expecting to coach and encourage her sister, yet Samantha had risen to every occasion. She had grown up so much in the past year, it was humbling to think that Liliah had missed it.

"Good, good. I've made all the arrangements necessary and Miss . . . Miranda will be leaving tomorrow morning with my wife's lady's maid. Her name is Emily, Miss Miranda. You'll love her, a more circumspect and gracious person you'll never meet. Believe me, she's endured my wife for nearly three decades." He gave a wink to Liliah's sister.

"He sounds like an old codger, but he loves his wife to distraction. Don't be fooled by his bluster." Lucas spoke to Samantha with a wicked grin.

Liliah was quite at ease with this new acquaintance, and she hoped her sister felt the same peace. She cast a glance to her sister, studying her face. A small bemused grin tipped her lips and her wide eyes had lost their edge.

"Now, since we've established the formalities and the particulars of the plan, Lord Barrot, by your leave, I'll let Miss Miranda remain in your care till tomorrow, while I take my wife and celebrate our marriage." Lucas spoke politely, however the underlying message was caught clearly by Liliah, who felt the anticipation of *celebrating* hit her in full force. Yet her heart lingered with her sister; would she be at ease with this arrangement?

"Miss Miranda." Lucas turned to face Liliah's sister, giving her his full attention. "Lord and Lady Barrot have my full trust. They have guarded many secrets throughout their lives, and are the most trustworthy of people. Are you at ease with this arrangement? I'm aware you're trusting your future to my, and their, hands. I haven't earned such trust, but I know you give it on account of the faith you have in your sister. For that, I thank you, and will endeavor to be worthy of such a gift."

Tears stung Liliah's eyes as she listened to her husband speak so kindly to her sister. Clearly moved, *Miss Miranda*—Liliah practiced her sister's new alias in her mind—nodded thoughtfully. "I thank you, for taking such a grave risk on my and my sister's behalf."

"The honor is all mine. After all, it takes a great risk to earn such a precious reward." Lucas inclined his head and then turned back to Liliah. "Do you wish to have some time to speak with your sister?"

Liliah nodded. "Yes." Lord Barrot and Lucas quit the room to give her and Samantha some privacy, and as the door clicked shut, Liliah rushed to embrace her sister. The familiar scent of rosewater floated through her senses and she wondered just how much time need pass before they could be reunited. She utterly trusted Lucas, but she knew that her sister must be struggling despite her brave demeanor.

"Are you truly well?" Liliah asked, studying Samantha's face.

"As well as can be, under the circumstances. I understand the risk, but I'm willing to take it. Apparently I'm more like you than I thought."

"Than either of us thought." Liliah reached up and smoothed Samantha's hair from her face.

"Go. And know you won't ever be far from my heart, and I hope we will be reunited soon." *Miss Miranda* spoke softly.

"It won't take much to travel to Scotland, my love. I'm sure you'll see me quite soon," Liliah assured her, and hugged her tightly again.

"If I haven't said it yet, I'm ever so happy for you, dear sister. You truly found a love match."

Liliah gave a soft giggle. "I did, most unexpectedly. And I have faith that you will as well, when the time is right."

"Let us survive one adventure at a time."

Liliah nodded in agreement, then released her sister from the embrace, taking several steps back and giving one last loving glance before opening the door. A very elegantly dressed lady with kind blue eyes was waiting expectantly.

"Lady Heightfield?" she asked with anticipation.

"Yes," Liliah replied, glancing at a beaming Lord Barrot.

"Allow me to introduce you to my wife, Lady Barrot, who is utterly beside herself to have a guest."

"Ah, Lady Barrot, a pleasure. Allow me to introduce—"

"Miss Miranda! How famously we shall get along! And your gown? I know that modiste's designs well. You'll have to help me look through my latest fashion plates from Paris, I just received them today!" Lady Barrot had grasped Samantha's hands and was pulling her down the hall, talking with a jubilant tone.

"And that, is my wife." Lord Barrot chuckled.

"I like her," Liliah remarked, grinning.

"And that is our exit cue," Lucas added, tugging on Liliah's hand.

Lord Barrot chuckled. "Don't let me halt your departure. We shall be in touch." He gave a sober glance to Lucas, then bowed and took his leave.

Lucas tugged on Liliah's hand, placing a soft kiss on her lips. "Finally," he breathed softly.

As he led her to the waiting carriage, she couldn't have agreed more.

Finally, she was free.

Finally, she had escaped.

Finally, Samantha had found her voice.

And finally, Liliah would be free to love Lucas for all her life.

All because she was willing to fall from grace—His Grace, her father—into the arms of one of the lords of temptation.

Sometimes sin was ever so sweet.

Epilogue

Liliah bit her lip as a wide smile spread across her face while reading the London *Times*. The news was surely a week old at least, being that she was not in residence in London, but visiting Scotland to keep a loving eye on her sister in hiding. But the delay in reading the news only added to her joy.

It was living proof that love always found a way.

Lord and Lady Grace wish to announce the betrothal of their daughter, Rebecca Grace, to Meyer Longfit, the Earl of Greywick.

Liliah read, then reread the short announcement. It had been more than a year since her own hasty marriage had set the London ton on its ear. She was quite certain that there was still titter about the duke's wayward daughters, not to mention the loss of the Earl of Greywick's Sussex estate to pay for his substantial gambling loss. He'd been found dead not two weeks after the estate was forfeit. The *Times* had said it was a failed heart. Regardless, the title had passed along to Meyer, who was surely taking his father's poor business decisions in hand and rectifying them. She was encouraged that Lord and Lady Grace had seen past the sins of the father and given their blessing to Meyer and Rebecca. There was no on-dit regarding her father's illicit acts, but she wasn't sure those whisperings would reach as far as Scotland.

Lord Barrot had ensured the privacy and delivery of Samantha's letter to the duke by that evening, to ensure that the authorities were not notified about a potential crime; however, Lord Barrot and Lucas had assumed that the duke would wish to try to resolve the issue quietly, without others being the wiser.

It was rumored that he had sent footmen to every dock, searching for his wayward daughter, only to come up empty—with a disgruntled elderly suitor, to boot.

Liliah was utterly unable to find any pity in her heart for either man.

As for her marriage to Lucas, they had spent the night in travel to keep one step ahead of her father. It wasn't the most romantic of nights if you were to look at it from a consummation perspective, but it was by far the most romantic in the aspect of love. She and Lucas had spent the night whispering, holding each other, and kissing in the carriage, anticipating the night's stay at the Hare and Hound. From there they took a short tour of the continent, with the expectation to return to Scotland within a fortnight.

Even though it was a year ago, she blushed at the memory of the enthusiastic ways they had partaken of their new freedom to love one another without restraint. And whether that sealed the deal, or if fate had already ensured it, no more than nine months later an heir to the Earldom of Heightfield was brought into the world.

Liliah glanced at the sleeping child in her beloved husband's arms, as he raised one hand to lift a teacup to his lips ever so carefully, so as not to wake the little boy.

Liliah met his warm gaze, smiling wide and feeling deep joy echo in her heart. Never had she dreamed that fate would be so kind to her.

"If you keep casting such joyful glances in my direction, I shall not be held responsible for my actions," Lucas whispered, arching a dark brow.

"And what if I encourage such actions?" Liliah replied just as softly.

Lucas chuckled, causing the little one to sigh.

"I do believe it's time to give him to the nurse," Lucas murmured, kissing his child's soft, downy head.

"I'll fetch her." Liliah made a move to stand from the breakfast table, but her husband lifted a hand for her to stop.

"I'll fetch her, you make your way back to our room." He grinned mischievously, and Liliah's body responded like wax to a hot flame as she awaited the pleasure she found so readily in her husband.

"Hurry." She leaned forward and kissed him softly on the cheek.

"I thought you liked it when I took it slow," he replied, then stood and quit the room, bouncing softly to soothe the little one as he walked away.

Liliah watched in rapture as the two most precious people in the world walked down the hall.

The third most precious person was only a few

miles away, established in a house that had sorely needed not only sunshine, but some direction as well.

As Liliah made her way to the bedroom she shared with Lucas, she thought over her sister's situation. She still kept the alias of Miranda, but the Viscount Kilpatrick had been notified of her real identity.

That had been an interesting night.

But she had a feeling that the man who was resentful of being "saddled" with another female—the man had been designated a ward—he was quite thrilled with the assistance that Liliah's dear sister had provided.

And maybe more, but that was a story in and of itself.

She padded into the room and closed the door, unpinning her hair and allowing the golden locks to fall freely. Not a moment later Lucas opened the door and closed it quietly.

"We don't have to be so careful anymore—he's with the nurse, is he not?" Liliah teased, watching as her husband straightened, then grinned as if realizing he was indeed being overly quiet. Their son, William, had conditioned them well.

"Minx, you're quite right."

"I do love hearing those words from your lips," Liliah teased, taking a few seductive steps toward him.

"Ah, I must admit having favorite certain words come from your lips . . . they include *more, deeper,* and my personal favorite . . . my name," Lucas replied, his grin as wicked as his reputation had been. "And since we have no need to be quiet . . ." He rushed at her, lifting her over his shoulder and plopping her onto the bed, covering her with his body and nipping at her ear and down her neck.

"Luc!" Liliah breathed, arching into him.

"Louder," Lucas commanded, lowering his mouth to the sensitive flesh of her breast. "More."

"More," she called, pulling at his clothing.

His growl against her lips was his only reply as he continued to love her deeply, passionately, and without reservation.

And afterward, as she rested in his warm arms, she was again thankful that she had risked it all to fall from grace, landing in the arms of love.

Don't miss the next book in the

GENTLEMEN OF TEMPTATION

Series!

ESCAPING HIS GRACE

Will be available in

February 2019

At your favorite bookseller and e-retailer!

Connect with Us

Visit us online at
KensingtonBooks.com
to read more from your favorite authors, see books
by series, view reading group guides, and more.

for sneak peeks, chances to win books and prize packs,
and to share your thoughts with other readers.

facebook.com/kensingtonpublishing
twitter.com/kensingtonbooks

Tell us what you think!

To share your thoughts, submit a review,
or sign up for our eNewsletters, please visit:
KensingtonBooks.com/TellUs.

Books by Bestselling Author
Fern Michaels

__**The Jury**	0-8217-7878-1	$6.99US/$9.99CAN
__**Sweet Revenge**	0-8217-7879-X	$6.99US/$9.99CAN
__**Lethal Justice**	0-8217-7880-3	$6.99US/$9.99CAN
__**Free Fall**	0-8217-7881-1	$6.99US/$9.99CAN
__**Fool Me Once**	0-8217-8071-9	$7.99US/$10.99CAN
__**Vegas Rich**	0-8217-8112-X	$7.99US/$10.99CAN
__**Hide and Seek**	1-4201-0184-6	$6.99US/$9.99CAN
__**Hokus Pokus**	1-4201-0185-4	$6.99US/$9.99CAN
__**Fast Track**	1-4201-0186-2	$6.99US/$9.99CAN
__**Collateral Damage**	1-4201-0187-0	$6.99US/$9.99CAN
__**Final Justice**	1-4201-0188-9	$6.99US/$9.99CAN
__**Up Close and Personal**	0-8217-7956-7	$7.99US/$9.99CAN
__**Under the Radar**	1-4201-0683-X	$6.99US/$9.99CAN
__**Razor Sharp**	1-4201-0684-8	$7.99US/$10.99CAN
__**Yesterday**	1-4201-1494-8	$5.99US/$6.99CAN
__**Vanishing Act**	1-4201-0685-6	$7.99US/$10.99CAN
__**Sara's Song**	1-4201-1493-X	$5.99US/$6.99CAN
__**Deadly Deals**	1-4201-0686-4	$7.99US/$10.99CAN
__**Game Over**	1-4201-0687-2	$7.99US/$10.99CAN
__**Sins of Omission**	1-4201-1153-1	$7.99US/$10.99CAN
__**Sins of the Flesh**	1-4201-1154-X	$7.99US/$10.99CAN
__**Cross Roads**	1-4201-1192-2	$7.99US/$10.99CAN

Available Wherever Books Are Sold!
Check out our website at **www.kensingtonbooks.com**

More by Bestselling Author
Hannah Howell